William Henry Holmes

Art in Shell of the Ancient Americans

William Henry Holmes

Art in Shell of the Ancient Americans

ISBN/EAN: 9783337392451

Printed in Europe, USA, Canada, Australia, Japan

Cover: Foto ©Andreas Hilbeck / pixelio.de

More available books at **www.hansebooks.com**

SMITHSONIAN INSTITUTION——BUREAU OF ETHNOLOGY.

ART IN SHELL

OF THE

ANCIENT AMERICANS.

BY

WILLIAM H. HOLMES.

179

CONTENTS.

ILLUSTRATIONS.

184   ILLUSTRATIONS.

ART IN SHELL OF THE ANCIENT AMERICANS.

By William H. Holmes.

INTRODUCTORY.

The student will find scattered throughout a wide range of archæologic literature frequent but casual mention of works of art in shell. Individual uses of shell have been dwelt upon at considerable length by a few authors, but up to this time no one has undertaken the task of bringing together in one view the works of primitive man in this material.

Works of ancient peoples in stone, clay, and bronze, in all countries, have been pretty thoroughly studied, described, and illustrated.

Stone would seem to have the widest range, as it is employed with almost equal readiness in all the arts.

Clay is widely used and takes a foremost place in works of utility and taste.

Metals are too intractable to be readily employed by primitive peoples, and until a high grade of culture is attained are but little used.

Animal substances of compact character, such as bone, horn, ivory, and shell, are also restricted in their use, and the more destructible substances, both animal and vegetable, however extensively employed, have comparatively little archæologic importance.

All materials, however, are made subservient to man and in one way or another become the agents of culture; under the magic influence of his genius they are moulded into new forms which remain after his disappearance as the only records of his existence.

Each material, in the form of convenient natural objects, is applied to such uses as it is by nature best fitted, and when artificial modifications are finally made, they follow the suggestions of nature, improvements being carried forward in lines harmonious with the initiatory steps of nature.

Had the materials placed at the disposal of primitive peoples been as uniform as are their wants and capacities, there would have been but little variation in the art products of the world; but the utilization of a particular material in the natural state gives a strong bias to artificial products, and its forms and functions impress themselves upon art products in other materials. Thus unusual resources engender unique arts

185

and unique cultures. Such a result, I apprehend, has in a measure been achieved in North America.

In a broad region at one time occupied by the mound-building tribes we observe a peculiar and an original effort—an art distinctive in the material employed, in the forms developed, and to some extent in the ideas represented. It is an age of shell, a sort of supplement to the age of stone.

It is not my intention here to attempt an extended discussion of the bearings of this art upon the various interesting questions of anthropologic science, but rather to present certain of its phases in the concrete, to study the embodiment of the art of the ancient American in this one material, and to present the results in a tangible manner, not as a catalogue of objects, but as an elementary part of the whole body of human art, illustrating a particular phase of the evolution of culture.

This paper is to be regarded simply as an outline of the subject, to be followed by a more exhaustive monograph of the art in shell of all the ancient American peoples.

Art had its beginning when man first gathered clubs from the woods, stones from the river bed, and shells from the sea-shore for weapons and utensils. In his hands these simple objects became modified by use into new forms, or were intentionally altered to increase their convenience. This was the infancy, the inception of culture—a period from which a tedious but steady advance has been made until the remarkable achievements of the present have been reached.

Rude clubs have become weapons of curious construction and machinery of marvelous complication, and the pebbles and shells are the prototypes of numerous works in all materials. Rude rafts which served to cross primeval rivers have become huge ships, and the original house of bark and leaves is represented by palaces and temples, glittering with light and glowing with color.

The steps which led up to these results are by no means clear to us; they have not been built in any one place or by any one people. Nations have risen and fallen, and have given place to others that in turn have left a heap of ruins. We find it impossible to trace back, through the historic ages into and beyond the prehistoric shadows, the pathway to culture followed by any one people. The necessity for groping increases with every backward step, and we pick up one by one the scattered links of a chain that has a thousand times been broken. So far our information is meager and fragmentary, and centuries of research will be required to round up our knowledge to such a fullness as to enable us to rehabilitate the ancient races, a result to be reached only by an exhaustive comparative study of the art products of all peoples and of all ages.

By collecting the various relics of art in shell I shall be able to add a fragment to this great work. Destructible in their character these relics are seldom preserved from remote periods, and it is only by reason of their inhumation with the dead that they appear among antiquities at all. A majority of such objects, taken from graves and tumuli, known to post-date even the advent of the white race in North America, are so far decayed that unless most carefully handled they crumble to powder.

It is impossible to demonstrate the great antiquity of any of these relics. Many of those obtained from the shell heaps of the Atlantic coast are doubtless very ancient, but we cannot say with certainty that they antedate the discovery more than a few hundred years.

Specimens obtained from the mounds of the Mississippi Valley have the appearance of great antiquity, but beyond the internal evidence of the specimens themselves we have no reliable data upon which to base an estimate of time. The age of these relics is rendered still less certain by the presence of intrusive interments, which place side by side works of very widely separated periods.

The antiquity of the relics themselves is not, however, of first importance; the art ideas embodied in them have a much deeper interest. The tablets upon which the designs are engraved may be never so recent, yet the conceptions themselves have their origin far back in the forgotten ages. Deified ancestors and mythical creatures that were in the earlier stages rudely depicted on bark and skins and rocks were, after a certain mastery over materials had been achieved, engraved on tablets of flinty shell; and it is probable that in these rare objects we have, if not a full representation of the art of the ancient peoples, at least a large number of their most important works, in point of execution as well as of conception.

Man in his most primitive condition must have resorted to the seashore for the food which it affords. Weapons or other appliances were not necessary in the capture of mollusks; a stone to break the shell, or one of the massive valves of the shells themselves, sufficed for all purposes.

The shells of mollusks probably came into use as utensils at a very early date, and mutually with products of the vegetable world afforded natural vessels for food and water.

For a long period the idea of modifying the form to increase the convenience may not have been suggested and the natural shells were used for whatever purpose they were best fitted. In time, however, by accidental suggestions it would be found that modifications would enhance their usefulness, and the breaking away of useless parts and the sharpening of edges and points would be resorted to. Farther on, as it became necessary to carry them from point to point, changes would be made for convenience of transportation. Perforations which occur naturally in some species of shell, would be produced artificially, and the shells would be strung on vines or cords and suspended about the neck; in this way, in time, may have originated the custom of wearing pendants for personal ornament. Following this would be the transportation of such articles to distant places by wandering tribes, exchanges would take place with other tribes, and finally a trade would be developed and a future commerce of nations be inaugurated.

Results similar to the foregoing would spring doubtless from the employment of substances other than shell, but that material most closely associated with the acquisition of food would come first prominently into use.

The farther these useful articles were carried from the source of supply the greater the value that would attach to them, and far inland the shell of the sea might easily become an object of unusual consideration. Having an origin more or less shrouded in mystery, it would in time become doubly dear to the heart of the superstitious savage, perhaps an object of actual veneration, or at least one of such high esteem that it would be treasured by the living and buried with the dead.

The material so plentiful on the sea-shore that it was thought of only as it proved useful for vessels and implements, became a valued treasure in the interior; its functions were gradually enlarged and differentiated; it was worked into varied shapes, such as pendants for the ears, beads for the neck, pins for the hair, and elaborate gorgets for the breast; it served its turn as fetich and charm; and was frequently used in the ceremonial jugglery of the mystic dance.

The slightest modification of these relics by the hand of man attracts our attention, and from that infant stage of the art until the highest and most elaborate forms are reached they have the deepest interest to the student of human progress.

UNWORKED SHELLS.

Some writers have suggested that the ancient peoples of the interior districts must have held shells from the sea in especial esteem, not only on account of their rarity, but also by reason of some sacred properties that had, from the mystery of their origin, become attached to them. It would appear, however, that shells were valued chiefly for their utility and beauty, and that fresh water as well as marine varieties were constantly employed. In their unworked state, for their beauty alone, they are treasured by peoples in all grades of culture, from the savage up through the barbarian stages to the most civilized state. As they are most conveniently shaped for utensils and implements, they have been of great service in the arts, and were thus of the greatest importance to primitive peoples.

It must not be supposed that the natural shells found in graves were always destined for use in an unworked state, but they should doubtless in many cases be regarded as highly-valued raw material intended for use in the manufacture of articles of utility and taste, in the tempering of potter's clay, or in effecting exchanges with neighboring tribes.

As vessels for food and drink, and as cups for paint, many species are most conveniently shaped. Good examples may be found in the *Haliotis*, so plentiful on the Pacific coast, the *Helcioniscus* of the Pacific islands, the *Pattelidæ* of Central and South America, or the *Pecten* of many seas.

In their natural state they have a twofold interest to us—as utensils they are the forerunners of many more elaborate forms that have been evolved in more advanced stages of culture, and in their distribution they give us important insight into the commerce and migrations of their aboriginal owners.

Pectens.—The Pectens are very widely distributed, and on account of their beauty of form and color have been in great favor with all peoples. They figure in the heraldic devices of the Middle Ages and in the symbolic paintings of the ancient Mexicans. They have been employed extensively by the ancient inhabitants of America as ornaments and rattles, and many examples exhumed from graves, mounds, and refuse heaps appear to have been used as utensils, cups for paint, and vessels for food and drink. They are especially plentiful in the cemeteries of the ancient Californians, from which Schumacher and Bowers have made excellent collections, and specimens may be found in the great museums of the country. A very good example of this shell (*Janira dentata*)[1] is shown in Fig. 3, Plate XXI, which represents a paint cup from Santa Barbara, Cal. This cup is still partially filled with dark, purplish, indurated paint. Some were receptacles for asphaltum, while others, which are quite empty, were employed probably for domestic purposes. The species chiefly used on the Atlantic coast are the *Pecten irradians* and *P. concentricus*. On the Pacific coast the *Pecten caurinus* and *P. hastatus* are employed by the Makah and other Indians for rattles, and it is probable that some of the rudely perforated specimens found in our collections were intended for the same purpose.

Clams.—Clams formed a very important part of the food of the ancient seaboard tribes, and the emptied shells have been utilized in a great variety of ways. The valves of many species are large and deep, and are available for cups and dishes, and as such are not scorned even by the modern clam-baker, who, like the ancient inhabitant, makes periodical visits to the sea-shore to fish and feast. They were also used as knives, scrapers, and hoes, and in historic times have been extensively used in the manufacture of wampum. The hard-shell clam, *Venus mercenaria*, on account of the purplish color of portions of the valves, has been most extensively used for this purpose. A southern variety, the *Mercenaria præparca*, is much larger and furnishes excellent dishes. The soft-shell clam, *Mya arenaria*, has been an important article of food, but the valves are not serviceable in the arts. The hen clam, *Mactra ponderosa*, which has large handsome valves, has also been used to some extent for utensils. On the Pacific coast the large clam, *Pachydesma crassatelloides*, is known also to be similarly used.

Unios.—Shells of the great family of the *Unios* have always held an important place in the domestic and mechanical arts of the savages of North America. Their chalky remains are among the most plentiful relics of the mounds and other ancient burial-places, and they come from kitchen middens and the more recent graves with all the pearly delicacy of the freshly emptied shell.

The valves of many varieties of these shells are well adapted to the use of man. Not large enough for food vessels, they make most satisfactory spoons and cups, and are frequently found to retain portions of the pigments left from the last toilet of the primeval warrior and destined for use in the spirit land. It is probable, however, that they were much more frequently employed as knives and scrapers, and as such have played their part in the barbaric feast of the primitive village, or have assisted in the bloody work of scalp-taking and torture. They are pretty generally distributed over the country, and their occurrence in the mounds will probably have but little importance in the study of artificial distribution. Very little trouble has been taken by explorers and writers to identify the numerous species collected.

---

[1] I am greatly indebted to Prof. W. H. Dall, of the Coast Survey, for assistance in the identification of Pacific coast varieties.

Haliotis.—The *Haliotis* affords one of the best examples of the varied uses to which the natural shell has been applied by savage peoples. Recent explorations conducted by the government exploring parties in California have brought to the notice of archæologists and the world the existence of a new field of research—the burial-places of the ancient tribes of the Pacific coast. Many of the interments of this region are probably post-Columbian. Several species of this beautiful shell were used and are taken from the graves in great numbers, the pearly lusters being almost perfectly preserved. Many were used as paint-cups, and still retain dark pigments, probably ochers; one of these, a fine example of the *Haliotis californianus*, is shown in Fig. 4, Plate XXI. Some had contained food, and in a few cases still retained the much-esteemed *chia* seed, while in others were found asphaltum, which was employed by these peoples in a variety of arts, the rows of eyes in the *Haliotis* usually being stopped with it, and in one case, as shown in a specimen in the National Museum, it has been used to deepen a cup by building up a rim around the edge of a shallow shell. Many others are quite empty, and doubtless served as bowls, dishes, and spoons, or were ready at hand for the manufacture of implements and ornaments. Buried with the dead, they were designed to serve the purposes for which they were used in life.

This shell probably formed as important a factor in the commerce of these tribes as did the large conchs of the Atlantic coast in that of the mound-builders and their neighbors. In recent times they are known to have a high value attached to them, and Professor Putnam states[1] that a few years ago a horse could be had in exchange for a single shell of the *Haliotis rufescens*. This species is a great favorite toward the south, and the *Haliotis Kamschatkana*, which furnishes a dark greenish nacre, is much used farther north.

The rougher and more homely oyster-shell has also enjoyed the favor of the mound-building tribes, and has probably served many useful purposes, such as would only be suggested to peoples unacquainted with the use of metal. Many species of the *Fissurella* and *Dentalium* shells were in common use, advantage being taken of the natural perforations for stringing, the latter being quite extensively used for money on the Pacific slope.

In Fig. 2, Plate XXI, a cut is given of a *Mytilus* shell paint-cup from an ancient Peruvian grave. It is copied from Plate 83 of the Necropolis of Ancon.[2] It is represented as still containing red paint, probably cinnabar.

A great variety of the larger univalve sea-shells were used in the unaltered state, the *Busycons* probably taking the most important place, species of the *Strombus*, the *Cassis*, the *Nautilus* and *Fasciolaria* following in about the order named.

---

[1] Putnam: in Surveys West of the 100th Meridian, Vol. VII, p. 251.

[2] Reiss and Stübel: Necropolis of Ancon, Peru, Plate 83.

The *Busycon perversum* has been more extensively used than any other shell, and consequently its distribution in one form or other is very wide. It is o'tained along the Atlantic and Gulf coasts from Massachusetts to Mexico, and within the United States it is artificially distributed over the greater part of the Atlantic slope. The uses to which this shell has been put by the ancient Americans are so numerous and varied that I shall not attempt to enumerate them here. They are, however, pretty thoroughly brought out in the subsequent pages of this paper.

From the employment of shells in their complete state their modification for convenience is but a slight step, and when once suggested is easily accomplished—holes are bored, handles are carved or added, margins are ground down, useless parts are broken away, and surfaces are polished. . The columellæ are removed from the large univalves, and the parts used for a great variety of purposes. The mechanical devices employed have been very simple, such as flint implements for cutting, and rough stones for breaking and grinding. Hand-drills were at first used for perforating; but later mechanically revolving drills were devised.

VESSELS.

I shall not attempt to take up the various classes of objects in shell in the order of their development, as it would be hard to say whether food utensils, weapons, or ornaments were first used. It is also difficult to distinguish weapons proper from implements employed in the arts, such as celts, knives, hammers, etc., as it is probable they were all variously used according to the needs of their possessors.

Having briefly treated of natural vessels, it seems convenient to go on with vessels shaped by art. Early explorers in many portions of the American continent record, in their writing, the use by the natives of shells of various kinds as vessels. We have in this case historic evidence which bears directly upon prehistoric customs. Indeed, it is not impossible that the very shells used by the natives first encountered by Europeans, are the identical ones exhumed so recently from burial places, as many of the finer specimens of shell objects have associated with them articles of undoubted European manufacture. A notice of the earliest recorded use of these objects naturally introduces the prehistoric use.

With many nations that were bountifully supplied with convenient earthen and stone vessels, as well perhaps as others of the hard shells of fruits, the sea-shell was nevertheless a favorite vessel for drinking. Herrera describes the use of silver, gold, shell, and gourd cups at the banquets of the elegant monarch Montezuma II, who "sometimes drank

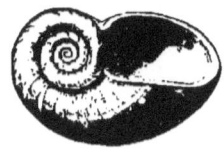

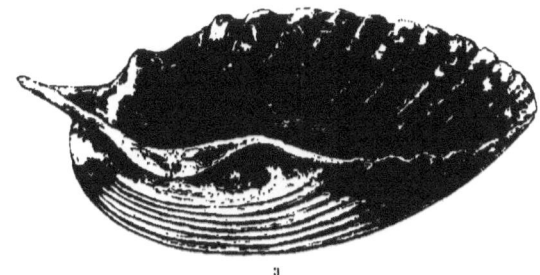

1. From a plate in De Bry.   3. Pecten, California grave. (⅓)
2. From a Peruvian grave.   4. Haliotis, California grave. (⅓)

SHELL VESSELS.

out of cocoas and natural shells richly set with jewels." Other authors make similar statements. Clavigero says that "beautiful sea-shells or naturally formed vessels, curiously varnished, were used." In many of the periodical feasts of the Florida Indians shells were in high favor, and it is related how at a certain stage of one of the dances two men came in, each bearing very large conch-shells full of black drink, which was an infusion of the young leaves of the cassine (probably *Ilex Cassine*, L.). After prolonged ceremonies, this drink was offered to the king, to the whites present, and then to the entire assembly.[1] It is a remarkable fact that a similar custom has been noticed among the Moquis of Arizona. Lieutenant Bourke witnessed the snake dance of that tribe a few years ago, and states that in front of the altar containing the snakes was a covered earthen vessel, which contained four large sea-shells and a liquid of some unknown composition, of which the men who handled the snakes freely drank. Vessels thus associated with important ceremonial customs of savages would naturally be of first importance in their sepulchral rites. De Bry, in the remarkable plates of his "Brevis Narratio," furnishes two instances of such use. Plate 19 shows a procession of nude females who scatter locks of their hair upon a row of graves, on each of which has been placed a large univalve shell, probably containing food or drink for the dead, and in Plate 40 we have another illustration of this custom, the shell being placed on the heap of earth raised above the grave of a departed chieftain. In Plate XXI, Fig. 1, an outline of the shell represented is given; it resembles most nearly the pearly nautilus, but, being drawn by the artist from memory or description, we are at liberty to suppose the shell actually used was a large *Busycon* from the neighboring coast, probably more or less altered by art. Haywood, Hakluyt, Tonti, Bartram, Adair, and others mention the use of shells for drinking vessels, and in much more recent times Indians are known to have put them to a similar use.

On account of the rapidity with which they decay, we can know nothing of surface deposits of shells by prehistoric or even by comparatively recent peoples. It is only through the custom of burying valued articles with the dead that any of these relics are preserved to us. When we consider the quantity of such objects necessarily destroyed by time, exposure, and use, we marvel at the vast numbers that must have been, within a limited period of years, carried inland. In the more recent mounds there may be found specimens obtained by the Indians through the agency of white traders, but the vast majority were derived doubtless from purely aboriginal sources. Many instances could be cited to show that the whites have engaged in the trade in shells. Kohl, in speaking of early trade with the Ojibways of Lake Superior, states that when the traders "exhibited a fine large shell and held it to the ears of the Indians, these latter were astonished, saying they heard the roaring

[1] De Bry: Collectio Pars 2. Brevis Narratio, 1591, Plate 29.

13 E

of the ocean in it, and paid for such a marvelous shell furs to the value of $30 or $40, and even more."[1]

Cabeça de Vaca[2] traded in sea-shells and "hearts" of sea-shells among the Charruco Indians of the Gulf coast nearly three hundred and fifty years ago.

The form of vessel of most frequent occurrence is made by removing the whorl, columella, and about one-half of the outer shell of the large univalves. The body of the lower whorl is cut longitudinally, nearly opposite the lip and parallel with it. The spire is divided on the same plane, a little above the apex, giving a result well illustrated in Fig. 1, Plate XXII. A very convenient and capacious bowl is thus obtained, the larger specimens having a capacity of a gallon or more. The work of dividing the shell and removing neatly the interior parts must have been one of no little difficulty, considering the compactness of the shell and the rudeness of the tools.

For nomadic peoples these vessels would have a great superiority over those of any other material, as they were not heavy and could be transported without danger of breaking.

In the manufacture of these vessels the *Busycon perversum* seems to have been a great favorite; this may be the result of the less massive character of the shell, which permits more ready manipulation. The spines are less prominent and the walls more uniform in thickness than in shells of most other varieties found along the Atlantic seaboard. Specimens of the *Strombus, Cassis,* and *Fasciolaria* were occasionally used. The specimen illustrated in Fig. 1, Plate XXII, is from a mound at Ritcherville, Ind., and is now in the National Museum at Washington. It is made from a *Busycon perversum,* and is ten and one-half inches in length by six and one-half in width at the most distended part. The body and spire have been cut in the manner described above, and the interior whorl and columella have been skillfully taken out. The rim is not very evenly cut, but is quite smooth. The outer surface of the shell has been well polished, but is now worn and scarred by use. The substance of the shell is very well preserved. A second example, now in the national collection, is from an ancient mound at Naples, Ill. It is very similar to the preceding, being made from the same species of shell. It is eleven inches in length by seven in width. The body of the shell is well preserved, the apex, however, being broken away. A small specimen, also in the National Museum, was obtained from a mound at Nashville, Tenn., by Professor Powell. It is three and a half inches in length, and very shallow, being but a small portion of the lower whorl of a *Busycon.*

Among the more recent acquisitions to the national collection are two very fine specimens of these *Busycon* vessels. One of these was obtained from a mound at East Dubuque, Ill. It is eleven inches in length by seven in width at the widest part; the exterior surface is

[1] Kohl: Kitschi-Gami, vol. I, p. 186, Rau, trans.
[2] Cabeça de Vaca: Relation et Naufrages. Paris, 1837, p. 121. Spanish ed., 1555.

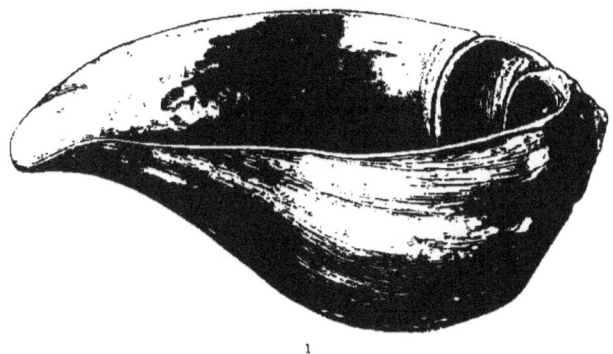

1

2

1. Shell vessel made from a *Busycon perversum*, Ind. (⅔)
2. Earthen vessel made in imitation of shell, Mo. (⅓)

VESSELS.

highly polished; the interior is less so, having suffered somewhat from decay; the beak is very long and slender, and has been used as a handle. The whole vessel has a dipper like appearance.

The finest example of these vessels yet brought to my notice was obtained from a mound at Harrisburg, Ark., by Dr. Palmer, in October, 1882. It differs from the other specimens described in having an elaborate ornamental design engraved on the exterior surface. In shape it corresponds pretty closely to the first specimen figured, no part of the spire, however, being cut away; the interior parts have been removed, as usual. The surface is quite smooth, and the ridges on the inner surface of the spire are neatly rounded and polished. Its length is eleven inches, and its width seven. Plate XXIII is devoted to the illustration of this specimen. The entire exterior surface, from apex to base, is covered with a design of engraved lines and figures, which are applied in such a manner as to accord remarkably well with the expanding spiral of the shell. The upper surface of the spire is unusually flat, and has been ground quite smooth. It will be seen by reference to Fig. 2, Plate XXIII, that a series of lines, interrupted at nearly regular intervals by short cross lines and rectangular intaglio figures, has been carried from the apex outward toward the lip. Another series of lines begins on the upper margin next the inner lip of the shell, passes around the circumference of the upper surface, and extends downward over the carina, covering, as shown in the other figure, the entire body of the vessel, excepting the extreme point of the handle. The base of the shell, which is perforated, has a small additional group of lines. The lines of the principal series are, on the more expanded portion of the body of the shell, about eight inches long, and are interrupted by two rows of short lines and two rows of incised rectangular figures. The space between the latter contains the most interesting feature of the design. Three arrow-head shaped figures, two inches in length by one and one-half in width, are placed, one near the outer lip, another near the inner lip, and the third in the middle of the body, a little below the center. These figures are neatly cut and symmetrical, and resemble a barbed and blunt-pointed arrow-head. Near the center of each is a small circle, which gives the figure a close resemblance to a variety of perforated stone implements, one specimen of which has been found near Osceola, Ark. Whatever may be the significance of this design, and it is undoubtedly significant, it is at least a very remarkable piece of work and a highly successful effort at decoration. The pottery of this region which is generally highly decorated with painted and incised lines, contains nothing of a character similar to this, and it is probable that what I have come to consider a rule in such matters applies in this case; the design on the shell is significant or ideographic, that on the pottery is purely ornamental.

For the purpose of showing the very wide distribution of vessels made from large seashells, especially the *Busycon perversum*, I introduce here descriptions of most of the specimens heretofore reported.

Dr. Rau, in his paper on ancient aboriginal trade in North America, states that in the collection of Colonel Jones, of Brooklyn, there is a vessel formed from a *Cassis* which is eight and a half inches long, and has a diameter of seven inches where its periphery is widest. It was obtained from a stone grave near Clarksville, Habersham County, Georgia.[1]

Two fine specimens of the *Cassis flammea* were taken from mounds in Nacoochee Valley, Georgia. They were nearly ten inches in length and about seven inches in diameter. The interior whorls and columellæ had been removed, so that they answered the purpose of drinking cups or receptacles of some sort.[2]

From a stone grave mound near Franklin, on the Big Harpeth River, Prof. Joseph Jones took two large sea-shells, one of which was much decayed. The interior surface of these shells had been painted red, and the exterior had been marked with three large circular spots.[3]

In the grave of a child, near the grave just mentioned, the following relics were found : " Four large sea-shells, one on each side of the skeleton, another at the foot, and the fourth, a large specimen, with the interior apartments cut out and the exterior surface carved, covered the face and forehead of the skull." [1]

In a small mound opposite the city of Nashville, Tenn., Professor Jones found "a large sea-conch." The interior portion or spiral of which had been carefully cut out; it was probably used as a drinking vessel, or as the shrine of an idol as in a case observed by Dr. Troost.[5]

Two large shells of *Busycon*, from which the columellæ had been removed, were obtained from the Lindsley mounds, sixty miles east of Nashville, by Professor Putnam.[6]

Professor Wyman, writing of the mounds of Eastern Tennessee, says that "among the implements are well-preserved cups or dishes, made of the same species of shell [*Busycon perversum*] as the preceding, but of much more gigantic size than those now found. One of them measures a foot in length, though the beak has been broken off. When entire its length could not have been less than fourteen or fifteen inches. These shells probably came from the Gulf of Mexico, and found their way into Tennessee as articles of traffic. The dishes are made in the same way, and not to be distinguished from those found in Florida at the time of the first visit of the Europeans, or from those, as will be seen further, found in the ancient burial mounds. The great similarity in the style and make of these dishes renders it quite probable that they were manufactured in Florida."[7] A number of similar dishes, made

[1] Rau, in Smithsonian Report for 1872, p. 376.
[2] Jones: Antiquities of the Southern Indians, p. 253.
[3] Jones: Aboriginal Remains of Tennessee, p. 59.
[4] Ibid., p. 60.
[5] Ibid., p. 45.
[6] Putnam, in Eleventh Annual Report, Peabody Museum, p. 355.
[7] Wyman, in Third Annual Report, Peabody Museum, p. 7.

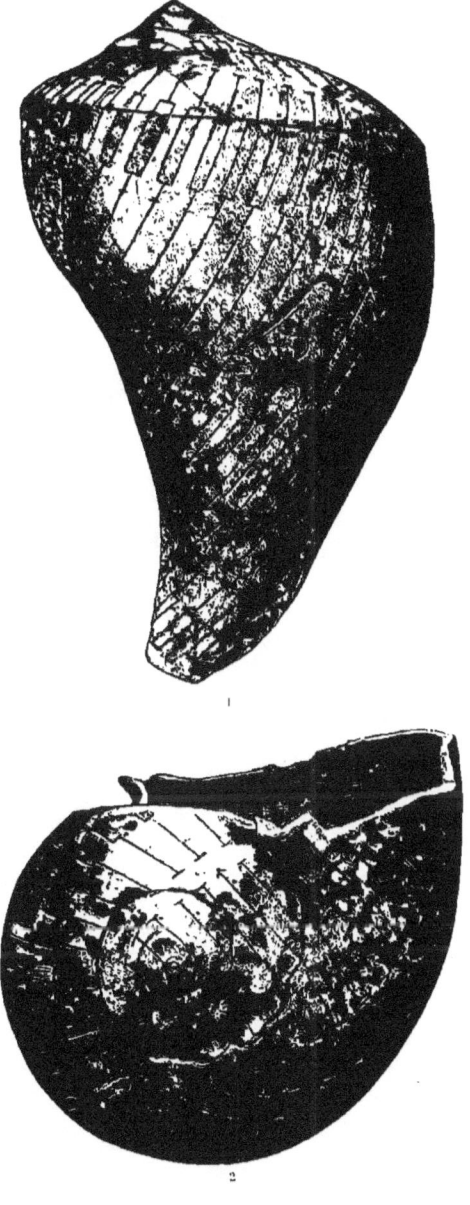

ENGRAVED VESSEL.
Harrisburg, Ark.

from the same shell, were obtained from mounds at Cedar Keys, Florida, by Professor Wyman.[1]

Francis Cleveland, C. E., who, in 1828, had charge of the excavation known as the "deep cut" on the Ohio Canal, informed Colonel Whittlesey that at the depth of twenty-five feet in the alluvium several shells belonging to the species *Busycon perversum* were taken out.[2]

Dr. Drake, writing of the Cincinnati mounds, mentions "several large marine shells, belonging, perhaps, to the genus *Buccinum*, cut in such a way as to serve for domestic utensils, and nearly converted into a state of chalk."[3]

Mr. Atwater states that "several marine shells, probably *Buccinum*, cut in such a manner as to be used for domestic utensils, were found in a mound on the Little Miami River, Warren County, Ohio."[4]

A *Cassis* of large size, from which the inner whorls and columella had been removed to adapt it for use as a vessel, was found in Clark's mound, on Paint Creek, Scioto Valley, Ohio.[5] This specimen is eleven and a half inches in length by twenty-four in circumference at the largest part. It is further stated that fragments of these and other shells are found in the tumuli and upon the altars of the mound-builders. In digging the Ohio and Erie Canal, there was found, near Portsmouth, its southern terminus on the Ohio River, a cluster of five or six large shells, which appeared to have been thus carefully deposited by the hand of man. They were about three feet beneath the surface. The columellæ of some large shells, probably the *Strombus gigas*, were also discovered.[6]

Several large marine shells were found in a mound near Grand Rapids, Mich. They were all hollowed out, apparently for carrying or storing water, and in one case perforated at the upper edge on opposite sides for suspension by a cord or thong.[7]

Mr. Farquharson mentions a vessel made from a *Busycon perversum*, obtained from a mound near Davenport, Iowa. The shell has been cut through about an inch above the center; it is thirteen inches in length by seven in width, and has a capacity of nearly two pints.[8] He also describes a large specimen of *Cassis* from a mound in Muscatine County, Iowa.[9]

Long, in his expedition from Pittsburgh to the Rocky Mountains in

[1] Wyman, in Third Annual Report, Peabody Museum, p. 8.
[2] Foster: Prehistoric Races of the United States, p. 78.
[3] Since the shell here named is quite small it is probable that the specimens found were *Busycons*.
[4] Long's Expedition to the Rocky Mountains, Vol. I, p. 361.
[5] Atwater, in Transactions American Antiquarian Society, Vol. I.
[6] Squier and Davis: Ancient Monuments of the Mississippi Valley, p. 283.
[7] Ibid., p. 284.
[8] Farquharson, in Proceedings of the Am. Association, 1875, page 296.
[9] Ibid., p. 297.

1819, speaks of a large shell which seems to have been reverenced as a kind of oracle. This may have been one of the large, brilliantly-colored fossil *Baculites* so common in the upper Missouri region. His description will be given in full in treating of the sacerdotal uses of shells.

In the Naturalist for October, 1879, Mr. Frey describes a sea-shell drinking vessel, somewhat modified by art, having a length of four and one-half inches. This, with other relics, among which were many shell beads, was found in ancient grave in eastern New York, probably in the Mohawk Valley.

These vessels of shell have also served as models for the primitive potter. The ancient peoples of the middle Mississippi district were extremely skillful in the reproduction of natural objects in clay, and it is not surprising that they should imitate the form of the shell.

In the Peabody Museum is an earthen vessel copied from a shell vessel of the class just described, the characteristic features being all well imitated. It is about nine inches wide, eleven long and four deep. It is neatly made, and ornamented with the red and white designs peculiar to the pottery of this region. It was taken from one of the Stanley mounds, Saint Francis River, Ark.

A small earthen vessel made in imitation of these shell vessels is illustrated in Fig. 2, Plate XXII. It is of the ordinary blackish ware so common in the middle Mississippi district. The general shape of the shell is well represented; the sides, however, are nearly symmetrical and the spire is represented by a central node, surrounded by four inferior nodes. It is four inches wide and five and one-half long. Three others represent shell vessels, somewhat less closely, the spires and beaks being added to the opposite sides of ordinary cups.

SPOONS.

As domestic utensils bivalve shells have held a place hardly inferior in importance to that of the large univalves. Marine and fluviatile varieties have been used indiscriminately, and generally in the natural state, but occasionally altered by art to enhance their beauty or add to their convenience. The artificial utensils do not, however, present a very great variety of form, the alteration consisting chiefly in the carving out of a kind of handle, by which device hot food could be eaten without danger of burning the fingers. The handle, which may be seen in all stages of development, is produced by cutting away portions of the anterior and basal margins of the shell, leaving the salient angle projecting; this angle is then undercut from the opposite sides so that it is connected with the body of the valve by a more or less restricted neck. The outer edge of the handle is frequently ornamented with notches, and in a few cases a round perforation has been made near the anterior tip for the purpose of suspension. In one case a rude design of small circular depressions has been added to the upper surface. In the finished implement the hinge, ligament, and teeth have been cut away, the thick dorsal margin carefully ground down, leaving a smooth, neat edge, and the anterior point, which was presented to the lips in eating or drinking, was well rounded and polished. The whole surface of the shell in the more finished specimens has been most carefully dressed. Altogether, the fashioning of these spoons must be regarded as a very ingenious performance for savages, and has cost much more labor than would the attachment of a handle, for which purpose it is not improbable the lateral notches may at times have been used. Our collections furnish no examples of marine univalves worked in this manner; a few slightly altered specimens, however, have been reported. Nearly all the specimens of carved spoons that have come to my notice are made from a few species of *Unio*.

It is a curious fact that most of these utensils have been made from the left valve of the shell, which gives such a position to the handle that they are most conveniently used by the right hand, thus indicating right-handedness on the part of these peoples. In the national collection there are two left-handed specimens, one from Nashville, Tenn., and one from Union County, Ky.

Professor Putnam states that he has " examined over thirty of these shell-spoons now in the museum [Peabody], and all are made from the right [left] valves of *Unionidæ*, and so shaped as to be most conveniently used with the right hand." [1]

By reference to Fig. I, Plate XXIV, the probable manner of grasping and using the spoon will be seen. It will also be observed that the left valve of the shell is used to make the right-handed spoon, supposing of course that the point of the spoon is presented to the lips, the hinge corner being much less convenient for that purpose.

In regard to the use of these objects, which have occasionally been taken for ornaments, it should be mentioned that very many of them have been found within earthen vessels placed in the graves with the dead. The vessels, in all probability, were the receptacles of food, the spoons being so placed that they could be used by the dead as they had been used by the living.

The specimen shown in Fig. 3, Plate XXIV, was obtained by Professor Powell, from a mound near Nashville, Tenn. It is made from the left valve of a very delicate specimen of the *Unio ovatus*,[2] and has been finished with more than usual care. The entire rim is artificially shaped, the natural shell being much reduced, and six notches ornament the outside of the handle. The bowl of the spoon is nearly four inches in length and two and one-half in width. Eight other specimens were obtained from the same locality by Professor Powell. All are made from the *Unio ovatus*, one only being left-handed. All are

---

[1] Putnam, in Eleventh Annual Report, Peabody Museum, p. 235.

[2] I am indebted to Dr. Charles A. White, of the Geological Survey, for the identification of the numerous specimens of *Unionidæ* mentioned in this paper.

inferior in finish to the specimen illustrated. The handles of a number are rudimentary, and the margins and surfaces are but slightly worked.

The spoon illustrated in Fig. 4, Plate XXIV, is made from the left valve of a *Unio alatus* (?) and was obtained from a mound at Madisonville, Ohio. It is an unusually well-finished and handsome specimen, and notwithstanding its fragile character, is well preserved. A portion of the point has, unfortunately, been broken away. The handle is ornamented with four shallow notches, the anterior point being neatly rounded and perforated for suspension. The edges of the utensil have been carefully finished, and both the inner and outer surfaces have been ground down and polished so that all the natural markings are obliterated, and the surface shows the pearly marbling of the foliation. This specimen is figured in an interesting paper,[1] prepared by Mr. Charles F. Low, as an ornament, this use being suggested by its finish and decoration; but as it was found in what was presumably a food vessel, and at the same time resembles so closely the spoons of other localities, I take the liberty of classifying it with them.

One of the most interesting collections of these utensils was made in Union County, Ky., by S. S. Lyon. Our information in regard to this lot of specimens is, unfortunately, quite meager, as Mr. Lyon's report gives them but casual mention.

Fig. 2, Plate XXIV, illustrates the finest of these specimens on a scale of one-half. The shell used is a large specimen of *Unio oratus*, the bowl of the spoon being about four inches long and three wide. As the right valve has been used, the utensil is left-handed. The handle is ornamented with two marginal notches; the basal point is long and spine-like, and is deeply undercut. The anterior point is beak-like in shape, the nicely made perforation holding, in relation to it, the position of an eye, which, together with the comb-like notches above, gives a pretty close resemblance to a bird's head. The point of the spoon is broken away.

The seven remaining spoons from this locality have a variety of handles, all of which are notched on the outer margin, while a few only are deeply undercut; all have been made from the left valve of the *Unio oratus* (?) and are of medium size and ordinary finish.

Another specimen in the national collection comes from Henderson County, Ky. The shell used is the *Unio oratus;* the handle is notched on the outer margin, but is only slightly under-cut; the thick margin of the shell about the hinge has not been removed.

A spoon made from the left valve of a *Unio siliquoideus* (?) has recently been obtained from a mound at Osceola, Ark.; it is but slightly worked, having a series of small notches cut in the basal margin, toward the front.

The Natural History Museum of New York contains a specimen of this

[1] Archæological Explorations by the Literary and Scientific Society of Madisonville, 1879.

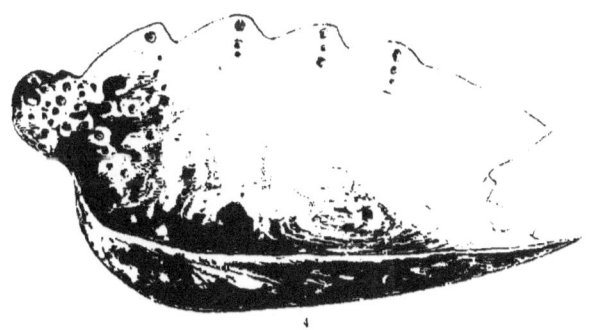

1. Manner of grasping spoon.
2. From a mound in Kentucky. (½).

3. From a mound near Nashville. (½)
4. From a mound in Ohio. (½)

SHELL SPOONS.

class, labeled as coming from Georgia. It has a rounded handle, without either perforation or notches.

The Peabody Museum contains a very superior collection, consisting of specimens from several localities. Six of these, made from *Unionidæ*, mostly from the *Unio ovatus*, were obtained from one of the Bowling mounds near Nashville, Tenn.; others crumbled on being handled and were lost. Several others were obtained in the same region.[1] Two more were found in an earthen vessel between two skeletons, in one of the Lindsley mounds at Lebanon, sixty miles east of Nashville.[2]

In a stone-cist mound on the Big Harpeth River, Prof. Joseph Jones found "a few large fresh-water mussel-shells, which were much altered by time. These mussel-shells appeared from their shape to have been artificially carved, and to have been used as ornaments and also as spoons or cups for dipping up food and drink."[3]

Three fine specimens have recently been obtained from graves at Harrisburg, Ark. They are but slightly worked as compared with the more elaborate specimens. The hinge, teeth, and ligaments have been ground down and a portion of the postero-dorsal margin removed, leaving the posterior point and basal margin projecting for a handle. The surfaces are well smoothed. The general outline of the shell is subtriangular; it is three inches wide by four and one half in length and is probably made from the *Unio cuneatus*.

Beverly gives a plate illustrating two Virginia Indians, man and wife, at dinner; on the mat by the woman is "a Cockle-Shell, which they sometimes use instead of a Spoon." "The Spoons which they eat with, do generally hold half a Pint; and they laugh at the English for using small ones, which they must be forc'd to carry so often to their Mouths, that their Arms are in Danger of being tir'd, before their Belly."[4]

KNIVES.

From a very early date shells must have been employed quite extensively by the ancient Americans as implements, as weapons for war and the chase, as appliances for fishing, as agricultural implements, and as knives, gouges, scrapers, perforators, etc., in a variety of arts. It is a noteworthy fact, however, that our collections do not abound in objects of these classes, and our literature furnishes but little information on the subject. Our interest lies chiefly in such of these objects as have been shaped by the hand of man, but to illustrate their use we will find it instructive to study the various ways in which the natural shells

[1] Putnam, in Eleventh Annual Report, Peabody Museum, p. 344.
[2] Ibid., p. 344.
[3] Jones: Antiquities of Tennessee, p. 64.
[4] Beverly: History of Virginia, 1722, pl. 10, p. 154.

have been employed. In this manner we may trace the origin and development of artificial forms.

As we have seen in the early modification of food utensils the beginning of the art of cutting and shaping shell, which in time led to the manufacture of objects of taste, and probably proved an important step in the evolution of native American art, so in this convenient and workable material, as employed in the mechanical arts, we witness the inception of many important human industries, and in the rude machines constructed from shell probably behold the prototypes of numerous works in stone and metal. It cannot be supposed that such of these objects as we do possess are of very ancient date, as the material is not sufficiently enduring. It is also improbable that such objects would, as a rule, be so frequently deposited in graves, as food vessels or objects of personal display, and objects not so deposited must soon have disappeared.

The early explorers of the American coast make occasional mention of the employment of shells in the various arts. As many of these notices are interesting, and have an important bearing upon the subject under consideration, I will present a number of them here. Among a majority of the American Indians, knives of stone, obsidian, jasper, and flint were in general use, but it would seem that shells artificially shaped and sharpened were also sometimes used for shaping objects in wood and clay, in preparing food, in dressing game, and in human butchery.

Strachey informs us, in volume VI of the Hakluyt Society, that when the omnipotent Powhatan "would punish any notorious enemy or trespasser, he causeth him to be tyed to a tree, and with muscle shells or reedes the executioner cutteth off his joints one after another, ever casting what is cutt off into the fier; then doth he proceede with shells and reedes to case the skyn from his head and face." [1]

Such knives were also used by Powhatan's women for cutting off their hair. [2]

A number of authors mention the use of shells as scalping-knives.

Kalm, speaking of the Indians of New Jersey, says that "instead of knives, they were satisfied with little sharp pieces of flint or quartz, or else some other hard kind of a stone, or with a sharp shell, or with a piece of bone, which they had sharpened." [3]

The Indians encountered by Henry Hudson during his first voyage, in making him welcome, "killed a fat dog, and skinned it in great haste with shells which they had." [4]

Beverly asserts that before the English supplied the Virginia Indians with metallic tools, "their Knives were either sharpen'd Reeds, or Shells,

[1] Strachey, in Hakluyt Society Publications, vol. VI, p. 52.
[2] Ibid., vol. VII, p. 67.
[3] Kalm's Travels, London, 1772, vol. I, p. 341.
[4] Collections New York Historical Society, vol. I, 2nd series, p. 198.

and their Axes sharp Stones bound to the end of a Stick, and glued in
with Turpentine. By the help of these they made their Bows of the
Locust Tree."[1]

Drake, in his "World Encompassed," speaking of some of the southern tribes of South America, probably the Patagonians, says that "their
hatchetts and knives are made of mussel-shells, being great and a foot
in length, the brickle part whereof being broken off, they grind them
by great labor to a fine edge and very sharpe, and as it seemeth, very
durable.[2] * * * Their working tools, which they use in cutting
these things and such other, are knives made of most huge and mon-
strous mussell shels (the like whereof have not been seen or heard of
lightly by any travelers, the meate thereof being very savourie and good
in eat'ng), which, after they have broken off the thinne and brittle
substance of the edge, they rub and grind them upon stones had for the
purpose, till they have tempered and set such an edge upon them, that
no wood is so hard but they will cut it at pleasure with the same."[3]

According to Sproat, shell knives were used by the Indians of Vancouver's Island in carving the curious wooden images placed over
graves.[4]

Ancient shell knives are very rarely found in collections. Such specimens as have come to my notice could as well be classed as scrapers
or celts. We will probably not be far wrong in concluding that such
implements were used for scraping and digging as well as for cutting.
As a rule, knives proper were simply sharpened bivalve shells. The
scrapers so frequently mentioned were doubtless often the same, but
probably more frequently portions of the lower whorl of the large univalves.

CELTS.

Implements of this class are generally made from the lower part of
large univalves. They were probably used in a variety of ways, with
handles and without. The spine-like base of the shell forms the shaft,
the blade being cut from the broadly expanded wall of the lower whorl.
Nearly all the specimens in the national collection have been obtained
in this way. In Plate XXV three very fine examples are figured. The
specimen illustrated in Fig. 1 is more than usually well fashioned, and
is extremely massive, having the proportions and almost the weight of
typical stone celts. It is five inches in length, two and three-fourths in
width, and nearly one inch through at the thickest part.

[1] Beverly: History of Virginia, 1722, p. 197.
[2] Drake, in Hakluyt Society Publications, vol. XVI, p. 74.
[3] *Ibid*, p. 78.
[4] Sproat's Savage Life, p. 86.

The edge is even and sharp, and but slightly rounded; the beveled faces are quite symmetrical, and meet at an angle of about 35°; the faces are curved slightly, following the original curvature of the shell, and the sides are evenly dressed and taper gently toward the upper end which shows some evidence of battering. The surface of the specimen is slightly chalky from decay. It has been made from a *Strombus gigas*, or some equally massive shell. It was collected at Orange Bluff, Fla., by T. S. Barber. A profile view of the same specimen is presented in Fig. 2. The specimen shown in Fig. 3 was found in Madison County, Ky., and is the only one in the national collection from the Mississippi Valley. It was obtained from a mound, but in what relation to the human remains I have not learned. It is fashioned much like the specimen just described; it is one and a half inches in width at the upper end, and two inches wide near the cutting edge. It has also been made from a very massive shell.

Fig. 4 illustrates a specimen from St. Michael's Parish, Barbadoes, West Indies. It is made from the basal portion of a *Busycon perversum*. The handle is curved and neatly rounded, and the edge is beveled or sharpened on the inside only.

In the national collection there are about twenty of these objects; six are from Tampa, Fla.; four of these are fragmentary; the remaining two are short and triangular, and have been made, one from a *Busycon perversum*, the other from a *Busycon* or *Strombus*. The cutting edge is wide and well sharpened. Two are from Cedar Keys, Fla., and are made from thin-walled specimens of the *Busycon perversum*. The larger is six and one-half inches in length by three in width toward the base; the other is about one-half as large. Both are rudely made, and show the effects of use. Five came from East Pass, Choctawhatchie Bay, Fla. Two of them are fragmentary; one of the entire specimens is very well made, and has a regularly beveled, oblique edge, while another is remarkable in having a curiously worn edge, which is deeply serrated by use or weathering. The majority of these specimens are from ancient shell heaps. Three are from St. Michael's Parish, Barbadoes, West Indies, one of which has already been described.

Professor Wyman, in the Naturalist for October, 1868, illustrates two of these celt-like implements from the fresh-water shell heaps near St. Johns, Fla. One is made from a triangular piece cut from a *Busycon carica*, so as to comprise a portion of the rostrum, which serves as a handle, and a portion of a swollen part of the body, which terminates in the cutting edge of the tool. The sides and apex are smoothed and rounded, while the base is regularly rounded and ground to an edge like that of a gouge, but with the bevel on the inside.

This author states that another specimen, obtained at Old Enterprise, shows clearly that it was detached from the shell by first cutting a groove and then breaking off the fragment. He also gives two views of a small shell celt which, from the exterior markings and the thick

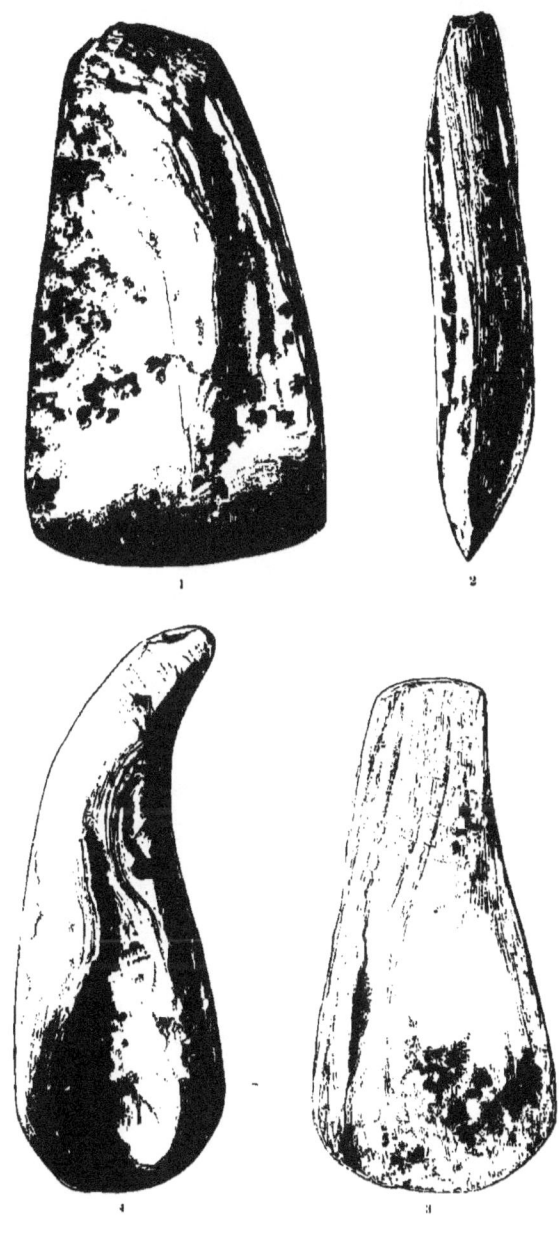

1. Orange Bluff, Fla. (⅔)
2. Orange Bluff, Fla. (⅔)
3. Madison County, Ky. (¼)
4. Barbadoes, W. I. (¼)

SHELL CELTS.

ridge on the inside, is thought to have been cut from the base of a *Strombus gigas*. "The broad end is ground to a blunt edge like that seen in most of the stone chisels from the other States, and the other is ground to a blunt point."

These implements are frequently mentioned by early explorers. In Plate 12 of the "Admiranda Narratio," an Indian is represented[1] with a shell implement, scraping away the charred portions from the interior of a canoe which is being hollowed out by fire. The same implement was employed for removing the bark from the tree trunks used.

Catlin, in speaking of the Klahoquat Indians of Vancouver's Island, says that "a species of mussel-shell of a large size, found in the various inlets where fresh and salt water meet, are sharpened at the edge and set in withes of tough wood, forming a sort of adze, which is used with one hand or both, according to its size; and the flying chips show the facility with which the excavation is made in the soft and yielding cedar, no doubt designed and made for infant man to work and ride in."[2]

Wood, speaking of the Indians of New England, says that "their Cannows be made either of Pine-trees, which before they were acquainted with *English* tooles, they burned hollow, scraping them smooth with Clamshels and Oyster-shels, cutting their out sides with stone-hatchets."[3]

The method of hafting these implements, when used for axes and adzes, was doubtless the same as that employed for stone implements of similar shapes. This is illustrated in Fig. 2, Plate XXVII, the handle being securely fastened by cords or sinews. It will be seen that but one of the specimens mentioned comes from the interior, and that from Madison County, Ky.

SCRAPERS.

The great majority of the scraping implements obtained from the mounds, graves, and shell heaps are simply valves of *Unio* or clamshells, unaltered except by use; yet there is a widely distributed class of worked specimens, which have been altered by making a rough perforation near the center of the valve, and by the grinding down and notching of the edges. A very fine specimen is illustrated in Fig. 3, Plate XXVI. It is formed of the left valve of a *Unio tuberculosus*. It was taken from a mound at Madisonville, Ohio, and is now in the national collection. A similar specimen from the same locality is illustrated in an account of the exploration conducted by the Scientific and Literary Society of Madisonville.[4] I have seen four other fine speci-

[1] De Bry: Collectio Pars 1. "Admiranda Narratio," Plate 12.
[2] Catlin: Indians of the Rocky Mountains and Andes, page 101.
[3] Wood: New England Prospect, p. 102.
[4] Archæological Explorations by the Literary and Scientific Society of Madisonville, Ohio, Part 1, p. 17.

mens from the same locality; all are made of the shell of the *Unio
tuberculosus* (?). It will be seen by reference to Fig. 3 that the posterior
point of the shell is much worn, as if by use, while at the opposite end,
near the hinge, the margin has been slightly notched. The large specimen, figured in the Madisonville pamphlet, as well as all other examples from this locality, are also much worn at the posterior end, and
slightly notched on the anterior margin. The perforations are roughly
made, and nearly one-half an inch in diameter.

I have carefully examined all the specimens of this class within my
reach, probably twenty-five in all, most of which are in the national
collection, and I find them all very much alike. They are from two to
five inches in length, have rude central perforations, and are worn by
use at the posterior point, and notched on the anterior margin. The
blunting of one end by use calls for no explanation, but the purpose of
the perforation is a little obscure. It may have been used for convenience in transportation, but more probably for attaching a handle. On
discovering that a notch had in all cases been made at the upper end, I
became convinced that the latter use was intended. Whether the supposed handle has been long or short, or attached longitudinally or
transversely, I am unable to determine.

In Plate XXVI, Figs. 4 and 5, two methods of hafting are illustrated.
If used for striking, the long handle would be the more suitable, but if
for scraping, dressing skins, scaling fish, or shaping wood or clay, the
handle suggested in Fig. 5 would be the most convenient. The clam-
shell agricultural implements, so frequently mentioned by explorers
along the Atlantic coast, were attached to handles in the manner of
hoes or adzes, as shown in Fig. 2, Plate XXVII. It is possible that the
specimens under consideration may have been hafted in this manner.

A perforated valve of a *Unio gibbosus*, which has probably been used
as a knife or scraper, is shown in Fig. 1, Plate XXVII. It was obtained
from a cave near Nashville, and is now in the national collection.

Another interesting variety of shell implement is shown in Fig. 1,
Plate XXVI. It was obtained from the Oconee River, near Milledge-
ville, Ga., and is made from the left valve of a *Unio rericosus*. Its
perfect state of preservation indicates that it is of quite recent manufacture. A deep, sharply cut groove encircles the beak and hinge of
the shell, and the posterior margins are considerably worn. A few shallow lines have been engraved on the smooth convex surface of the
valve. The position of the groove suggests the method of hafting shown
in Fig. 2.

Fig. 6, Plate XXVI, represents a perforated *Pecten*, which may have
been used as an implement or as part of a rattle. It was collected by
Mr. Webb on the west coast of Florida.

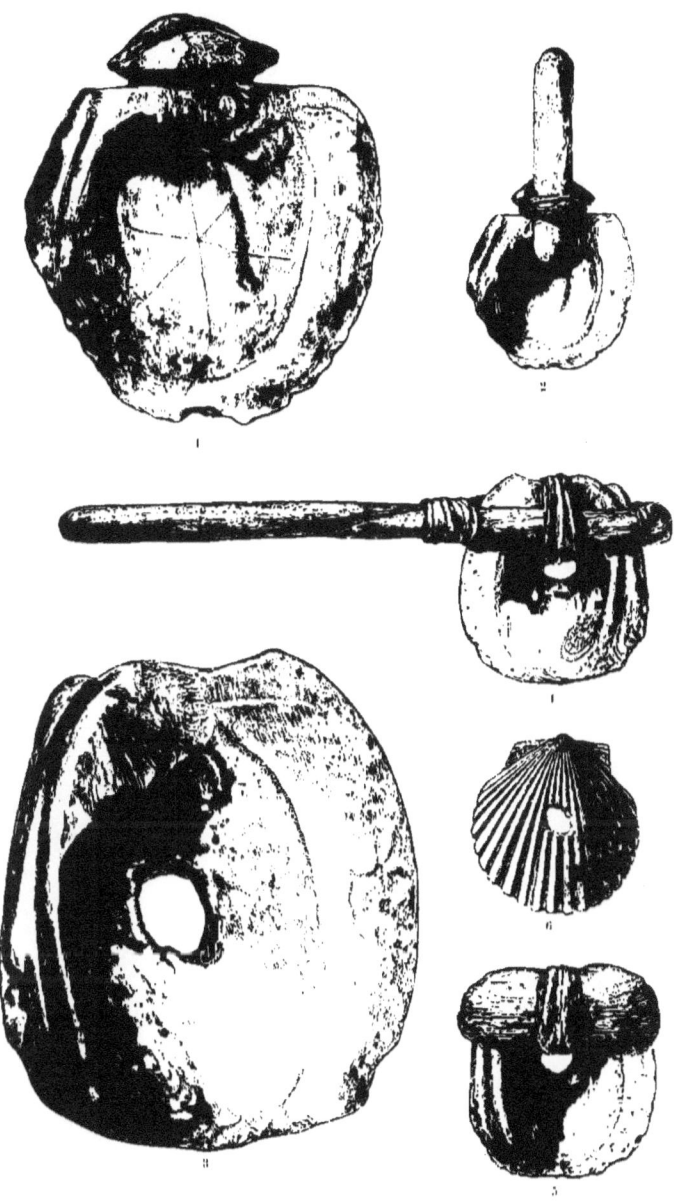

1. Scraper, Georgia. (½)
2. Probable manner of hafting.
3. Implement from a mound, Ohio. (½)
4. Probable manner of hafting.
5. Probable manner of hafting.
6. Perforated pecten, Florida. (½)

SHELL IMPLEMENTS.

AGRICULTURAL IMPLEMENTS.

The first explorers of the Atlantic seaboard found many of the tribes cultivating the soil to a limited extent, corn being the chief product. The methods and appliances were exceedingly primitive, and the implements employed, whether wood, bone, stone, or shell, possess but little interest to art.

Unworked shells, lashed to rude handles, served all the purposes as well as if wrought out in the most fanciful manner. The large, firm valves of clam-shells were most frequently used, as the following extracts will show.

"Before the Indians learned of the English the use of a more convenient instrument, they tilled their corn with hoes made of these shells, to which purpose they are well adapted by their size."[1]

A further reference to this shell is found in Wood's New England Prospect: "The first plowman was counted little better than a Juggler: the *Indians* seeing the plow teare up more ground in a day, than their Clamme shels could scrape up in a month, desired to see the workemanship of it, and viewing well the coulter and share, perceiving it to be iron, told the plowman, hee was almost *Abamocho*, almost as cunning as the Devill."[2]   And again the same author says: "An other work is their planting of corne, wherein they exceede our *English* husband-men, keeping it so cleare with their Clamme shell-hooes, as if it were a garden rather than a corne-field, not suffering a choking weede to advance his audacious head above their infant corne, or an undermining worme to spoile his spurnes."[3]

Other writers make but the most casual mention of this subject. De Bry gives, in Plate XXI, Vol. II, a picture in which a number of natives are engaged in cultivating their fields. In Fig. 3, Plate XXVII, I give an enlarged cut of one of the implements employed; the original drawing has probably been made from memory by the artist, and the cut serves no purpose except to give an idea of the general shape of the implement and to suggest the manner of hafting, if indeed the implement is not made wholly from a crooked stick.

FISHING APPLIANCES.

The use of shell in the manufacture of fishing implements seems to have been almost unknown among the tribes of the Atlantic coast, and with the exception of a few pendant-like objects, resembling plummets

[1] Mass. Hist. Soc. Coll., vol. VII, p. 193.
[2] Wood: New England Prospect, p. 87.
[3] Wood: New England Prospect, p. 106.

or sinkers of stone, nothing has been obtained from the ancient burial mounds of the Mississippi Valley. Hooks of shell, however, are very plentiful in the ancient burial-places of the Pacific coast, and are frequently so well shaped as to excite our admiration. Hooks and other fishing apparatus, in whole or in part made of shell, are extensively employed by the present natives of the Pacific islands and among the numerous tribes of the northwest coast, although bone and ivory are in much higher favor for these purposes.

We cannot say with certainty for what purpose the various sinker-like objects of shell were used. In all cases they are so perforated or grooved as to be suspended by a string; but it is the custom of all savage peoples to employ very heavy pendants as ornaments for the ears or for suspension about the neck, and where stone could be secured for such ordinary uses as the sinking of nets or lines, it seems improbable that objects of shell, which form superb ornaments, would be so employed.

That hooks were used to some extent by the Atlantic coast Indians is proved by the association of bone hooks with other ancient relics. I am not aware that their use has been noticed by early writers, who describe at length, however, the capture of fish by means of arrows, spears, and nets. The ancient Mexican manuscripts contain many drawings showing the use of nets in fishing, but the use of hooks and lines is not suggested.

In the absence of positive proof as to the exact manner in which the plummet-like objects were utilized, I shall for the present follow the custom of the best authors and classify the heavier specimens as sinkers. The smaller specimens will be described as pendant ornaments.

In Fig. 8, Plate XXVIII, a very handsome specimen from a refuse heap on Blennerhasset Island, Ohio River, is shown. It has been cut from the columella of a *Busycon perrersum*, the reverse whorl being indicated by the well-preserved spiral groove, and was suspended by means of a small, well-made perforation near the upper end. The surface is weathered and chalky with age.

Another specimen, from the same locality, differs but slightly from this; the perforated end is broken away; the surface is deeply weathered, and the more compact laminae stand out in high relief.

Two specimens from Sarasota Bay, Fla., resemble these very closely in shape and size; instead of a perforation, however, they are grooved near the upper end. They are made from the columella of the *Busycon perrersum*. One of them is shown in Fig. 9, Plate XXVIII.

It is possible that a number of the small shells usually supposed to be perforated for use as ornaments have been used for sinkers. One such specimen, collected by Professor Velie in Florida, is preserved in the national collection. It is made from an almost entire specimen of a small but compact univalve—a dextral-whorled *Busycon* or a *Strombus*. A shallow groove has been cut near the basal point for the purpose of attaching a line.

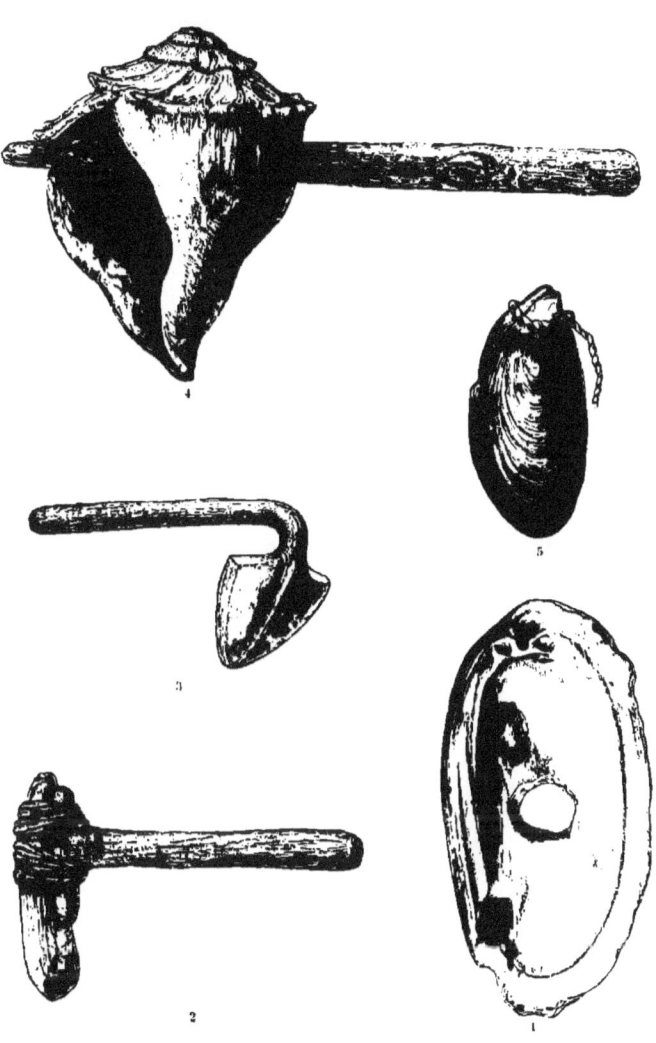

1. Shell implement, Tennessee.
2. Probable manner of hafting celt.
3. Implement illustrated in De Bry.
4. Shell club-head, Florida.
5. Shell implement, Peru.

SHELL IMPLEMENTS.

A fourth specimen, from Florida, is represented by a cast presented by Professor Velie; it is three inches in length and nearly one inch in diameter, and has been derived from the columella of a *Busycon perversum*. It has a broad groove near the upper end, with a long, sloping shoulder, the body being somewhat conical below. Other specimens of similar character have recently been added to the national collection. A grooved specimen of medium size was obtained from a mound at Madisonville, Ohio, and is figured by the explorers.[1] A few smaller specimens come from New York, and others from Kentucky, but they were probably intended for ornaments, and as such I prefer to class them.

From the Pacific coast we have a large number of examples, one of the finest being illustrated in Fig. 7, Plate XXVIII. It is a flattish, somewhat pear-shaped pendant, and has a neatly cut groove near the upper end. It was collected by Bowers on the island of Santa Rosa, Cal., and was probably made from a *Pachydesma* or *Amiantis*.

A new-looking specimen from Santa Barbara, carved from a flat bit of pearly *Haliotis*, represents a fish, the mouth, gills, body, and tail being distinctly shown. It may have been used as a bait.

By far the most interesting examples of fishing implements of ancient date have been obtained from graves in California ; these are well represented in the collections made by Schumacher and Bowers. A number of specimens may be seen in the National Museum; one sinker from this collection has already been described. Fish-hooks, however, constitute the great majority of the specimens, and many of them are of such unprecedented forms that they have been mistaken for ornaments. The marked peculiarity consists in the great width of the body of the hook, and the deeply involuted character of the barbless point, making it seem impossible that a fish should be impaled at all. It may be that this hook was intended only as a contrivance for securing bait, and that the fish, having swallowed this, was unable to disgorge it, and in this way was secured by the fisherman.

In Plate XXVIII, three of these hooks are illustrated. The method of fastening them to the line is not well known, and the form does not suggest it, except in a few cases in which the shaft is enlarged slightly at the upper end. The head is never perforated, but is frequently pointed, and may have been inserted in a head of some other material and secured by means of asphaltum. The fact that portions of this material still adhere to the upper part of the shaft confirms this conjecture. None of these hooks are barbed. Similar hooks of bone, exhibited in the national collection, have barbs on the outside, near the point. Hooks resembling these are used by some tribes to secure the ends of strings of beads.

Prof. F. W. Putnam has described a number of these hooks which belong to the Peabody Museum. The largest is two and three-fourths

---

[1] Archæological Explorations by the Literary and Scientific Society, part II, p. 38, fig. 31.

14 E

inches in length and one inch wide at the middle of the shank. These came from San Clemente, San Miguel, and Santa Cruz islands, and the mainland about Santa Barbara, and are accompanied by stone implements used in their manufacture.[1]

The natives of Tahiti had fish-hooks made of mother of pearl, and every fisherman made them for himself. They generally served for the double purpose of hook and bait. "The shell is first cut into square pieces, by the edge of another shell, and wrought into a form corresponding with the outline of the hook by pieces of coral, which are sufficiently rough to perform the office of a file; a hole is then bored in the middle; the drill being no other than the first stone they pick up that has a sharp corner; this they fix into the end of a piece of bamboo and turn it between the hands like a chocolate mill; when the shell is perforated, and the hole sufficiently wide, a small file of coral is introduced, by the application of which the hook is in a short time completed, few costing the artificer more time than a quarter of an hour."[2]

The specimens illustrated are made from the thicker portions of species of the *Haliotis* or of the valves of the dark purplish *Mytilus californianus*. They are handsome objects, their surfaces being well rounded and polished. In the collection there are specimens which illustrate very well the process of manufacture. A series of these is given in Plate XXVIII. Fig. 1 shows a small fragment broken out roughly from the shell, probably by a stone or shell implement. Fig. 2 shows a similar specimen in which an irregular perforation has been made. In Fig. 3 we see a considerable advance toward completion; the hole has been enlarged by rubbing or filing with some small implement, and the outline approximates that of the finished hook. Figs. 4, 5, and 6 represent typical examples of the completed hooks. These range in size from one-half to three inches in length, the width being but slightly less. The skill acquired in the manufacture of such objects of use is of the greatest importance in the development of art. It is only through the mastery of material thus engendered that the arts of taste become possible.

WEAPONS.

It would hardly seem at first glance that shells or shell substance could be utilized for weapons to any advantage. A close examination, however, of some of the more massive varieties will convince us that they could be made available. The specific gravity of some varieties, such as the *Strombus* and *Busycon*, is equal to that of moderately compact stone, and with their long, sharp beaks they would, with little modification, certainly make formidable weapons.

Dr. Charles Rau seems to have been the first to call attention to the

[1] Putnam, in Explorations West of the 100th Meridian, vol. VII, p. 223.
[2] Cook: Voyage Around the World, 1770, vol. II, p. 212.

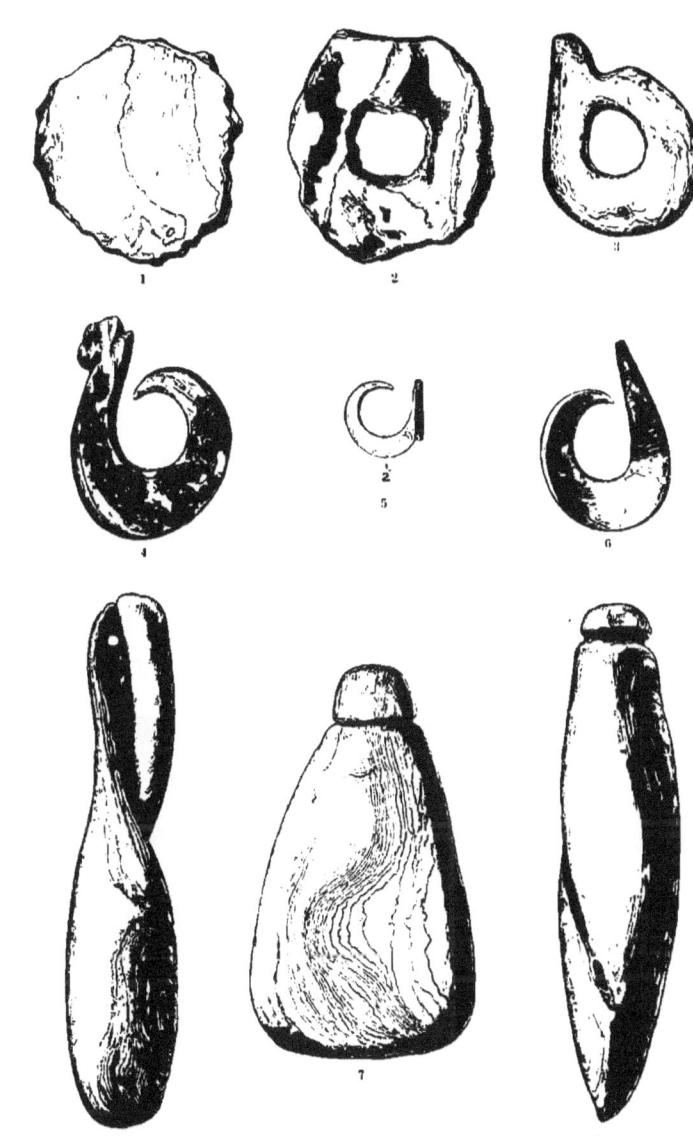

1, 2, 3. Manufacture of hooks.
4, 5, 6. Hooks from graves, California.

7. Pendant or sinker, California.
8, 9. Pendants, Atlantic slope.

SHELL FISHING APPLIANCES.

use of shells as club-heads by the tribes of Florida. In his valuable paper on the archæological collections of the National Museum he gives a very good description, which I copy in full:

"It further appears that the Florida Indians applied shells of the *Busycon perversum* as clubs or *casse-tetes* by adapting them to be used with a handle, which was made to pass transversely through the shell. This was effected by a hole pierced in the outer wall of the last whorl in such a manner as to be somewhat to the left of the columella, while a notch in the outer lip, corresponding to the hole, confined the handle or stick between the outer edge of the lip and the inner edge of the columella. The anterior end of the canal, broken off until the more solid part was reached, was then brought to a cutting edge nearly in the plane of the aperture. A hole was also made in the posterior surface of the spire behind the carina in the last whorl, evidently for receiving a ligature by means of which the shell was more firmly lashed to the handle."[1]

Mention of these objects is also made by Knight in a recent pamphlet, the method of hafting being illustrated.[2]

Professor Wyman, in the Naturalist for 1878, describes and illustrates an object of this class, made from a *Busycon*, which he is inclined to regard as one of the conch-shells said to have been used by the Indians for trumpets. It is presumably from one of the shell heaps on the St. Johns River, Fla.[3]

In Fig. 4, Plate XXVII, I illustrate one of the National Museum specimens. The posterior point is much reduced by grinding, the apex and nodes are somewhat battered, and the whole surface of the shell is worn and discolored. There are about a dozen specimens in the National collection; in nearly all cases they are made from heavy walled specimens of the *Busycon perversum*, and range from three to eight inches in length. They are described as coming from three localities, St. Johns River, Clearwater River, and Sarasota Bay, Fla. All were probably obtained from shell heaps, and although ancient, two of the specimens still retain rude and insignificant-looking handles of wood.

It will be seen from the foregoing that shells have actually been employed as weapons, a use, however, which would probably never have been suggested but for the great scarcity of stone along the southern coast.

TWEEZERS.

A rather novel use of shells by the ancient Indians is mentioned by early writers. The two valves of small mussels or clams were made to do service as tweezers for pulling out their hair.

[1] Rau: Archæological Collection of the National Museum, page 67.
[2] Knight: Savage Weapons at the Centennial Exhibition, page 10.
[3] Wyman: American Naturalist for October, 1878, p. 453.

Adair, speaking of the Choctaws, says that "both sexes pluck all the hair off their bodies with a kind of tweezers, made formerly of clam shells."[1]   Strachey states that shells were used by the Virginian Indians for cutting hair.   Beverly says of the Virginia Indians that they "pull their Beards up by the Roots with Muscle-shells, and both Men and Women do the same by the other Parts of their Body for Cleanliness sake."[2]   Heckewelder states that "Before the Europeans came into the country their apparatus for performing this work consisted of a pair of mussel-shells, sharpened on a gritty stone, which answered the purpose very well, being somewhat like pincers."[3]

Fig. 5, Plate XXVII, reproduced from a plate in the Necropolis of Ancon[4] represents two small *Mytilus* shells pierced at the beak and bound together with a cord.   They were found in one of the ancient graves of Peru, and may have been used for a similar purpose.

[1] Adair: History of the American Indians, p. 6.
[2] Beverly: History of Virginia, p. 140.
[3] Heckewelder's Indian Nations, p. 205.
[4] Reiss and Stübel: Necropolis of Ancon, Plate 83, fig. 17¼.

PINS.

Having studied the application of shell material to the various utilitarian arts, I turn to the consideration of what may, with more or less propriety, be called the arts of taste.

The skill acquired by the primitive artisan in shaping the homely spoon or the rude celt served a good purpose in the more elegant arts, and opened the way to a new and unique field for the development and display of the remarkable art instincts of these savages. It probably required no great skill and no very extended labor to fashion the various utensils and implements of the outer walls of the univalves or the thin valves of clams and mussels; but to cut out, grind down, and polish the columellæ of the large conchs required a protracted effort and no little mechanical skill. Of the various objects shaped from the columellæ, beads are probably the most important; but a large class of pin-shaped articles naturally come first, as they consist of entire or nearly entire columellæ dressed down to the desired shape.

The use of these objects is still problematical. As they are found in most cases deposited with human remains, they were doubtless highly valued. They must have served a definite purpose in well-established and wide-spread customs, as they are found distributed over a district almost co-extensive with that occupied by other shell vestigia of marine origin.

Let us first study the process of manufacture. A considerable number of the larger species of marine univalves have been brought into requisition. Various species of *Busycon, Strombus,* and *Fasciolaria* offer almost equal facilities; the former, however, seems to have been decidedly the favorite, the *Busycon perversum* having furnished at least three-fourths of the columns used. This result may be attributed, however, to the fact that, for reasons already mentioned, the *perversum* was so universally employed for vessels, the axes extracted from these being then ready for further manipulation. The outer case of the shell being somewhat fragile it is probable that the sea has very frequently broken it away, leaving the dismantled columella to be washed ashore in a shape convenient for manufacture or for inland trade. If the demand for these objects was very great, it is to be presumed that on shores where they abound these shells were broken open and the columns extracted for purposes of traffic. The State of Tennessee is found to be the great store-house of these as well as other ancient objects of shell. This is probably owing to two causes: first, that far inland, where they were difficult to procure, and very costly, they were highly esteemed,

213

and hence consecrated to the use of the dead; and, second, the conditions under which they were buried had much to do with preserving them from rapid decay, while on the coast or when exposed to the atmosphere they soon disappeared.

An interesting series of specimens illustrating the various stages of manufacture of articles from the columella is presented in Plate XXIX. In Fig. 1 a section of a *Busycon perversum* is given. The position of the columella and its relations to the exterior parts may be clearly seen. The reverse whorl of the spire will be noticed, and the consequent sinistral character of the groove. Fig. 2 illustrates the extracted columella in its untrimmed state. A similar specimen is shown in Fig. 3, Plate XXXI. It was obtained from the site of an old Indian lodge on the island of Martha's Vineyard. This, with a number of smaller specimens, may be seen in the National Museum. They show no signs of use, and were probably destined for manufacture into pins or beads.

Columellæ in this state are very frequently found in the mounds and graves of the interior States; a majority probably belong to the *Busycons*, but a considerable number are derived from the *Strombidæ*. A few specimens of large size may be seen in the national collection.

Fig. 3 represents a roughly dressed pin, of a type peculiar to the Pacific coast.

Fig. 4 illustrates a completed pin of the form most common in the middle Mississippi province.

Fig. 5 shows a rather rare form of pin, pointed at both ends. Bone pins of this form are quite common.

Fig. 6 represents a nearly symmetrical cylinder.

Fig. 7 illustrates the manner of dividing the cylinders into sections for beads.

In 1881 some very important additions to the National Museum were made, from the mounds of Tennessee. These include a great wealth of objects in shell. From the McMahon mound at Sevierville, Tenn., there are a dozen shell pins, all made from the *Busycon perversum*. The entire specimens range from three to six inches in length; two are fragmentary, having lost their points by decay. In shape these objects are quite uniform, being, however, as a rule, more slender in the shaft than the average pin. The heads range from one-half to one inch in length, and are generally less than one inch in diameter. They are somewhat varied in shape, some being cylindrical, others being conical above. The shaft is pretty evenly rounded, but is seldom symmetrical or straight. It is rarely above one-half an inch in diameter, and tapers gradually to a more or less rounded point. The groove of the canal shows distinctly in all the heads, and may often be traced far down the shaft. In a number of cases the surface retains the fine polish of the newly-finished object, but it is usually somewhat weathered, and frequently discolored or chalky. These specimens were found in the mounds along with deposits of human remains, and generally in close proximity to the head; this fact suggests their use as ornaments for the hair.

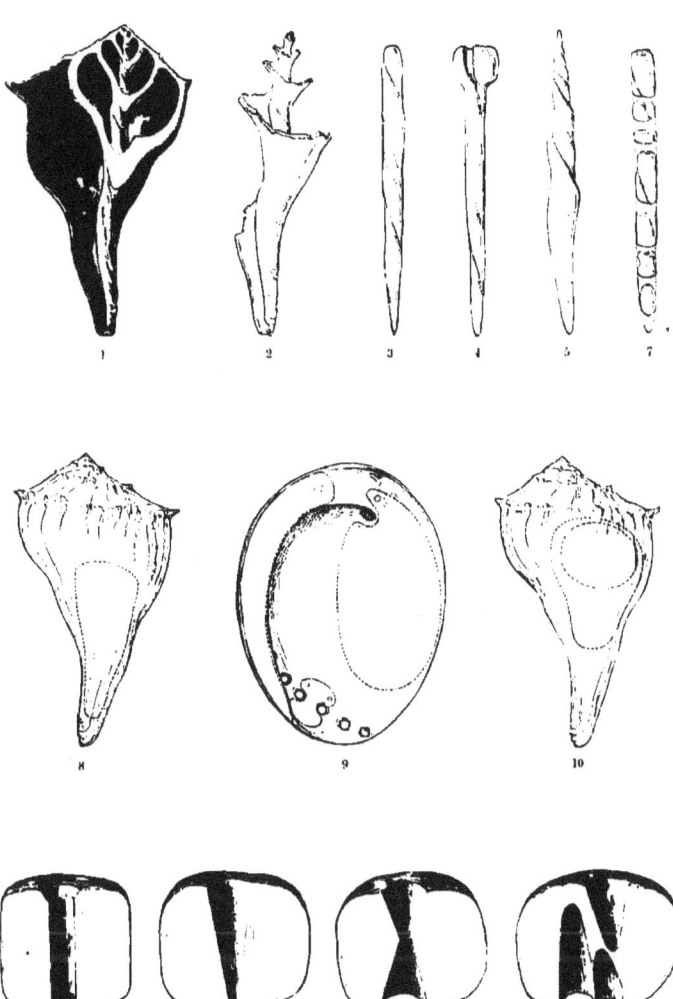

MANUFACTURE OF IMPLEMENTS AND ORNAMENTS.

Two illustrations are given in Plate XXX. Fig. 1 represents a fine example, six and a quarter inches in length. The head is deeply grooved, and is apparently cut from the middle part of the columella, the shaft being formed from the spine-like basal point. The spiral canal, which is clearly defined, makes but one revolution in the entire length of the pin. In Fig. 5 a somewhat similar specimen is represented. Two fine specimens come from a mound on Fain's Island, Tennessee River. The larger one is made from the columella of some heavy shell, probably the *Strombus gigas*. The head is cylindrical, and the shaft large, but imperfect. The smaller is a little more than two inches in length, the head being small and conical, and the point more than usually blunt. Another specimen was obtained from a mound at Taylor's Bend, near Dandridge, Tenn. The head is almost spherical, and the point broken off; the whole surface is new looking and highly polished. A number of bone pins pointed at both ends were obtained from Fain's Island, besides many perforators and other well-made implements of bone.

Prof. C. C. Jones describes[1] a number of shell pins without mentioning localities, stating, however, that such pins have been obtained from a mound on the Chattahoochie River, below Columbus, Ga. He publishes illustrations of two varieties. One, of the ordinary type, is five and a half inches in length, one inch of that distance being occupied by the head, which is an inch and a quarter in diameter. The shank is an inch and a half in circumference, and, while tapering somewhat, is quite blunt at the point. The other is of somewhat rare occurrence, being pointed at both ends. An example of this variety is given in Fig. 4, Plate XXX. They are usually small and short, seldom exceeding three inches in length.

In the national collection there are ten fine pins, obtained by C. L. Stratton from a mound on the French Broad River, fifteen miles above Knoxville, Tenn. Four only are made from the *Busycon perversum*. The largest specimen has a very large, cylindrical head, with an extremely deep groove. The shaft has been at least five inches long, and is nearly one-half an inch in diameter. Another fine specimen is five inches long, very slender, and nearly symmetrical. A small, almost headless pin, not quite one and a half inches in length, is peculiar in having a longitudinal perforation. It has probably been strung as a bead. A fourth specimen is five and three-quarters inches in length. The head is well rounded above, and the shaft tapers gradually to a slender symmetrical point. The other specimens from the same locality are in an advanced stage of decay, the points being entirely destroyed.

The Peabody Museum contains a large number of very fine specimens of this class. The most important of these were obtained from the Brakebill, Lick Creek, and Turner mounds of Tennessee, by the Rev. E. O. Dunning. The largest of these is upward of six inches in length. An unusually symmetrical and well-preserved specimen from the Lick

[1] Jones: Antiquities of the Southern Indians, pp. 234, 518.

Creek mound is nearly seven inches in length. One specimen only in this collection differs from the type already described; this has been made from a dextral-whorled shell; the head is somewhat spherical, but is unusual in having an umbonate projection at the top. It is illustrated in Fig. 6, Plate XXX.

Another small pin, which is about one and one-half inches in length, has a poorly defined head, and would seem useless for the purposes ordinarily suggested for the larger specimens.

A recent collection from Pikeville, Tenn., includes a number of specimens made from the spike-like base of the *Busycon perversum*. They are roughly finished, and taper to a point at both ends. The larger ones are six inches in length and nearly one inch in diameter. All are perforated longitudinally. This perforation is neatly made and about one-eighth of an inch in diameter. In one specimen which has been broken open two perforations may be seen running almost parallel with each other, as if they had been bored from opposite ends and had failed to meet. The length of these perforations is quite remarkable, and it is difficult to understand how, with the primitive tools at the disposal of these people, a uniform diameter could be given throughout. One of these objects is shown in Fig. 3, Plate XXX.

Other States besides Tennessee have furnished a limited number of shell pins. Their occurrence in a mound near Columbus, Ga., has already been mentioned.

The national collection contains a fine specimen from Macon, Ga., collected by J. C. Plant. The Peabody Museum has a number from mounds on the Saint Francis River, Ark. One of these is illustrated in Fig. 8, Plate XXX. They differ from the pins heretofore described, being in all cases unsymmetrical. The shaft is flat and somewhat curved, and joins the mushroom-shaped head near one edge. This results from the peculiar shape of the portion of the shell from which the pin is derived, the head being cut from the peripheral ridge and the shaft from the body below or the shoulder above. Two specimens of this class have recently been obtained from a mound at Osceola, Ark. A profile view of one is shown in Fig. 10, Plate XXX.

A pin of this class, from a burial mound at Black Hammock, Fla., is described and illustrated by Professor Wyman.[1] From the fact of its being perforated at the point, he regards it as a pendant ornament. He states that it is cut from the suture, where a whorl joins the preceding one. In this respect it resembles the specimens from Arkansas. It is made from a *Busycon perversum*.

In the National Museum we have two specimens from Florida. One of these, from Pensacola, is illustrated in Fig. 2, Plate XXX, and is of the ordinary form. The other is a short, broad-headed specimen, illustrated in Fig. 7, Plate XXX.

In the Peabody Museum are two small specimens of the ordinary type,

[1] Wyman, in the American Naturalist, November, 1868, Plate X, p. 455.

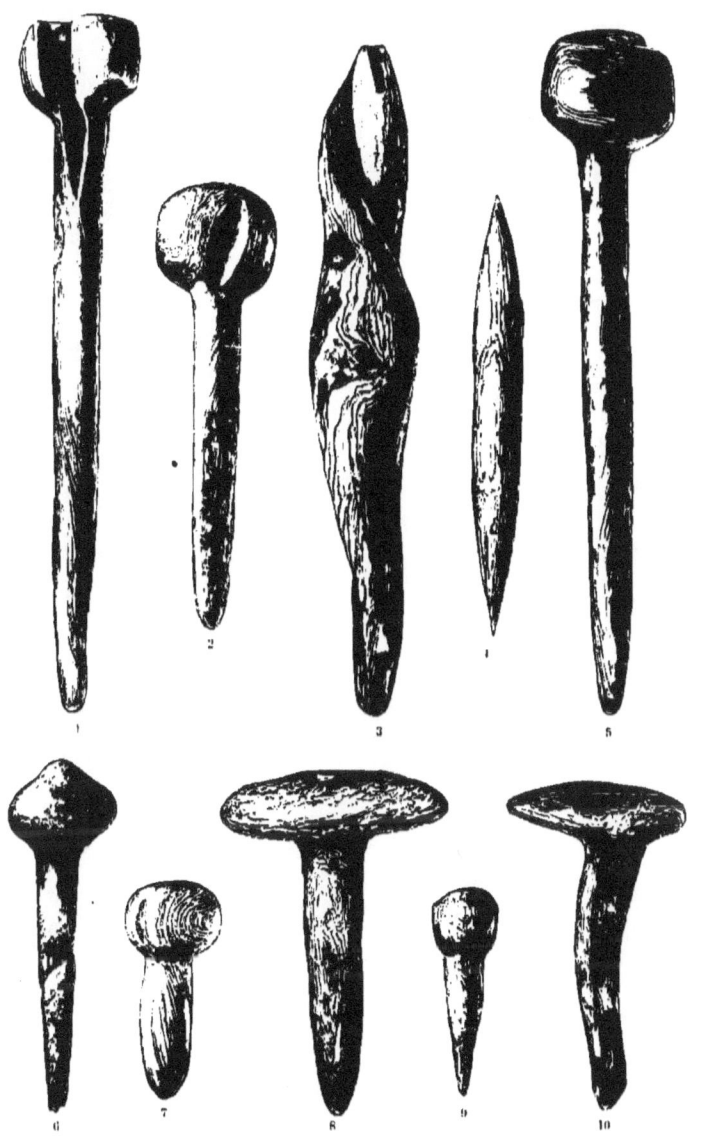

PINS—EASTERN FORMS.

from a mound near Jamestown, Va. One of these, a small, pointed variety, is given in Fig. 9, Plate XXX.

In Volume VI of Schoolcraft's Indian Tribes, a pin, probably of shell, is shown in a plate illustrating relics from South Carolina.

A few localities have furnished bone, stone, and clay pins similar to these in shape. Specimens of the latter may be found both in the National and Peabody museums. They were probably intended as stoppers for bottle-shaped earthen vessels. Bone pins are generally headless, and have in most cases been intended as implements for perforating and for sewing. Mr. Schumacher found a pin-like object of bone on the island of San Clemente, Cal. It resembles the shell pins pretty closely, having a somewhat spherical head. It is figured by Professor Putnam in a recent work.[1]

As already stated, the exact uses to which these pins were applied by the mound-building tribes are unknown; various uses have been suggested by archaeologists. The favorite idea seems to be that they were hair-pins, used by the savages to dress and ornament the hair. It would seem that many of them are too clumsy for such use, although when new they must have been very pretty objects. The shorter and headless varieties would certainly be quite useless. Similar objects of bone or ivory, often tastefully carved, are used by the natives of Alaska for scratching the head, although it seems improbable that this should have been their most important function.

Professor Dall suggests that some of the shell pins may have been used as were the "blood-pins" of the Indians of the northwest coast. When game is killed by an arrow or bullet, the pin is inserted in the wound, and the skin drawn and stitched over the flat head, so that the much valued blood may be prevented from escaping. A small, very tastefully carved specimen of these pins is given in Plate XXXI, Fig. 4. It was obtained from the Indians of Oregon. A similar specimen comes from San Miguel Island, Cal.

It is possible that they may have served some purpose in the arts or games of the ancient peoples; yet when we come to consider the very great importance given to ornaments by all barbarians, we return naturally to the view that they were probably designed for personal decoration.

From the Pacific coast we have shell pins of a very different type They also are made from the columellæ of large marine univalves, and were probably used as ornaments, doubtless to a great extent as pendants. These objects have been obtained in great numbers from the ancient graves of the California coast, at Santa Barbara, at Dos Pueblos, and on the neighboring islands of Santa Clara, Santa Catalina, San Clemente, and Santa Rosa. Professor Dall is of the opinion that the shell mostly used is the *Purpura crispata*, the smaller specimens probably being derived from the *Mitra maura*.

---

[1] Putnam, in Surveys West of the 100th Meridian, Vol. VII, p. 230.

Such a very concise description of these objects is given by Prof. F. W. Putnam in a recent paper that I beg leave to quote it here, omitting his references to figures: "A columella was ground down to the required size and shape, and made into a pendant by boring a hole through the larger end. In order to make this pendant still more attractive, the spiral groove is filled with asphaltum, or a mixture of that material and a red pigment. Sometimes the spiral groove was so nearly, or even wholly, obliterated in the process of grinding the columella into shape as to make it necessary to enlarge or even recut the groove in order to make a place for the much-loved asphaltum." Another form, made from another shell, is described, the whorls of which are "loose and open, so that a natural tube exists throughout the length of the spire; at the same time the spiral groove in the central portion is very narrow; consequently it has to be artificially enlarged for the insertion of the asphaltum, which thus winds spirally about the shell. As the natural orifice at the large end of the shell seems to have been too large for properly adjusting and confining the ornament as desired, this difficulty was overcome by inserting a small shell of *Dentalium*, or by making a little plug of shell, which is carefully fitted and bored." [1]

The national collection contains upward of fifty of these pins, which come from ancient graves at Santa Barbara and Dos Pueblos, Cal., and from the islands of Santa Cruz and San Miguel. These vary in length from one to five inches, the well-finished specimens seldom reaching one half an inch in diameter. At the upper end they round off somewhat abruptly to an obtuse point, but taper to a sharp point at the lower end, something like a cigar. Two fine examples are shown in Figs. 1 and 2, Plate XXXI. All show the spiral groove, and nearly all have portions of the asphaltum remaining. The columellæ from which they are made may be to some extent naturally perforated, but are certainly not sufficiently so to permit the ready passage of a cord. The points are seldom sharp, and are often broken off. A bit of *Dentalium* inserted into the perforation and set with asphaltum helps to enforce the point and to guard against further breakage. The larger specimens are seldom perforated transversely at either end, while the smaller ones are almost always perforated at the larger end, which is slightly flattened. A good example is shown in Fig. 5, Plate XXXI.

A peculiar bulb-pointed specimen is illustrated in Fig. 6, Plate XXXI. The bulb is made from the upper end of the columella. There are six of these pins in the collection.

The consideration of these pins leads naturally to the presentation of other classes of objects manufactured from the columellæ of marine univalves among which beads are the most numerous and important.

[1] Putnam, in Surveys West of the 100th Meridian, Vol. VII, p. 259.

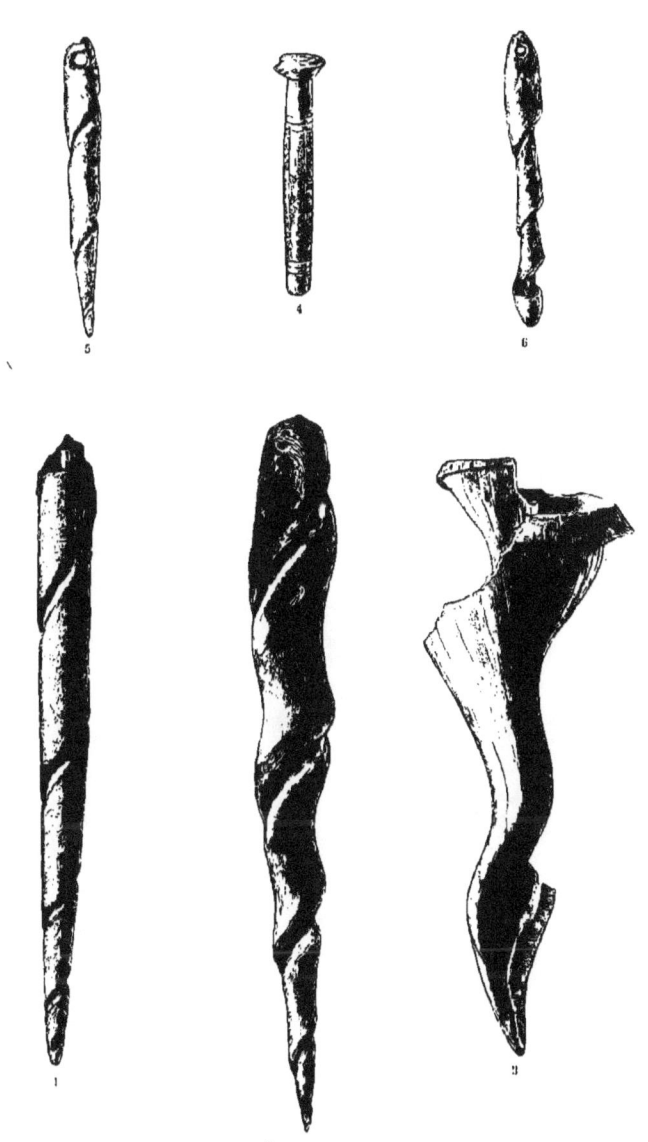

1. Shell pin from San Miguel Island.
2. Shell pin from Dos Pueblos, Cal.
3. An untrimmed columela.
4. Bone pin from Oregon.
5. Shell pin from San Miguel Island.
6. Shell pin from San Miguel Island.

PINS—PACIFIC COAST FORMS.

BEADS.

I shall not attempt within the limits of this paper to give more than an outline of this important division of my subject.

The use of beads seems to have been almost universal with peoples of all times and of all grades of culture, and the custom of wearing them is a relic of barbarism that promises to be carried a long way into the future. All suitable natural objects have been brought into requisition—animal, vegetable, and mineral. Shells from the sea, precious stones from the mountains, and fruits from the forest have been utilized; and claws of birds, teeth of animals, and even the nails of the human hand have been worked into ornaments to gratify the barbaric vanity of the "untutored savage." The flinty substance of the shells of mollusks has been a favorite material at all times and with all peoples. Especially is this true of the shell-loving natives of North America, among whom shell beads have been in use far back into the prehistoric ages, and who to-day, from Oregon to Florida, burden themselves to discomfort with multiple strings of their favorite ornament; and this, too, without reference to their value as money or their service as charms. On the necks of brawny and unkempt savages I have seen necklaces made of the highly glazed *Oliva*, or of the iridescent nacre of the pearly *Haliotis*, that would not shame a regal wardrobe, and have marveled at the untaught appreciation of beauty displayed.

Beads made of shell may have three divisions based upon derivation, and three based upon function.

First, they consist of all smaller varieties of natural shells, pierced for suspension, or only slightly altered, to add to beauty or convenience; second, they are made of the shells of bivalves and the outer walls of univalves; or, third, of the columellæ of the larger univalves cut to the desired sizes, and shaped and polished to suit the savage taste.

As to function, they may be classed as personal ornaments, as money, and as material for mnemonic records.

PERFORATED SHELLS.

Under this head I shall examine briefly the manner of piercing or altering the smaller varieties of shells preparatory to stringing. The multitudes of perforated shells exhumed from the graves of our ancient tribes afford a fruitful field of study, and our large collections of more recent specimens serve to illustrate the manner in which they were employed.

In Plate XXXII illustrations are given showing the various methods of manipulation and perforation. In North America the *Marginella*, the *Oliva*, and the *Cyprea* seem to lead in importance.

Fig. 1 represents an *Oliva*, the apex of which has been broken away and the rough edge ground down, producing a passage for a thread, which may be introduced through the natural aperture below. This is a common method of perforation in many widely separated districts, and with a considerable variety of shells. The specimen figured is from a mound in Cocke County, Tenn. It is an *Oliva literata* from the Atlantic coast.

Fig. 2 shows a very usual method of treating small univalves. The most prominent part of the lower whorl is ground down until the wall is quite thin, and a small round hole is then drilled through it. The specimen illustrated is a large *Olivella biplicata*, obtained from the island of Santa Rosa, Cal.

Figs. 3 and 4 illustrate specimens from Mexico. Some thin-bladed implement, probably of stone, has been used to saw a slit or notch in the first convolution of the shell near the inner lip. Fig. 3 has one of these perforations, and Fig. 4 has two. The shell is the *Oliva literata*, from the Atlantic coast.

Fig. 5 is simply one-half of an *Olivella biplicata* with the interior parts extracted. It is made by cutting the shell longitudinally and drilling a central perforation. The specimen figured is from San Miguel Island, Cal.

Fig. 6 illustrates the manner of breaking out a disk preparatory to making a bead. This disk, when perforated, is frequently used by the Indians of the Pacific coast without additional finish.

Fig. 7 shows two examples of beads made from small specimens of the *Olivella biplicata;* both extremities are ground off, leaving a rather clumsy cylinder. The originals are from graves on the island of Santa Rosa. Such beads are frequently worn at the present time.

One of the specimens shown in Fig. 8 is from a grave in Monroe County, New York, and the other is from a mound in Perry County, Ohio. The shell is the *Marginella conoidalis*, which has a wide distribution in the ancient burial places of the Atlantic slope. In making the perforation the shoulder is often ground so deeply as to expose the entire length of the interior spiral.

Fig. 9 represents a perforated *Cerrithidea sacrata*, from Santa Rosa Island, Cal. The method of perforating employed is a usual one with small shells of this form. Similar specimens come from many parts of the United States. Beads of this and the preceding variety are said to have constituted the original wampum of the Atlantic seaboard.

Fig. 10 illustrates a rude bead made from the spire of a univalve, probably a small specimen of *Busycon perversum*. Most of the body of the shell has been removed and a perforation made near the border. Three of these specimens were found in a burial mound at Murphysboro, Ill.

Fig. 11 illustrates a perforated *Cyprea* from the Pacific coast. This is a recent specimen which illustrates an ancient as well as a modern method of perforation.

Fig. 12 shows a rather peculiar method of treating *Cyprea* shells by

PERFORATED SHELL BEADS.

(½)

the tribes of the Pacific coast and the Pacific islands. The prominent
part of the back is cut or ground away, and the columella is partially
or wholly removed, a passage the full size of the natural aperture being
thus secured. This is also an ancient as well as a modern method of
treatment.

Small bivalve shells are prepared for stringing by drilling one or
more holes in the center or near the margin, according to the manner
in which they are to be strung. Such beads have been in almost universal use by primitive peoples, both ancient and modern.

Shells with natural perforations, such as the *Fissurellas* and *Dentalia*,
are extensively employed by the west coast peoples, and foreign varieties
of the latter have been largely imported by Europeans, and from very
early times have been used by the tribes of all sections. The natural
perforation of the *Fissurella* is often artificially enlarged, and additional perforations are made near the margin. Examples may be seen
in Plate XLIX.

I shall include under the head of beads all small objects having a
central or nearly central perforation, made for the purpose of stringing
them in numbers. In shape, they range from straw-like cylinders, three,
four, and even five inches long, with longitudinal perforations, to thin,
button-like disks, two or more inches in diameter. In general the cylinders are made from the columellæ of univalves, and the disks from
the outer walls of the same, or from the shells of bivalves. Of course,
there are forms that fall under no classification, such as disks with perforations parallel with the faces, or cylindrical forms with transverse
perforations, while many small, pendant-like objects, of varied shapes,
are strung with the beads, and might be classed with them; but these
are exceptions, and can be described along with the classified objects
most nearly resembling them.

The grinding down and the perforating of natural shells is easily
accomplished, so that any savage could afford to decorate his person
with this jewelry in profusion. But the class of beads illustrated in
Plates XXXIII, XXXIV, and XXXV could not have been made without the expenditure of much time and labor, and doubtless owe their
existence, in a measure, to mercenary motives. As they were made
from the walls or columellæ of massive shells, they must have been
broken or cut out, ground smooth about the edges, and perforated; this,
too, with most primitive tools.

DISCOIDAL BEADS.

In shape discoidal beads range from the concavo-convex sections of
the curved walls of the shell to totally artificial outlines, in such forms
as doubly-convex disks, cylinders, and spheroids. In size the disks
vary from very minute forms, one-tenth of an inch in diameter and one-
thirtieth of an inch in thickness, to two inches in diameter and nearly
one-half an inch in thickness. The thickness of the finished beads is

governed in a great measure by the thickness of the shell from which they are manufactured.

The *Venus mercenaria* of the Atlantic coast and the heavier *Unios* of the Mississippi Valley give a general thickness of from one-eighth to three-eighths of an inch, while others, such as the heavy clams of the Pacific, are very much thicker. The walls of univalves, especially near the base, are often extremely heavy, while the smaller varieties of shells furnish specimens of wafer-like thinness.

In Plate XXXIII a series of beads of this class is given, beginning with the smaller disks and ending with those of large, though not the largest, size.

In fig. 1 I present two views of a minute disk, obtained, with many others of similar shape and size, from a mound on Lick Creek, Tenn. The perforations in these specimens, as well as in most of those that follow, are bi-conical, and sufficiently irregular in form to indicate that they are hand-made. Beads of this general appearance have been found in a multitude of graves and mounds, distributed over a large part of North as well as of South America. A vast majority of these beads are doubtless of aboriginal make, as they are found in the oldest mounds.

Fig. 2 represents a minute form from Santa Cruz Island, Cal. The peripheral surface is ornamented with a net-work of incised lines.

Fig. 3 illustrates a small cylindrical bead, with large perforation, from a mound near Prairie du Chien, Wis. It was found, with a number of others, near the neck of the skeleton of a child.

Fig. 4 represents a small spheroidal bead from the great mound near Sevierville, Tenn.; it is neatly made and well preserved.

Figs. 5 and 6 illustrate specimens of roughly finished concavo-convex disks, much used by both ancient and modern tribes of California, Arizona, and New Mexico.

I essayed at one time to purchase a long necklace of these homely ornaments from a Navajo Indian in Arizona, but soon discovered that it was beyond my reach, as my best mule was hardly considered a fair exchange for it. These beads are made from the *Olira* chiefly, but to some extent from small bivalves.

This bead is not common in the mounds of the Mississippi Valley, but is used by many modern savages. It seems to be the form called, by the Indians of Virginia, "roenoke," which, according to Beverly, is made of the cockle-shell, broken into small bits, with rough edges, and drilled through in the same manner as beads.

Fig. 7 represents a smoothly cut bead of medium size, said to have been obtained from a grave at Lynn, Mass. It has been cut from the curved wall of some large univalve, and is very similar to modern specimens in use over a greater part of the United States.

Fig. 8 belongs to a necklace brought from the northwest coast, and is very much like the specimen shown in Fig. 7.

Fig. 9 is a well-made specimen from Sevierville, Tenn. The sides are

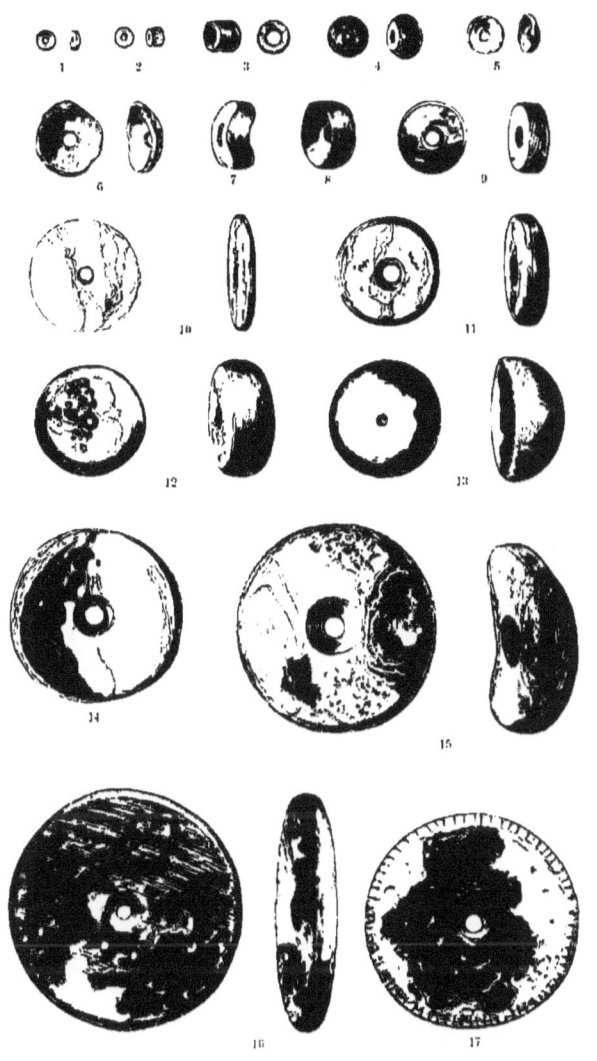

DISCOIDAL BEADS.

(⅓)

ground perfectly flat and the edges are well rounded. The shell is very
compact, and well preserved, and bears a close resemblance to bone or
ivory.

Fig. 10 represents a thin, fragile disk, from a mound in Southern Illinois. It is made of a *Unio*, and separates into thin sheets or flakes, like
mica.

Figs. 11 and 12 illustrate two compact, nearly symmetrical specimens
from a mound at Paint Rock Ferry, Tenn.

Fig. 13 is from the same locality, and is hemispherical in shape.

Fig. 14 represents a button-like disk, with large conical perforation,
from a mound at Paint Rock Ferry, Tenn. It has probably been made
from the wall of a large marine univalve.

The fine specimen shown in Fig. 15 comes from a mound in Cocke
County, Tenn., and is unusually well preserved. It is very compact,
having the appearance of ivory, and has probably been made from the
basal portion of a large univalve. The perforation is extremely large,
and is conical, having been bored entirely from one side.

Figs. 16 and 17 represent two fine specimens from California. They
are nearly symmetrical, the faces being flat or slightly convex. The
smaller one has been coated with some dark substance—the result,
probably, of decay—which has broken away in places, exposing the
chalky shell. The edges are ornamented with shallow lines or notches.
Such disks, when used as ornaments, probably formed the central piece
of a necklace, or were fixed singly to the hair, ears, or costume. As
long as these larger specimens retained the color and iridescence of the
original shell, they were extremely handsome ornaments, but in their
present chalky and discolored state they are not prepossessing objects.

This plate will serve as a sort of key for reference in the study of
beads of this class, as the specimens are typical.

MASSIVE BEADS.

Beads made from the columellæ of univalves have generally a number
of distinguishing characteristics. They are large and massive, and
rarely symmetrical in outline, being sections of roughly dressed columns.
They are somewhat cylindrical, and often retain the spiral groove as
well as other portions of the natural surface. In cases where the form
is entirely artificial they may be distinguished by the sinuous character
of the foliation. The perforation is nearly always with the axis of the
bead, and is in most cases bi-conical. In Plate XXIX a series of cuts
is given which illustrates the various methods of perforation and shows
very distinctly the differences between the rude work of savages and the
mechanically perfect work of modern manufacturers. Beads of this class
are more decidedly aboriginal in character than those of any other group,
and are without doubt of very ancient origin. They are widely distributed, and have been found in graves and mounds covering an area

outlined by Massachusetts, Canada West, Minnesota, Missouri, and the Gulf and Atlantic coasts.

Figs. 1, 6, 7, 11, and 14 of Plate XXXIV represent typical specimens of this class. In every case they are considerably altered by decay, rarely retaining any of the original polish. All come from ancient burial mounds, some of the interments of which probably antedate, while others post-date, the coming of the whites.

The bead shown in Fig. 1 is made from the columella of a *Busycon perversum*. It is a rude, tapering cylinder, with rounded ends and deep spiral groove. The perforation is bi-conical and somewhat irregular. This, with many similar beads, made of both dextral and sinistral shells, was associated with human remains in the great mound at Sevierville, Tenn.

The bead illustrated in Fig. 6 has been made from the column of some dextral whorled shell. It was obtained from a mound on Lick Creek, East Tenn. It is a typical specimen of average size, and illustrates very well the large collection of this class of relics made by Dr. Troost.

Fig. 7 was obtained from a mound at Franklin, Tenn. It is cut from the columella of a *Busycon perversum*, and is of the usual form, being a heavy, short cylinder, rounded at the ends until it is somewhat globular. The perforation is very large, and has been made almost entirely from one end. The surface is much weathered, the firmer *laminæ* being distinctly relieved. Other specimens from the same locality are much smaller.

Fig. 11 is from a grave in an ancient cemetery at Swanton, Vt., and is similar to the preceding, having been cut, however, if correctly represented, from a dextral whorled shell. The cut is copied from a paper by G. H. Perkins.[1]

Fig. 14 illustrates a very large specimen of these beads from the Lick Creek Mound, East Tenn. The surface is encrusted, stained, and decayed. It has been made from the broad beak of a *Strombus* or dextral whorled *Busycon*. The perforation is symmetrical and bi-conical. Specimens upwards of two inches in length and one and one-fourth in width come from the same place. The larger perforations are three-eighths of an inch in diameter at the ends and quite small in the middle.

Fig. 12 represents a large bead of symmetrical outline, made from the columella of a *Busycon perversum*. The shape is artificial, with the exception of a small portion of the spiral canal. The surface retains much of the original polish, but exfoliation has commenced on one side. The perforation is about three-sixteenths of an inch in diameter at the ends and one-sixteenth in the middle. There is a slight offset where the perforations meet. It is from a burial mound at Harrisburg, Ark.

The bead shown in Fig. 9 is one of a large number obtained from a

[1] Perkins, on An Ancient Burial-Ground in Swanton, Vt., Proceedings of the American Association, 1873.

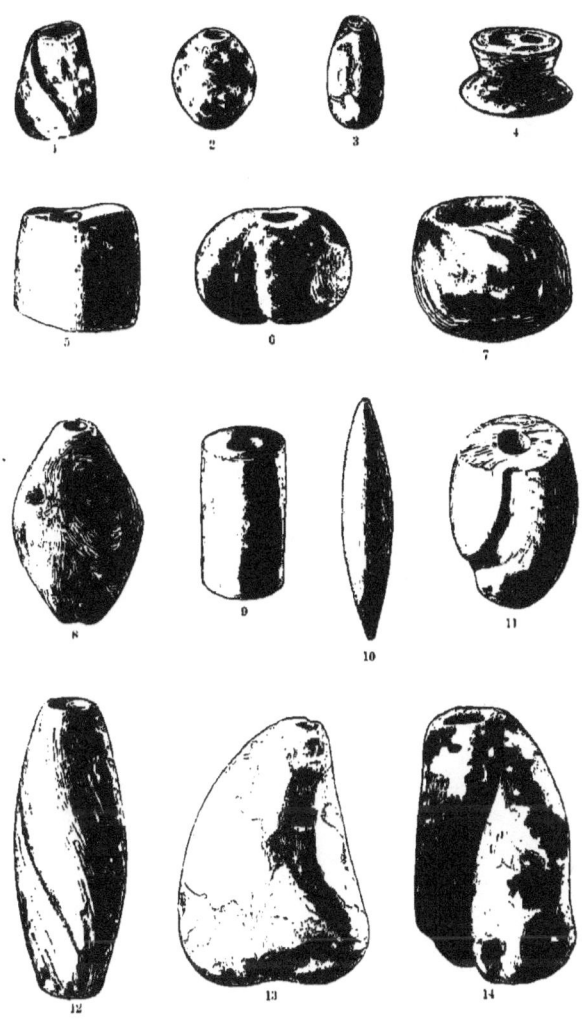

MASSIVE BEADS AND PEARLS.

(1)

mound at East St. Louis, Ills. It is a symmetrical, well-polished cylinder. The small portion of the spiral groove which remains indicates that it is derived from a *Busycon perversum*. The perforation is neatly made and doubly conical in shape. The symmetry, finish, and fine condition of this bead lead to the suspicion that it may be of recent manufacture. Its form is by no means a common one among ancient mound relics.

The bead represented in Fig. 10 is described and illustrated by Squier and Davis.[1] This, with many similar specimens, was taken from a mound in the Ohio Valley. It is made from the columella of some marine univalve, and is well wrought and symmetrical.

Fig. 5 is a flattish, highly polished bead from Monroe County, New York. The material, which resembles ivory, may have been obtained from the tusk of some animal. It is slightly concave on one side and convex on the other. The perforation is neatly made and of uniform diameter throughout.

In Fig. 4 I present a bead of unusual shape; it is made from the basal portion of some heavy univalve. The axis and perforation are at right angles to the plane of lamination. The middle portion of the bead has been excavated, producing a form resembling a labret or lip-block, in common use by many tribes. It is from a mound on French Broad River, Tenn. We have a bead of similar shape, but which has a lateral perforation, from a mound at Nashville, Tenn.

Fig. 2 illustrates a spheroidal bead obtained from an ancient grave on Santa Rosa Island, Cal. The form is unusually symmetrical and the perforation neatly made, being small, doubly conical, and slightly countersunk at one end. The surface is smooth and retains a little of the original purplish hue of the shell, probably a *Heanites giganteus*. Others of the same shape from this locality exhibit like characteristics. A few similar specimens come from San Miguel Island.

Another large specimen from this locality is shown in Fig. 8. It is somewhat flat, and is quite wide in the middle portion, tapering rapidly towards the ends. The perforation is small and regular. The lines of foliation are distinctly marked, but are not sufficiently characteristic to indicate the part of the shell from which the bead is derived.

Pearls.—Two of the most remarkable beads in the national collection are illustrated in Figs. 3 and 13. The latter is an enormous pearl, probably derived from the *Haliotis Californianus*. It is somewhat pear-shaped, the base being rounded and the apex a little bent. The transverse section is subtriangular. Having been buried for an unknown period in the soil or sand, it has suffered greatly from decay, and has probably lost considerably by exfoliation. The thin, chalky lamellæ come away readily in concentric scales, exposing the iridescent *nacre* beneath. The perforation is about one-sixteenth of an inch in diameter, and seems to pass through a natural cavity in the interior of the pearl. The smaller specimen given in Fig. 3 is in many respects similar to the

[1] Squier and Davis: Ancient Monuments of the Mississippi Valley, p. 232.

15 E

large one. Another, of about the same size as Fig. 3 bears quite a marked resemblance to a lima bean, and is pierced laterally, giving a button like appearance.

These specimens were obtained from graves on San Miguel Island, by Stephen Bowers.

TUBULAR BEADS.

In Plate XXXV I have arranged a number of cylindrical beads, together with a few others of unclassified form.

Figs. 1 and 2 illustrate the most common form of the ancient wampum, the white example being made from the columella of a small univalve, and the dark one from the purple portion of a *Venus mercenaria*. The specimens represented belong to the celebrated "Penn belt," preserved in the rooms of the Historical Society of Pennsylvania.

It is not known positively that beads of this particular shape were employed in pre-Columbian times; but it is certainly one of the earliest historical forms, and one which has been manufactured extensively by the Indians as well as by the whites. They may be found both in very old and in very recent graves, in widely separated parts of the United States and British America, and have always formed an important part of the stock of the Indian trader.

Figs. 3 and 4 represent a very large class of Pacific coast forms. These are from the island of San Miguel. They are simple white cylinders, with somewhat irregular bi-conical perforations. Many examples may be found which taper slightly toward the ends. They are coated with a rusty-looking deposit, which breaks away easily, exposing the chalky substance of the shell. They range from one-half to three inches in length, and from one-eighth to three-eighths in diameter. They are probably made from the thick valves of the *Pachydesma crassatelloides* or the *Amiantis callosa*. They were probably used as beads for the neck and as pendant ornaments for the ears. The longer specimens may have been worn in the nose. It is also said that beads of this class were used as money.

Fig. 5 illustrates a very long, tubular bead found at Piscataway, Md. It has been made from the columella of some large univalve. It is four and a half inches long and one-fourth of an inch in diameter. The surface is smooth, but a little uneven, and the ends taper slightly. The perforation which has apparently been made from both ends, as there is an offset near the middle, is quite regular, though slightly enlarged near the ends.

A large number of beads of the class illustrated in Fig. 6, Plate XXXV, were obtained from the ancient graves of San Miguel Island, Cal. They have been made from one of the large bivalve shells of the Pacific coast, probably the *Pachydesma crassatelloides*. The curvature of the bead is the result of the natural curve of the valve from which it is fashioned. The larger specimens are nearly five inches in length. In the middle portion they are three-eighths of an inch in diameter. They taper gradually towards the ends to the size of the perforation,

1, 2. Beads from the Penn Belt.
3, 4. Pacific coast forms.
5. Bead from Maryland.
6. A Pacific coast form.
7. A Pai-Ute nose ornament (bone).

8. Bead made from a Haliotis.
9, 10, 11. Beads made from hinge of Henuites.
12. Bead made from a Dentalium.
13. Bead from mound, Tenn.

BEADS.

(1)

which averages about one-sixteenth of an inch. The curvature of the bead is so great that there has been much difficulty in making the perforations from opposite ends meet, and none of the larger specimens will permit the passage of a wire, although the perforations lap considerably and water passes through quite freely. It will be observed that the surface of these objects is coated with a dark, rough film, which, when broken away, exposes the natural shell. Such beads may have been used as nose ornaments, but more probably formed parts of some composite ornament for the neck or ear.

Fig. 7 represents a bone nose ornament obtained from the Pai-Ute Indians by Professor Powell. Its shape is not unlike that of the curved bead just described.

The large rude bead given in Fig. 8 is made from the thick lip or rim of the *Haliotis Californianus*. This, with a number of similar specimens, was obtained from an ancient grave at Dos Pueblos, Cal. The perforations are all large and symmetrical. In one case the hole has been reduced at the ends by inserting small bits of shell, through which minute passages have been made.

In Figs. 9 and 10 I give two illustrations of a bead of rather remarkable form. A large number of similar specimens have been brought from Dos Pueblos, La Patera, and the islands of San Miguel and Santa Cruz. They are made from the hinge of the *Hinnites giganteus*, a large bivalve, having a delicate purplish tinge. The shape results from the form of the hinge; the curve is the natural curve of the shell; and the notch near the middle of the convex side is the natural pit, often somewhat altered by art to add to the appearance or to assist in completing the perforation. The holes are generally very small, and have been made with much difficulty, owing to the curvature of the bead. Where by accident the perforation has become enlarged at the end, it has been bushed by setting in a small piece of shell. The specimen figured is perforated near the end for suspension, no longitudinal perforation having been attempted.

Fig. 11 shows one of these beads in an unfinished state, the portion of the hinge used being roughly broken out and slightly rounded. We have in the national collection specimens of this class in all stages of manufacture. Professor Haldeman has described and illustrated a number of similar beads. He describes the rounded notch near the middle as artificial, and considers it a device to help out the perforation or facilitate the stringing. Professor Putnam, in the same work,[1] states that the "notches were subsequently filled with asphaltum even with the surface of the shell."

The curved bead illustrated in Fig. 12 is made from a *Dentalium indianorum* (?) by removing the conical point. These shells, either entire or in sections, are much used by the Indians of the northwest, both as ornaments and as a medium of exchange.

---

[1] Putnam, in Surveys West of the 100th Meridian, Vol. VII, p. 266.

BUTTONS.

In Plate XXXVI I present a number of illustrations of a class of relics which have occasionally been mentioned in literature, and which are represented to some extent in our collections. As these objects resemble beads rather more closely than pendants, I shall refer to them in this place, although Mr. Schoolcraft considers them badges of honor or rank, and treats them as gorgets. He describes them as consisting of a "circular piece of flat shell, from one and a half to two inches in diameter, quartered with double lines, having the devices of dots between them. This kind was doubly perforated in the plane of the circle."[1]

In "Notes on the Iroquois," by the same author, we have a much fuller description. He says that "this article is generally found in the form of an exact circle, rarely a little ovate. It has been ground down and repolished, apparently, from the conch. Its diameter varies from three-fourths of an inch to two inches; thickness, two-tenths in the center, thinning out a little towards the edges. It is doubly perforated. It is figured on the face and its reverse, with two parallel latitudinal and two longitudinal lines crossing in its center, and dividing the area into four equal parts. Its circumference is marked with an inner circle, corresponding in width to the cardinal parallels. Each division of the circle thus quartered has five circles, with a central dot. The latitudinal and longitudinal bands or fillets have each four similar circles and dots, and one in its center, making thirty-seven. The number of these circles varies, however, on various specimens. In the one figured there are fifty-two."[2]

Figs. 1 and 2 are copied from Plate 25 of Schoolcraft. The smaller was obtained from an ancient grave at Upper Sandusky, Ohio, and the larger from an Indian cemetery at Onondaga, N. Y. Others have been found at Jamesville, Lafayette, and Manlius, in the latter State. The Indians, according to Mr. Schoolcraft, have no traditions respecting this class of objects, and we are quite in the dark as to their significance or the manner in which they were used.

Mr. W. M. Beauchamp, of Baldwinsville, N. Y., has very kindly sent me sketches of two of these objects. The originals were obtained from an ancient village site at Pompey, N. Y. One is almost a duplicate of the smaller specimen copied from Schoolcraft, but the other, which is illustrated in Fig. 4, Plate XXXVI, presents some novel features. The central portion of the face is occupied by a rosette-like design, which consists of six sharply oval figures that radiate from the center like the spokes of a wheel. These rays are ornamented with a series of oblique lines, arranged in couplets. The margin is encircled by a narrow band, similarly figured. Mr. Beauchamp expresses the opinion that these specimens are of European origin.

The specimen shown in Fig. 3 belongs to a necklace now in the

[1] Schoolcraft : History of the Indian Tribes, Vol. III, p. 79, Plate 25.
[2] Schoolcraft : Notes on the Iroquois, p. 233.

1. New York.
2. New York.
3. Arizona.

4. New York.
5, 6. Sections.
7. Manner of wearing.

RUNTEES.

(†)

national collection. This necklace was obtained from the Indians of
New Mexico by Lieutenant Whipple, and consists of three of these
shell ornaments, together with about fifty small porcelain beads. The
shell beads are strung at regular intervals. The specimen illustrated
is ornamented with a design in minute conical pits, arranged precisely
as are the circlets in the crosses and encircling bands of the New York
and Ohio specimens. The edges and surfaces are much worn by use.
The substance of the shell is well preserved, and has an ivory-like appearance although in the specimen shown in the cut the lamination
of the shell is distinctly seen. The perforations in these three specimens are quite symmetrical, and suggest the use of machinery. The
method of perforation is identical in all these specimens, and will be
readily understood by reference to the two sections given in Figs. 5
and 6. All of these specimens are nearly circular; but the regularity of
the outline is in some cases marred by shallow notches produced by
wear at the perforations. This wear has been accelerated by the abrasion of the small beads with which the disks have probably been strung.

It will be noticed that there is quite a close resemblance between
these objects and the "runtees" of the early writers. Beverly gives an
illustration of an Indian boy who is described as wearing a necklace of
these "runtees," which "are made of the Conch Shell, as the Peak is,
only the Shape is flat and like a Cheese, and drill'd Edge-ways."[1] A
portion of this illustration is copied in Fig. 5, Plate XXXVI. It will
be seen by reference to this cut that the manner of stringing corresponds with the method in which the objects under consideration would
have to be strung.

It is probable that the signification of the designs engraved upon
these ornaments will remain forever a matter of conjecture. It cannot
be affirmed that the cross, which occurs on the faces of most of the
specimens, has any particular significance, although it may represent
the points of the compass. That it may have some emblematic meaning is, however, not impossible. I have counted the number of circlets
on all of the specimens with which I am acquainted. The result is
shown in the following table:

	In the cross.		In the circle, ex-clusive of cross.	Total.
	Longitudi-nal arm.	Transverse arm.		
No. 1 (Fig. 1)	10	9	23	41
No. 2 (Fig. 3)	10	12	27	48
No. 3 (Fig. 2)	11	9	23	42
No. 4[1]	9	9	20	37
No. 5[2]	12	11	29	51
No. 6[2]	9	9	20	37

[1] Schoolcraft: Notes on Iroquois, p. 233.   [2] From sketch by Mr. Beauchamp.

The central circlet having been counted with each arm of the cross, the
total number of circlets in each specimen will be one less than the sum
of the three columns.

[1] Beverly: History of Virginia, p. 145, Plate VI.

These circlets may be numerals. The design may be significant of some rank, the badge of a secret order, or the totem of a clan. The general arrangement of the figures upon the face of these disks suggests an incipient calendar.

These beads are doubtless American in origin, as nothing of a similar form, so far as I can learn, occurs in European countries. The fact that they are found in widely separated localities indicates that they were probably used in trade since the advent of the whites. This is possibly some form of bead held in high esteem by tribes of the Atlantic coast when first encountered by the whites who have taken up its manufacture for purposes of trade.

BEADS AS ORNAMENTS.

I have already spoken casually of the use of beads for personal ornament, but it will probably be better to enlarge a little upon the subject at this point.

Beads are generally found in the graves of ancient peoples in a loose or disconnected state, the strings on which they were secured having long since decayed. We cannot, therefore, with certainty, restore the ancient necklaces and other composite ornaments; but we can form some idea of their character by a study of the objects of which they were made and the positions held by these objects at the period of exhumation. Much can also be learned by a study of the ornaments of modern peoples in similar stages of culture.

As a rule, the combinations in the pendant ornaments of the ancient American seem to have been quite simple. Being without glass, and practically without metals, they had few of the resources of the modern savage. Their tastes were simple and congruous, not having been disturbed by the debasing influence of foreign innovation, which is the cause of so much that is tawdry and incongruous in the art of modern barbarians.

A curious example of a modern necklace is given by Professor Haldeman,[1] who had in his possession an Abyssinian necklace "composed of European beads, cowries (*Cyprea* shell), a triangular plate of glass, two small copper coins, small spheric brass buttons, cornelian, date-seeds, numerous cloves pierced through the sides, a fragment of wood, a bit of cane, and an Arab phylactery."

Something can be learned of the practices of the ancient Americans in the use of beads and pendant ornaments generally, by a study of the remains of their paintings and sculptures—such, for instance, as may be found in the Goldsborough manuscripts or the superb lithographs of Waldeck, examples of which are given in Plate XLV.

In a number of cases necklaces of the mound-builders have been found upon the necks of skeletons, just as they were placed at the time of burial.

[1] Haldeman, in Surveys West of the 100th Meridian, Vol. VII, p. 268.

Captain Atwater in describing the contents of a mound at Marietta, Ohio, makes the statement that on the breast of a skeleton "lay a stone ornament, with two perforations, one near each end, through which passed a string, by means of which it was suspended around the wearer's neck. On the string, which was made of sinew, and very much injured by time, were placed a great many beads made of ivory or bone."[1]

A similar necklace is described by Mr. Matson, in the Ohio Centennial Report, p. 127. It was found on the skeleton of a little girl, and was so made as to be larger in the center of the neck in front, tapering almost to a point at the middle of the back. On page 129 of the same volume much more varied uses of bead ornaments are suggested. Mr. Matson describes four skeletons, on each of which shell beads were found. In three cases they had been placed about the neck only; in the fourth, nearly thirty yards of beads had been used. There were four strands about the neck, crossing over on the breast and back and passing down between the legs. Strings passed down the legs to the feet, and were also found along the arms and around the wrists.

The arrangement of the various parts of a necklace or string of pendants is found to be much alike the world over, consisting of a strand of beads, small toward the ends and increasing in size toward the middle, where a central bead or pendant of peculiar form or unusual size is placed.

The practices of modern barbarians in the employment of beads as ornaments are extremely varied. They are employed in dressing the hair, in head-dresses and plumes, and pendants to these; as pendants to the hair, ears, nose, and lips; as necklaces and bracelets; as belts for the waist and sashes to be thrown across the shoulders; and as anklets and pendent ornaments to all parts of the costume.

Father Rasles, writing of the Abnaki Indians of Canada in 1723, says: "If you wish to see him in all his finery, you will find he has no other ornaments but beads; these are a kind of shell or stone, which they form into the shape of little grains, some white and others black, which they string together in such a way as to represent different showy figures with great exactness. It is with these beads that our Indians bind up and plait their hair on their ears and behind; they make of them pendants for the ears, collars, garters, large sashes of five or six inches in breadth, and on these kinds of ornaments they pride themselves much more than a European would on all his gold and jewelry."[2]

It is related of the New England Indians that more than a hundred years ago, they "hung strings of money about their necks and wrists, as also upon the necks and wrists of their wives and children. They also curiously make girdles, of one, two, three, four, and five inches thickness, and more, of this money; which, sometimes, to the value of ten pounds or more, they wear about their middle, and as a

---

[1] Atwater: Western Antiquities, p. 85. In the early days of mound exploration shell was usually mistaken for bone or ivory.

[2] Kip: Jesuit Missions, p. 25.

scarf about their shoulders and breasts. Yea, the princes make rich caps and aprons, or small breeches of these beads, thus curiously strung into many forms and figures; their black and white finely mixed together."[1]

It is further recorded that the New England Indians "wore ear-rings and nose-jewels; bracelets on their arms and legs, rings on their fingers, necklaces made of highly polished shells found in their rivers and on their coasts. The females tied up their hair behind, worked bands round their heads and ornamented them with shells and feathers, and wore strings of beads round several parts of their bodies. Round their moccasins they had shells and turkey spurs, to tinkle like little bells as they walked."[2]

The Indian women of the New Netherlands also gave great attention to personal decoration. One writer states that they ornamented the lower border of their skirts "with great art, and nestle the same with strips, which are tastefully decorated with wampum. The wampum with which one of these skirts is ornamented is frequently worth from one to three hundred guilders. * * * Their head-dress forms a handsome and lively appearance. Around their necks they wear various ornaments, which are also decorated with wampum. Those they esteem as highly as our ladies do their pearl necklaces. They also wear bead hand-bands, or bracelets, curiously wrought, and interwoven with wampum. Their breasts appear about half covered with an elegantly wrought dress. They wear beautiful girdles, ornamented with their favorite wampum, and costly ornaments in their ears."[3]

Smith states, in writing of Powhatan, that he found him "reclining proudly upon a Bedstead a foote high, upon tenne or twelve Mattes, richly hung with manie Chaynes of great Pearles, about his necke, and covered with a great Couvering of Rahaughcums,"[4] and the young women who surrounded him wore "a great Chaine of white Beades over their shoulders."[5]

The following is from Wood, whose quaint and graphic descriptions of the New England Indians are always interesting: "But a Sagamore with a Humberd in his eare for a pendant, a black hawk on his occiput for his plume, Mowhackees for his gold chaine, a good store of Wampompeage begirting his loynes, his bow in his hand, his quiver at his back, with six naked Indian spatterlashes at his heels for his guard, thinkes himselfe little inferior to the great Cham; he will not stick to say he is all one with King Charles. Hee thinkes hee can blow down Castles with his breath and conquer kingdomes with his conceit."[6]

Du Pratz, in speaking of the Louisiana Indians, says: "The women's ear-rings are made of the center part of a large shell called bingo, which

[1] Collections of the Massachusetts Historical Society, 1794, Vol. III, pp. 231, 292.
[2] Worsley, View the American Indians, p. 65.
[3] Collections of the New York Historical Society, 1841; vol. 1, 2nd Series, p. 194.
[4] Thought to be raccoon skins.
[5] Smith: True Relation of Virginia, pp. 33, 34.
[6] Wood: New England Prospect, p. 74.

is about the thickness of one's little finger, and there is a hole in the ear about that size for holding it."[1]

Lewis and Clark found the Shoshone Indians of the Upper Missouri using shells of the pearl oyster to decorate the collars of their fur tippets. The children wore beads around their necks; grown persons suspended them in little bunches from the ears, and the collars of the men were formed either of sea-shells from the southwest or from twisted grass with porcupine quills.[2]

Among the Carrier Indians of the Northwest both sexes perforate their noses, and from them the men often suspend an ornament consisting of a piece of an oyster shell or a small piece of brass or copper. The women, particularly those who are young, run a wooden pin through their noses, upon each end of which they fix a kind of shell bead, which is about an inch and a half long, and nearly the size of the stem of a common clay pipe. These beads they obtain from their neighbors, the At-e-nás, who purchase them from another tribe that is said to take them from the sea-shore, where they are reported to be found in plenty.

It is also stated of the same Indians that "the young women and girls wear a parcel of European beads, strung together and tied to a lock of hair directly behind each ear. The men have a sort of collar of the shell beads already mentioned, which they wind about their heads or throw around their necks."[3]

The absurd extreme to which this passion for ornament is carried is well illustrated by an example given by Swan, who, speaking of the tribes north of the Columbia River, says that "some of these girls I have seen with the whole rim of their ears bored full of holes, into each of which would be inserted a string of these shells that reached to the floor, and the whole weighing so heavy that, to save their ears from being pulled off, they were obliged to wear a band across the top of the head."[4]

When, however, beads are found in the graves in quantity, by thousands or tens of thousands, we shall probably have to attribute to them other than ornamental uses.

Captain Tom, of the Nishinam tribe of California, according to Powers,[5] had nearly a half bushel of shell beads and trinkets. One string of these, worn by his wife on special occasions, contained sixteen hundred pieces; but these treasures were hoarded because of their value as money rather than as ornaments.

The wampum belts used by many of the tribes of Indians are known to contain enormous numbers of beads. One of the historical belts kept by the Onondagas among their treasures contains nearly ten thousand beads. The famous belt of William Penn has about three thousand.

[1] Du Pratz: History of Louisiana, p. 364.
[2] Lewis and Clark: Expedition up the Missouri, &c., p. 537.
[3] Harmon's Journal, p. 287.
[4] Swan: The Northwest Coast, p. 158.
[5] Powers: Contributions to North American Ethnology, Vol. III, p. 363.

Sir John Lubbock, in his "Prehistoric Times," expresses surprise at the great number of beads sometimes found, instancing the Grave Creek mound of Virginia, which contained between three and four thousand. This number will, however, appear very insignificant when compared with a collection such as the costume of the great King Philip could have furnished.

Drake relates that Philip had a coat "made all of wampampeag," which, when in need of money, he "cuts to pieces, and distributes it plentifully among the Nipmoog sachems and others, as well to the east-ward as southward, and all round about."[1] By adding to this store of beads the contents of two belts, one of which was nine inches in breadth, and so long that when placed upon the shoulders it reached to the ankles, we conclude that the greatest collection ever taken from a prehistoric mound could not compare for a moment with the treasure of this one historic chieftain.

A great deal of art is shown in the stringing and mounting of beads. The simplest form is a single strand, a twisted string of vegetable fiber, a strip of buckskin, or a bit of sinew being passed through the perfora-tions. Again, rows of strands are placed side by side and fastened at intervals in such a manner as to keep them approximately parallel, or the beads when long are put on equidistant cross strands, the longitu-dinal strands serving to keep them in place; they are also woven into the fabric by being mounted upon one of the strands before twisting. It is also a very usual practice to sew them on strips of cloth or buckskin, patterns being produced by using beads of different colors. The man-ner of stringing in the manufacture of belts will be given in detail under Mnemonic Uses of Beads.

BEADS AS CURRENCY.

It will probably be impossible to prove that the prehistoric peoples of North America employed a medium of exchange in a manner corre-sponding to our use of money. It is a well-known fact, however, that a currency of shell beads was in general use throughout the Atlantic coast region very early in the historic period.

Of all objects within the reach of savage peoples, shells, either in their natural forms or in fragments artificially fashioned for convenience of use, are the best adapted for such a purpose.

In examining the contents of ancient cemeteries and mounds where all objects of value were to some extent deposited, we find no other relics that could have been conveniently used for such a purpose.

It is not probable that objects subject to rapid decay, such as wood, fruits, and seeds, could ever have come into general use for money, although such objects are employed to some extent by savages in dif-ferent parts of the world. The unlimited supply or easy manufacture of these objects would be against their use for this purpose, whereas the difficulty of shaping and perforating the flinty substance of shells would prevent such a plentiful production as to destroy the standard of value.

[1] Drake: Book of Indians, p. 27.

Objects and substances having a fairly uniform value, resulting from
their utilitarian attributes, have been employed by primitive peoples
as standards of value; as, for instance, cattle, in ancient Rome; salt, in
Assyria; tin, in Britain, and cocoa, in Mexico. But such mediums of
exchange are local in use. With these articles this function is only
accidental. The utilization of shells for money would naturally orig-
inate from the trade arising from their use as utensils and ornaments
in districts remote from the source of supply. Yielding in the worked
state a limited supply, and at the same time filling a constant demand,
they formed a natural currency, their universal employment for purposes of ornament giving them a fixed and uniform value. They have
undoubtedly been greatly prized by the ancient peoples, but on the part
of the open-handed savage they were probably valued more as personal
ornaments than as a means of gratifying avaricious propensities.

Lewis H. Morgan, who had access to all the sources of information on
the subject, says that "wampum has frequently been called the money
of the Indian; but there is no sufficient reason for supposing that they
ever made it an exclusive currency, or a currency in any sense, more
than silver or other ornaments. All personal ornaments, and most
other articles of personal property, passed from hand to hand at a fixed
value; but they appear to have had no common standard of value until
they found it in our currency. If wampum had been their currency it
would have had a settled value, to which all other articles would have
been referred. There is no doubt that it came nearer to a currency than
any other species of property among them, because its uses were so
general, and its transit from hand to hand so easy, that everyone could
be said to need it." Yet he admits that "the use of wampum reaches
back to a remote period upon this continent"; and further, that it was
an original Indian notion which prevailed among the Iroquois as early at
least as the formation of the League. He goes on to state that "the
primitive wampum of the Iroquois consisted of strings of a small fresh-
water spiral shell called in the Seneca dialect *Ote ko-á*, the name of
which has been bestowed upon the modern wampum."[1]

Loskiel says that "before the Europeans came to North America, the
Indians used to make strings of wampom chiefly of small pieces of wood
of equal size, stained either black or white. Few were made of muscle,
which were esteemed very valuable and difficult to make: for, not having proper tools, they spent much time in finishing them, and yet their
work had a clumsy appearance."[2]

Hutchinson is of the opinion that "the Indians resident northeastward
of the province of New York had originally no knowledge of this sort of
money or medium of trade."[3]

The great body of our historical evidence goes to show, however, that

[1] Morgan, in Fifth Annual Report on the New York State Cabinet of Natural History, pp. 71, 73.
[2] Loskiel: Mission of the United Brethren, Latrobe trans., p. 34.
[3] Hutchinson: History of Mass., Vol. I, p. 406.

a currency of shell was in use among the Atlantic coast tribes when first encountered by the Europeans. Thomas Morton, in speaking of the Indians of New England as far back as 1630, says that "they have a kinde of beads in steede of money to buy withal such things as they want, which they call wampampeak; and it is of two sorts, the one is white and the other is a violet colour. These are made of the shells of fishe; the white with them is as silver with us, the other as our gould, and for these beads they buy and sell, not only amongst themselves, but even with us. We have used to sell them any of our commodities for this wampampeak, because we know we can have beaver again from them for it: and these beads are current in all parts of New England, from one end of the coast to the other, and although some have endeavoured by example to have the like made, of the same kinde of shels, yet none has ever, as yet, obtained to any perfection in the composure of them, but the Salvages have found a great difference to be in the one and the other; and have knowne the counterfett beads from those of their owne making and doe slight them." [1]

According to Roger Williams also, the Indians of New England, as far back as his observations extend, were engaged in the manufacture of shell money as a well-established industry. It seems altogether impossible that such a custom should have been successfully introduced by the English, as the Indian is well known to be averse to anything like labor excepting in his traditional occupations of war and the chase, and if the whites had introduced it, would certainly have looked to them for a supply by means of trade in skins and game rather than apply himself to a new and strange art. Roger Williams says that "they that live upon the Sea side generally make of it, and as many as they will. The Indians bring downe all their sorts of Furs, which they take in the countrey, both to the Indians and to the English for this Indian Money: this Money the English, French and Dutch, trade to the Indians, six hundred miles in severall parts (north and south from New England) for their Furres, and whatsoever they stand in need of from them." Their methods were also aboriginal, another indication that the art was not of European introduction; and Williams states that "before ever they had awle blades from Europe, they made shift to bore their shell money with stones." [2]

That wampum was also manufactured farther south we learn from Lindström, who is writing of the Indians of New Sweeden: "Their money is made of shells, white, black, and red, worked into beads, and neatly turned and smoothed; one person, however, cannot make more in a day than the value of six or eight stivers. When these beads are worn out, so that they cannot be strung neatly, and even on one thread, they no longer consider them good. Their way of stringing them is to rub the whole thread full of them on their noses; if they find it slides

[1] Thomas Morton, in Historical Tracts, Vol. II, p. 29.
[2] Williams: A Key into the Language of America, p. 144.

smooth and even, like glass beads, then they are considered good, otherwise they break and throw them away."[1]

Although Beverly did not write until the beginning of the eighteenth century, his statements are probably based upon accurate information. Speaking of the Virginia Indians, he says that they "had nothing which they reckoned riches before the English went among them, except *Peak, Roenoke,* and such-like trifles made out of the *Cunk Shell.* These past with them instead of Gold and Silver, and serv'd them both for Money and Ornament. It was the *English* alone that taught them first to put a value on their Skins and Furs, and to make a Trade of them."[2]

From Lawson, who wrote in 1714, but whose statements deserve consideration, we also learn that the money of the Carolina Indians is "all made of shells which are found on the coast of Carolina, which are very large and hard so that they are very difficult to cut. Some English smiths have tried to drill this sort of shell-money, and thereby thought to get an advantage ; but it proved so hard that nothing could be gained."[3]

Speaking of its use and value in New York, he remarks that "an Englishman could not afford to make so much of this wampum for five or ten times the value; for it is made out of a vast great shell, of which that country affords plenty; where it is ground smaller than the small end of a tobacco pipe, or a large wheat straw." * * * "This the Indians grind on stones and other things until they make it current, but the drilling is the most difficult to the Englishman, which the Indians manage with a nail stuck in a cane or reed. Thus they roll it continually on their thighs with their right hand, holding the bit of shell with their left ; so, in time, they drill a hole quite through it which is a very tedious work; but especially in making their ronoak, four of which will scarce make one length of wampum. The Indians are a people that never value their time, so that they can afford to make them, and never need to fear the English will take the trade out of their hands. This is the money with which you may buy skins, furs, slaves, or anything the Indians have; it being their mammon (as our money is to us) that entices and persuades them to do anything, and part with everything they possess, except their children for slaves. As for their wives, they are often sold and their daughters violated for it. With this they buy off murders; and whatsoever a man can do that is ill, this wampum will quit him of and make him, in their opinion, good and virtuous, though never so black before."[4]

Adair confirms the statements made by these writers, and adds emphasis to the fact that the shell beads had, among the Cherokees and other southern Indians, a fixed value as currency. "With these they

[1] Penna. Historical Society, Vol. III, p. 131.
[2] Beverly: History of Virginia, p. 195.
[3] Lawson: History of North Carolina ; Raleigh reprint, 1860, p. 315.
[4] On this point, however, the author quoted is apparently at fault, as there is abundance of proof that the whites often engaged successfully in the manufacture of this shell money.

bought and sold at a stated current rate, without the least variation for circumstances either of time or place; and now they will hear nothing patiently of loss or gain, or allow us to heighten the price of our goods, be our reasons ever so strong, or though the exigencies and changes of time may require it."[1]

We find plentiful evidence in the stories of the early Spanish adventurers that beads made from sea shells were held in high esteem by the Indians of the south, but, so far as I am aware, there is no statement indicating that they formed a well regulated medium of exchange.

In regard to the manufacture of wampum by the whites, the following quotations will be instructive:

"Many people at *Albany* make the *wampum* of the *Indians*, which is their ornament and their money, by grinding some kinds of shells and muscles; this is a considerable profit to the inhabitants."[2]

"Besides the *Europeans*, many of the native *Indians* come annually down to the sea shore, in order to catch clams, proceeding with them afterwards in the manner I have just described. The shells of these clams are used by the *Indians* as money, and make what they call their wampum; they likewise serve their women as an ornament, when they intend to appear in full dress. These wampums are properly made of the purple parts of the shells, which the *Indians* value more than the white parts. A traveller, who goes to trade with the *Indians*, and is well stocked with them, may become a considerable gainer; but if he take gold coin, or bullion, he will undoubtedly be a loser; for the *Indians*, who live farther up the country, put little or no value upon these metals which we reckon so precious, as I have frequently observed in the course of my travels. The *Indians* formerly made their own wampums, though not without a deal of trouble: but at present the *Europeans* employ themselves that way; especially the inhabitants of *Albany*, who get a considerable profit by it. In the sequel I intend to relate the manner of making wampum.[3]

"The article was highly prized as an ornament, and as such constituted an article of traffic between the sea-coast and the interior tribes. * * *

"The old wampum was made by hand, and was an exceedingly rude article. After the discovery, the Dutch introduced the lathe in its manufacture, polished and perforated it with exactness, and soon had the monopoly of the trade. The principal place of its manufacture was at Hackensak, in New Jersey. The principal deposit of sea shells was Long Island, where the extensive shell banks left by the Indians, on which it is difficult to find a whole shell, show the immense quantities that were manufactured."[4]

The name *wampum* is often applied to shell beads indiscriminately,

[1] Adair: History of the American Indians, p. 170.
[2] Kalm's Travels, London, 1772, Vol. II, p. 100.
[3] Ibid., Vol. I, pp. 190, 191.
[4] Ruttenber: Indian Tribes of the Hudson River, p. 26.

but frequently has a more restricted significance, referring to the small cylindrical varieties used in strings and belts. It was known first in New England as *wampumpeag, wampompeage, peag, wompam* and *wampum*; the Dutch of New Sweden knew it as *sewan, sewant,* and *seawant,* while on the Virginia coast, it was called *peak,* a roughly made discoidal variety being known as *ronouk* or *roenoke,* and heavy flattish beads pierced edgeways were called *runtees.* It is probable that all of these names are American in origin, although there is some difference of opinion as to their derivation. Loskiel says that *wampom* is an Iroquois word meaning muscle, but according to Morgan, who is probably the best modern authority on this subject, the word *wampum* is not Iroquois in origin but Algonkin, as it was first known in New England as *wampumpeage.*

Roger Williams, speaking of the money of the New England Indians, probably the Narragansetts (Algonkin), says that "their white they call *Wompam* (which signifies white); their black *Suckauhock* (*Sücki,* signifying black)." In another place he gives the word *wompi* for white. Wood mentions two varieties of beads known in New England *wampompeage* and *mowhackees.* The latter is probably derived from *mowésu,* which, according to Williams, also signifies black.

It would seem that we have but little evidence of the ancient use of shell money amongst the tribes of the Mississippi Valley or the Pacific coast; yet we are not without proofs that it came into use at a very early date throughout the entire West, and even today the custom is by no means obsolete. The ancient burial places of the Pacific coast are found to contain large quantities of beads precisely similar to those now used as money by the coast tribes.

Lewis and Clark, speaking of traffic among the Indians of the Columbia River, state that shell beads are held in very high esteem by these people, and that to procure them they will "sacrifice their last article of clothing or their last mouthful of food. Independently of their fondness for them as an ornament these beads are the medium of trade by which they obtain from the Indians still higher up the river, robes, skins, chappeled bread, bear grass."[1]

The *Dentalium* shell has always been the favorite currency of the peoples of the Northwest and is highly valued, especially by the inland tribes. It is frequently found in ancient graves at great distances from the sea-shore. A few specimens have been found in burial places in the Ohio Valley, but we have no means of determining the source from which they were derived. As the modern use of this currency has but little archæologic interest, I will not enlarge upon the subject here. For further information the reader is referred to the following authors: J. K. Lord, The Naturalist in British Columbia, Vol. II, pp. 20 to 26; R. E. C. Stearns in the American Naturalist, Vol. III, No. 1, and in proceedings of the California Academy of Sciences, Vol. V, Part II, p. 113; W. H. Pratt in proceedings of the Davenport Academy of Natural

[1] Lewis and Clark: Expedition up the Missouri, p. 73.

Sciences, Vol. II, Part 1, p. 38; and Stephen Powers in Vol. 3, Contributions to North American Ethnology, pp. 21, 24, 30.

MNEMONIC USE OF BEADS.

One of the most remarkable customs practiced by the American Indians is found in the mnemonic use of wampum. This custom had in it a germ of great promise, one which must in time have become a powerful agent in the evolution of art and learning. It was a nucleus about which all the elements of culture could arrange themselves. I shall not at present undertake to divest the custom of adventitious features such as have been introduced by contact with European influence. Yet there is no reason to fear that any of the important or essential features have been derived from outside sources. It is not possible from any known records to demonstrate the great antiquity of this use of wampum. It does not seem probable, however, that a custom so unique and so wide-spread could have grown up within the historic period; nor is it probable that a practice foreign to the genius of tradition-loving races could have become so well established and so dear to their hearts in a few generations.

Mnemonic records are known to have come into use among many nations at a very early stage of culture. Picture writing as developed in the north is but another form of mnemonic record, a fact, a thought, a verse of a song being associated with an ideographic design, more or less suggestive of the subject. The Peruvians had their *quipus*, in which the record was made by associating things to be remembered with knots made in cords of different colors, each combination having a fixed association. The Mexicans had gone further and had achieved a system of picture writing that was very unique and curious, in which a phonetic element had already made its appearance, while the Mayas could boast the discovery of a true phonetic system with an alphabet of twenty-seven sounds.

The mnemonic use of wampum is one which, I imagine, might readily develop from the practice of gift giving and the exchange of tokens of friendship, such mementos being preserved for future reference as reminders of promises of assistance or protection. In time the use of such mementos would develop into a system capable of recording affairs of varied and complicated nature; particular facts or features of treaties would be assigned to particular objects, or portions of objects. With this much accomplished, but one step was necessary to the attainment of a hieroglyphic system—the permanent association of a single object or sign with a particular idea.

The wampum records of the Iroquois were generally in the form of belts, the beads being strung or woven into patterns formed by the use of different colors. By association simply they were made to record history, laws, treaties, and speeches—a fact, a law, a stipulation, or a declaration being " talked into " a particular part or pattern of the design with which it was ever afterwards associated, thus giving addi-

USE OF WAMPUM BELTS IN INDIAN COUNCIL.

Fac-simile of a plate in Lafitau.

tional permanency to tradition and bringing it one step further forward
in the direction of written records. Such records were, of course,
quite useless without the agency of an interpreter. Among the Iroquois, according to Morgan, one of the Onondaga sachems was made
hereditary "keeper of wampum," whose duty it was to be thoroughly
versed in its interpretation. But knowledge of the contents of these
records was not confined to the keeper, or even to the sachems. At
a certain season each year the belts were taken from the treasure-house
and exposed to the whole tribe, while the history and import of each
was publicly recited. This custom is kept up to the present day. It is
recorded by Ruttenber that among the Mohicans a certain sachem had
charge of the bag of peace which contained the wampum belts and strings
used in establishing peace and friendship with the different nations.[1]

Aside from records wampum was used in the form of strings and
belts for a variety of purposes; some of them were probably mnemonic,
others only partially so, being based either upon its association with
the name of some chief or clan, or upon a semi-sacred character resulting from its important uses. It was employed in summoning councils,
and the messenger who journeyed from tribe to tribe found in it a
well recognized passport. When a council was called it was presented
by the delegates from the various tribes as their credentials; it was
used in the ceremony of opening and closing councils, as was also
the calumet; it assisted in solemnizing oaths and in absolving from
them; white, it was a messenger of peace; black, it threatened war,
and covered with clay, it expressed grief. "White wampum was the
Iroquois emblem of purity and faith, it was hung around the neck of
the white dog before it was burned; it was used before the periodical
religious festivals for the confession of sins, no confession being regarded as sincere unless recorded with white wampum; farther than
this, it was the customary offering in condonation of murder, although
the purple was sometimes employed. Six strings was the value of a
life, or the quantity sent in condonation, for the wampum was rather
sent as a regretful confession of the crime, with a petition for forgive-
ness, than as the actual price of blood."[2] We readily recognize the influence of the Christian missionary in a number of these symbolic uses
of wampum.

The literature of wampum would fill a volume, but I forbear presenting more than will give an outline of the subject, confining myself to
such quotations as will serve to show clearly the extent and importance
of this ancient custom and its attendant practices.

The method of handling the belts of wampum in the presence of ceremonial assemblies is extremely interesting, and cannot be better presented than in the words of eye-witnesses.

---

[1] Ruttenber: Indian Tribes of the Hudson River, page 43.
[2] Morgan, in Fifth Annual Report on the condition of the New York State Cabinet
of Natural History, page 73.

The following is quoted from Brice, who is describing a council held in the Muskingum Valley in 1764:

"An Indian council, on solemn occasions, was always opened with preliminary forms, sufficiently wearisome and tedious, but made indispensable by immemorial custom, for this people are as much bound by their conventional usages as the most artificial children of civilization. The forms were varied, to some extent, according to the imagination of the speaker, but in all essential respects they were closely similar throughout the tribes of the Algonkin and and Iroquois lineage.

"They run somewhat as follows, each sentence being pronounced with great solemnity, and confirmed by the delivery of a wampum belt: 'Brothers, with this belt I open your ears that you may hear; I remove grief and sorrow from your hearts; I draw from your feet the thorns that pierced them as you journeyed thither; I clean the seats of the council-house, that you may sit at ease; I wash your head and body, that your spirits may be refreshed; I condole with you on the loss of the friends who have died since we last met; I wipe out any blood which may have been spilt between us.' This ceremony, which, by the delivery of so many belts of wampum, entailed no small expense, was never used except on the most important occasions; and at the councils with Colonel Bouquet the angry warriors seem wholly to have dispensed with it. * * * And his memory was refreshed by belts of wampum, which he delivered after every clause in his harangue, as a pledge of the sincerity and truth of his words.

"These belts were carefully preserved by the hearers as a substitute for written records, a use for which they were the better adapted, as they were often worked in hieroglyphics expressing the meaning they were designed to preserve. Thus at a treaty of peace the principal belt often bore the figure of an Indian and a white man holding a chain between them."[1]

From an account of a council held by the Five Nations at Onondaga nearly two hundred years ago, to which the governor of Canada sent four representatives, I make the following extract: "During the course of the proceedings Cannehoot, a Seneca sachem presented a proposed treaty between the Wagunhas and the Senecas, speaking as follows: 'We come to join the two bodies into one. * * * We come to learn wisdom of the Senecas (giving a belt). We by this belt wipe away the tears from the eyes of your friends, whose relations have been killed in the war. We likewise wipe the paint from your soldiers' faces (giving a second belt). We throw aside the ax which Yonondio put into our hands by this third belt.' A red marble sun is presented—a pipe made of red marble. 'Yonondio is drunk; we wash our hands clean from his actions (giving a fourth belt). * * * We have twelve of your nation prisoners; they shall be brought home in the spring (giving a belt to confirm the promise). We will bring your prisoners home when the strawberries

---

[1] Brice: History of Fort Wayne, 1868, page 28.

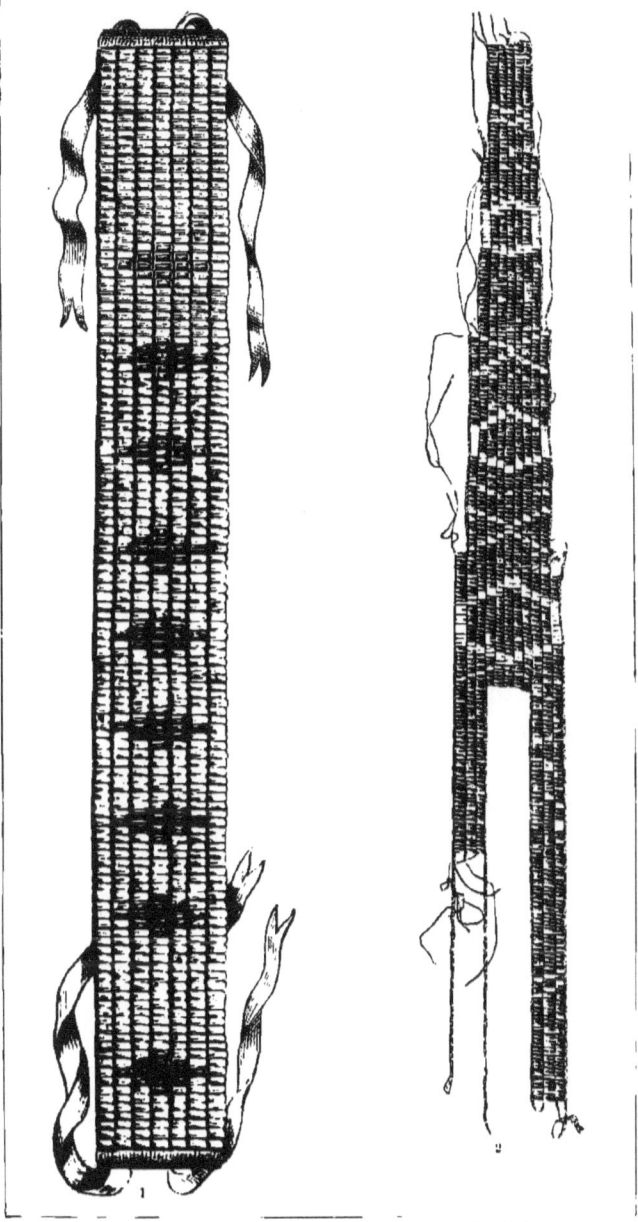

1. Mohawk Belt   2. Mohawk Belt.

WAMPUM BELTS.

shall be in blossom, at which time we intend to visit Corlear (the governor of New York), and see the place where wampum is made.'

"The belts were accepted by the Five Nations, and their acceptance was a ratification of the treaty. A large belt was also given to the messengers from Albany as their share. A wampum belt sent from Albany was, in the same manner, hung up and afterwards divided."[1]

This indicates a most extravagant use of belts; but since it is probable that as many were received in return this was a matter of little importance. The great profusion of wampum used in some of the later treaties is a matter of surprise. In a council held between four Indian ambassadors from New England and the French thirty-six fine large belts were given by the ambassadors to thank them that their people had not been treated with hostility.[2]

"The appendix to the second volume of Proud's History of Pennsylvania contains the journals of Frederick Christian Post, who was sent by Governor Denny, in 1758, to make a treaty with the Alleghany Indians; and in delivering the governor's answer to the chiefs, on his second visit in the same year, after proposing to them to unite in a treaty of peace which had lately been concluded with the Indians at Easton, and producing sundry belts, one of which was marked with figures representing the English and the Indians delivering the peace-belt to one of the commissioners, he proceeds to say: 'Brethren on the Ohio, if you take the belts we just now gave you, as we do not doubt you will, then by *this belt*'—producing another and using their figurative style of speech—'I make a road for you, and invite you to come to Philadelphia, to your first old council-fire, which we rekindle up again, and remove disputes, and renew the first old treaties of friendship. This is a clear and open road for you; therefore, fear nothing, and come to us with as many as can be of the Delawares, Shawanese, or the Six Nations; we will be glad to see you; we desire all tribes and nations of Indians who are in alliance with you may come.' Whereupon a large white belt, with the figure of a man at each end and streaks of black representing the road from the Ohio to Philadelphia, was then given to them."[3]

Lafitau, whose statements are considered unusually trustworthy, as they were based chiefly on personal observation of the Indian tribes of Canada, gives the following very instructive account of the mnemonic use of wampum:

"All affairs are conducted by means of branches [strings] and necklaces [belts] of porcelain [wampum] which with them take the place of compacts, written agreements, and contracts. * * * The shell, which is used for affairs of state, is worked into little cylinders of a quarter of an inch in length and large in proportion. They are distributed in two ways, in strings and in belts. The strings are composed

[1] Events in Indian History, Lancaster, Pa., 1841, page 143.
[2] History and description of New France, Vol. II, page 256.
[3] Penn, in Memoirs Hist. Soc. Penn'a, Vol. VI, p. 222.

of cylinders threaded without order one after another, like the beads of a rosary; the beads are usually quite white, and are used for affairs of little consequence, or as a preparation for other more considerable presents.[1]

"The belts are large bands, in which little white and purple cylinders are disposed in rows, and tied down with small thongs of leather, which makes a very neat fabric. The length and size and color are proportioned to the importance of the affair. The usual belts are of eleven rows of a hundred and eighty beads each.

"The 'fisk,' or public treasure, consists principally of these belts, which, as I have said, with them, take the place of contracts, of public acts, and of annals or registers. For the savages, having no writing or letters, and therefore finding themselves soon forgetting the transactions that occur among them from time to time, supply this deficiency by making for themselves a local memory by means of words which they attach to these belts, of which each one refers to some particular affair, or some circumstance, which it represents while it exists.

"They are so much consecrated to this use that besides the name *Gaïonni*, which is their name for the kind of belts most used, they bestow that of *Garihona*, which means a transaction; that of *Gaouenda*, voice or word, and of *Gaïanderenfera*, which means grandeur or nobility; because all the affairs dignified by these belts are the endowment and province of the *agoïanders* or nobles. It is they who furnish them; and it is among them that they are redivided when presents are made to the village, and when replies to the belts of their ambassadors are sent.

"The *agoïanders* and the ancients have, besides this, the custom of looking over them often together, and of dividing among themselves the care of noting certain ones, which are particularly assigned to them; so that in this way they do not forget anything.

"Their wampum would soon be exhausted if it did not circulate; but in almost all affairs, either within or without, the law requires a reply, word for word, that is to say, for one belt one must give another, to be of about the same value, observing, however, a slight difference in the number of beads, which must be proportioned to the rank of the persons or nations with which they treat.

"They do not believe that any transaction can be concluded without these belts. Whatever proposition is made to them, or reply given them, by word of mouth alone, the affair falls through, they say, and they let it fall through very effectually, as though there had been no question about it. Europeans little informed or little concerned about their usages have slightly inconvenienced them on this point in retaining their belts without giving them a similar response. To avoid the inconvenience which might arise from this they acquired the style of giving only a small quantity, excusing themselves on the plea that their

[1] In order to make the authors meaning quite clear, a free translation has been given of such words as *porcelaine, branches, colliers*, etc., as his use of them is somewhat confusing.

1

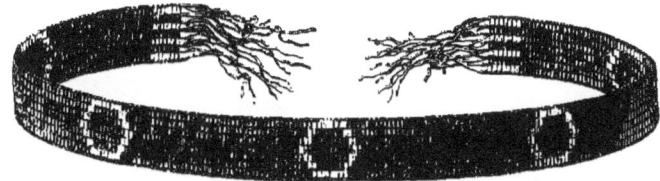

2

3

WAMPUM BELTS BELONGING TO THE ONONDAGAS.

wampum was exhausted ; and they supplied the rest with packages of
deer-skin, in return for which they were given trinkets of small value,
so that transactions between the Europeans and them have become a
sort of trade.

"Although all the savage nations of America make various kinds of
ornaments of shells, I believe that it is only those of North America
who employ them in transactions. I cannot even affirm that all of
these do."[1]

A very complete account of wampum is given by Loskiel, from whose
work the following extract is made :

" Four or six strings joined in one breadth, and fastened to each other
with fine thread, make a *belt of wampom*, being about three or four
inches wide, and three feet long, containing, perhaps, four, eight, or
twelve fathom of wampom, in proportion to its required length and
breadth. This is determined by the importance of the subject which
these belts are intended either to explain or confirm, or by the dignity
of the persons to whom they are to be delivered. Everything of moment
transacted at solemn councils, either between the Indians themselves
or with Europeans, is ratified and made valid by strings and belts of
wampom. Formerly, they used to give sanction to their treaties by delivering a wing of some large bird ; and this custom still prevails among
the more western nations, in transacting business with the Delawares.
But the Delawares themselves, the Iroquois, and the nations in league
with them, are now sufficiently provided with handsome and well-
wrought strings and belts of wampom. Upon the delivery of a string,
a long speech may be made and much said upon the subject under consideration, *but when a belt is given few words are spoken :* but they must
be words of great importance, frequently requiring an explanation.
Whenever the speaker has pronounced some important sentence, he de-
livers a string of wampom, adding, 'I give this string of wampom as a
confirmation of what I have spoken'; but the chief subject of his dis-
course he confirms with a belt. The answers given to a speech thus delivered must also be confirmed by strings and belts of wampom, of the
same size and number as those received. Neither the colour nor the
other qualities of wampom are a matter of indifference, but have an
immediate reference to those things which they are meant to confirm.
The brown or deep violet, called black by the Indians, always means
something of severe or doubtful import ; but the white is the colour of
peace. Thus, if a string or belt of wampom is intended to confirm a
warning against evil, or an earnest reproof, it is delivered in black.
When a nation is called upon to go to war, or war declared against it,
the belt is black, or marked with red, called by them, the *colour of blood*,
having in the middle the figure of an hatchet in white wampom. * * *
They refer to them as public records, carefully preserving them in a
chest made for that purpose. At certain seasons they meet to study
their meaning, and to renew the ideas of which they were an emblem

---

[1] Lafitau : Mœurs des Sauvages Ameriquains, 1724, tom. II, pp. 502-'3 and 505-'7.

or confirmation. On such occasions they sit down around the chest, take out one string or belt after the other, handing it about to every person present, and that they may all comprehend its meaning, repeat the words pronounced on its delivery in their whole convention. By these means they are enabled to remember the promises reciprocally made by the different parties; and it is their custom to admit even the young boys, who are related to the chiefs, to their assemblies; they become early acquainted with all the affairs of the State: thus the contents of their documents are transmitted to posterity, and cannot be easily forgotten."[1]

It is to be presumed that if a treaty or a promise were broken, the belt would be released from its office and in the same form, or worked into another, could again be used. Otherwise the records, if properly kept, would in time become extremely cumbersome.

The repudiation of a treaty and of the wampum which accompanied it is recorded by Brice. It was at a council held at Miami, in 1790, between Mr. Gamelin and a number of tribes. Mr. Gamelin in beginning his speech presented each nation with strings of wampum, but "the Indians were displeased with the treaty, and after consultation returned the wampum, saying: 'From all quarters we receive speeches from the Americans and not one is alike. We suppose that they intend to deceive us. Then take back your branches of wampum.' The Pottawatomies were better pleased with the speeches and accepted the wampum."[2]

Another good example which illustrates the manner of canceling treaties, confirmed by wampum, is given by Mr. Gilpin:

"When Washington, then but a youth of twenty-one, was intrusted by the colonial governor of Virginia with a mission to the western wilds of Pennsylvania, where the French from Canada were then penetrating and had already established, as was believed, four posts within our limits and were seeking to unite the natives in alliance against us, * * * he found that such an alliance had indeed been formed. He found that they had exchanged with the French, as its symbol, a wampum belt on which four houses were rudely embroidered—the representations of the posts which were to be defended, even at the risk of war. Influenced by his remonstrances, the Indian sachems consented to withdraw from the alliance; but they declared that the belt of wampum must be returned before the agreement could be abolished; and one of the sachems repaired to the French commander in order to restore to him the token of the warlike compact, and to proclaim the intention of the red men to take no part in the impending struggle."[3]

Heckewelder relates that "it once happened that war messengers endeavored to persuade and compel a nation to accept the belt by laying it on the shoulders or thigh of the chief, who, however, after shaking it

---

[1] Loskiel: Missions of the United Brethren. Trans. by La Trobe, Book 1, p. 26.
[2] Brice: History of Fort Wayne, p. 118.
[3] Gilpin, in Memoirs of the Hist. Soc. of Penna. Vol. VI, p. 248.

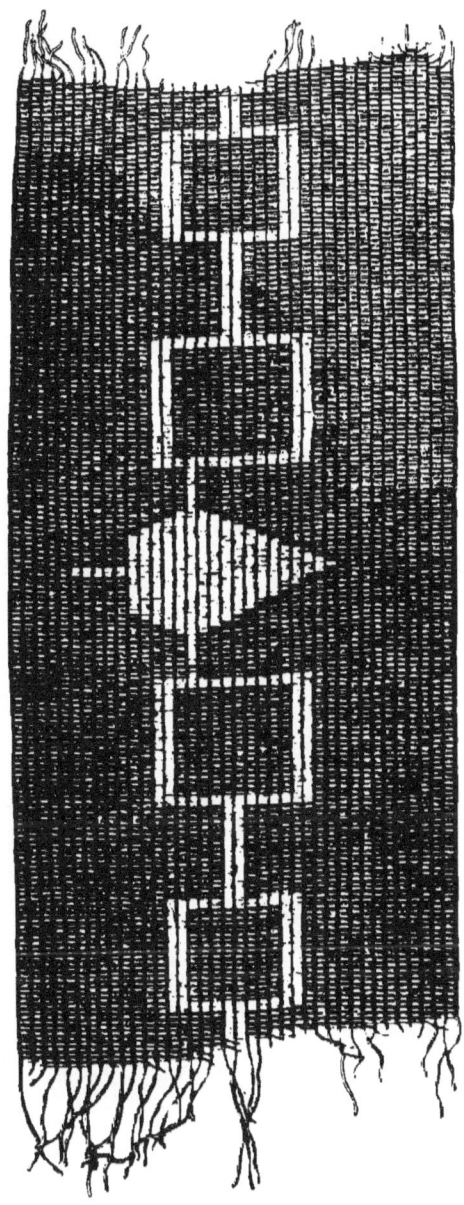

WAMPUM BELT BELONGING TO THE ONONDAGAS.

off without touching it with his hands, afterwards, with a stick, threw it after them, as if he threw a snake or toad out of his way."[1]

It is remarkable that other objects were not more frequently used for mnemonic records. We can only explain the partiality shown to wampum on the supposition that the idea of value was not entirely lost sight of and that importance was attached to a record which in itself merited preservation. Yet instances of the use of other objects are often met with. Parkman states that "the figures on wampum belts of the Iroquois were for the most part simply mnemonic. So also were those carved in wooden tables, or painted on bark or skin, to preserve in memory the songs of war, hunting, or magic."[1]

At one of the councils at Onondaga in 1690, a treaty was pledged and recorded in wampum by all the contracting parties but the New England colonies, which sent a wooden model of a fish as a token of their adherence to the terms of the treaty.[3]

Hunter, speaking of the manners and customs of the Osages, states that "they use significant emblems, such as the wing of the swan and wild goose, wampum, and pipes, in overtures for peace, while arrows, war clubs, and black and red painting, are used as indications or declarations of war. Any article, such as a skin painted black, or the wing of a raven, represents the death of friends, and when colored or striped with red, that of enemies. Amongst the Canada Indians when peace was conceded, a reddened hatchet was buried as a symbol of the oblivion of all past hostility between the contracting parties. A mutual exchange of neck ornaments sealed the treaty after its terms were debated and determined. But all was not yet over, for the chiefs on each side proffered and accepted presents of rare articles, such as calumets of peace, embroidered deer skins, &c. This kind of ceremonial barter being terminated to their mutual satisfaction, or otherwise, the conference broke up."[4]

Gumilla says that the Oronoco Indians ratify their treaties with sticks which they give reciprocally,[5] and the Araucanians, according to Molina, carry in their hands, when they conclude a peace, the branches of a tree, regarded as sacred by them, which they present to each other.[6]

I have already enumerated the various kinds of beads and shown the sources from which they were derived and the uses to which they were applied. I have yet to describe the manner in which they are strung or combined in strings and belts.

The beads chosen as most convenient for stringing or weaving into fabrics were small cylinders from one-eighth to one-quarter of an inch in diameter, and from one-quarter to one-half an inch in length. White strings or belts were sufficient for the expression of simple ideas or the

[1] Heckewelder: Indian Nations, 1876, p. 110.
[2] Parkman: Jesuits in North America, p. xxxiii.
[3] Events in Indian History, Lancaster, Pa., 1841, p. 143.
[4] Hunter: Indian Manners and Customs, p. 192.
[5] Gumilla: Histoire de Orinoque, Vol. III, p. 91.
[6] Molina: History of Chili, Vol. I, p. 119.

association of simple facts, but the combinations of colors in patterns rendered it possible to record much more complicated affairs. In belts used for mnemonic purposes the colors were generally arranged without reference to the character of the facts or thoughts to be intrusted to them, but in a few cases the figures are ideographic, and are significant of the event to be memorized. Strings cannot be utilized in this way.

Wampum in strings.—From Mr. Beauchamp's notes I have compiled the following brief account of the use of strings of wampum among the modern Iroquois. Six strings of purple beads united in a cluster represent the six nations. When the tribes meet the strands are arranged in a circle, which signifies that the council is opened. The Onondagas are represented by seven strings, which contain a few white beads; the Cayugas by six strands, all purple, and the Tuscaroras by seven strands, nearly all purple. The Mohawks have six strings, on which there are two purple beads to one white. These are illustrated in Fig. 2, Plate XLIV. There are four strings in the Oneida cluster; these contain two purple to one white bead. The Senecas have four strings, with two purple beads to one white. The three nations which were brothers are represented by similar clusters.

When a new chief is installed the address delivered on the occasion is "talked into" ten very long strings of white wampum. Three strings, mostly white, represent the name of the new chief. One of these clusters is shown in Fig. 1, Plate XLIV.[1] When a chief dies he is mourned on ten strings of black wampum. If he has merely lost his office, six short strings are used.

According to Mr. Beauchamp, possession of beads gives authority, and they are also used as credentials, or, as the Indians express it, "Chief's wampum all same as your letter." Such of these strings as remain in existence are still in use among the Iroquois, and are considered very precious by them, being made of antique hand-made beads.

In the literature relating to our Indian tribes we find occasional reference to the use of strings of wampum in ways that indicate that they were invested with certain protective and authoritative qualities, doubtless from their association with the name of some chief, clan, or tribe.

It is recorded that on one occasion Logan, the Mingo chief, saved a captive white from torture by rushing through the circle of Indians and throwing a string of wampum about the prisoner's neck. Through the virtue of this string he was enabled to lead him away and adopt him into his family.

A somewhat different use is mentioned by Pike, to whom a Chippewa chief made a speech, during which he presented his pipe to Mr. Pike to bear to the Sioux. Attached to the pipe were seven strings of wampum, which signified that authority was given by seven chiefs of the Chippeway to conclude peace or make war.[2]

Wampum belts.—In the manufacture of belts a great deal of skill and

[1] From an original sketch by Mr. Beauchamp.
[2] Pike: Travels through the Western Territories of N. A., 1805–'7, p. 103.

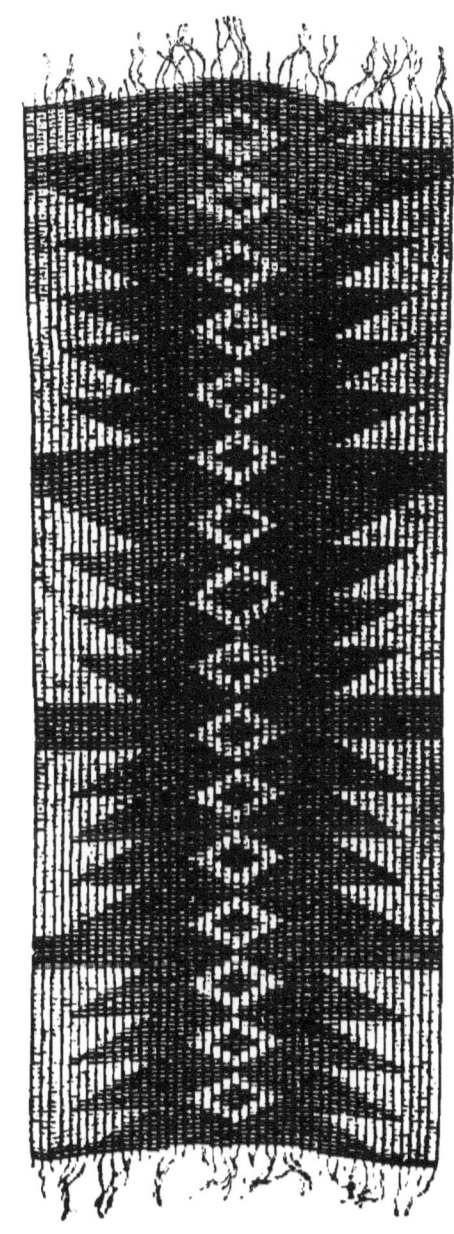

WAMPUM BELT BELONGING TO THE ONONDAGAS.

taste have been shown. The large figured varieties were intricate in design and extremely pleasing in color. Belts of wampum beads were probably used simply as a part of the costume long before they became the vehicles of tradition, and beads were doubtless used in other parts of the costume in a similar manner. It is said that in New England they were made by the women; in later times it is probable that the whites engaged to some extent in their manufacture.

Mr. Morgan gives such a good account of the details of belt making that I beg leave to quote him in full:

"In making a belt no particular pattern was followed; sometimes they are of the width of three fingers and three feet long, in other instances as wide as the hand and over three feet in length; sometimes they are all of one color, in others variegated, and in still others woven with the figures of men to symbolize, by their attitudes, the objects or events they were designed to commemorate. The most common width was three fingers, or the width of seven beads, the length ranging from two to six feet. In belt making, which is a simple process, eight strands or cords of bark thread are first twisted, from filaments of slippery elm, of the requisite length and size; after which they are passed through a strip of deer-skin to separate them at equal distances from each other in parallel lines. A piece of splint is then sprung in the form of a bow, to which each end of the several strings is secured, and by which all of them are held in tension, like warp threads in a weaving machine. Seven beads, these making the intended width of the belt, are then run upon a thread by means of a needle, and are passed under the cords at right angles, so as to bring one bead lengthwise between each cord and the one next in position. The thread is then passed back again along the upper side of the cords and again through each of the beads; so that each bead is held firmly in its place by means of two threads, one passing under and one above the cords. This process is continued until the belt reaches its intended length, when the ends of the cords are tied, the end of the belt covered and afterward trimmed with ribbons. In ancient times both the cords and the thread were of sinew." [1]

In another place Mr. Morgan states that belts were also made by covering one side of a deer-skin belt with beads, probably by sewing them on; [2] a method which is everywhere common in the use of glass beads in modern work, but is not noticed in any of the mnemonic belts now extant. It is a remarkable as well as a lamentable fact that none of the great collections of the country can boast the possession of a wampum belt. Considering their importance in our early history, and the great numbers that at one time must have been in existence, this is rather extraordinary. I have taken considerable pains to collect accurate representations of a number of examples of the ancient belts for

[1] Morgan, in Fifth Annual Report on the Condition of the New York State Cabinet of Natural History, 1852, p. 72.

[2] Morgan: League of the Iroquois, p. 387.

this work, and am only sorry that I am unable to present them in color—
the only method by which they can be adequately shown. As those
which have come to my notice represent but a few localities, I shall in-
sert descriptions of a number from regions as remote as possible. There
is, however, great uniformity in design and method of construction; the
result, probably, of their international character. From Heckewelder
I quote the following:

"Their belts of wampum are of different dimensions, both as to the
length and breadth. White and black wampum are the kinds they use;
the former denoting that which is good, as peace ,friendship, good-will,
&c.; the latter the reverse; yet occasionally the black also is made use
of on peace errands, when the white cannot be procured ; but previous
to its being produced for such purpose, it must be daubed all over with
chalk, white clay, or anything which changes the color from black to
white. * * * A black belt with the mark of a hatchet made on it
with red paint is a war belt, which, when sent to a nation, together with
a twist or roll of tobacco, is an invitation to join in a war. * * *
Roads from one friendly nation to another are generally marked on the
belt by one or two rows of white wampum interwoven in the black, and
running through the middle, and from end to end. It means that they
are on good terms, and keep up a friendly intercourse with each other."[1]

A belt accepted by the Indians of Western Pennsylvania from the
French in a treaty which secured to the latter four forts within English
territory had embroidered upon it four houses, pictographic representations of the forts.

Another example of the belts used in Pennsylvania, upwards of a
century ago, is described in Beatty's Journal. The Delawares, in ex-
plaining to Beatty a former treaty with Sir William Johnson, "showed
a large belt of wampum of friendship which Sir William Johnson had
given them. On each edge of this were several rows of black wampum,
and in the middle were several rows of white wampum. In the middle
of the belt was a figure of a diamond, in white wampum, which they
called the council fire. The white streak they called the path from him
to them and them to him."[2]

Loskiel states that "the Indian women are very dexterous in weaving the strings of wampom into belts, and marking them with different
figures, perfectly agreeing with the different subjects contained in the
speech. These figures are marked with white wampom upon black,
and with black upon the white belts. For example, in a belt of peace,
they very dexterously represent, in black wampom, two hands joined.
The belt of peace is white, a fathom long and a hand's breadth."[3]

In Plate XXXVII I present a fac-simile reproduction of a plate from
the well known work of Lafitau,[4] in which we have a graphic yet

[1] Heckewelder: Indian Nations, 1876, pp. 108-'9-'10.
[2] Beatty: Journal of Two Months Tour, 1768, p. 67.
[3] Loskiel: Missions of the United Brethren. Trans. by La Trobe, 1794. Book 1, p. 26.
[4] Lafitau: Mœurs des Sauvages Ameriquains, Tome, II, p. 314.

highly conventional representation of a council or treaty in which
wampum belts were used. It is probably drawn from description and
is far from truthful in detail. The more important facts are, however,
very clearly presented. No information is given either of the people
or the locality. The scene is laid in the middle of a broad featureless
plain, the monotony of which is broken by three highly conventionalized trees. The parties to the treaty are ranged in two rows, placed,
face to face. The chief who speaks stands at the farther end holding a belt
in his right hand. Three other belts lie upon the mat at his feet, while
a fifth is shown on a large scale in the foreground. The patterns can
not be clearly made out, but in a general way resemble very closely the
designs woven into the belts of the Irqouois.

The small belt shown in Fig. 1, Plate XXXVIII, is probably one of
the most recent examples. The cut is copied from Plate 1 of the Fifth
Annual Report of the Regents of the University of New York on the
condition of the State Cabinet of Natural History, p. 72. The beads of
which it is composed formerly belonged to the celebrated Mohawk chief,
Joseph Brant. They were afterwards purchased from his daughter by
Mr. Morgan. In 1850 they were taken to Tonawanda, in the State of New
York, and made into this belt. The trimmings are apparently of ribbons, and the symmetry and uniformity of the whole work give it a new
look not noticeable in the other specimens. The design consists of a row
of dark diamond-shaped figures upon a white ground. It is now preserved in the State Cabinet of Natural History at Albany.

A belt of unusual form is shown in Fig. 2, Plate XXXVIII. It
was kindly lent by Mrs. E. A. Smith, of Jersey City, by whom it
was obtained from the Mohawks. It is 26 inches (251 beads) in
length and in width varies from three inches (11 beads) at one end
to about one inch (5 beads) at the other. It is bifurcated at the
wide end, five rows having been omitted from the middle of the belt
for about one-third of the length. Near the middle of the belt one
row of beads is dropped from each side. Between this and the smaller
end at nearly equal intervals it is twice depleted in a like manner.
The beads are quite irregular in shape and size, but rather new looking and are strung in the usual manner, the longitudinal strings being
buckskin and the transverse small cords of vegetable fiber. The ends
and edges are all neatly finished by wrapping the marginal strings
with a thin fillet of buckskin. The figures are in white beads upon a
ground of purple. The form of this belt indicates that it has been
adapted to some particular use, the placing of cords at the corners
and shoulders suggesting its attachment in a fixed position to some part
of the person or costume.

In Plates XXXIX, XL, XLI and XLII, I present a series of illustrations of the wampum belts belonging to the Onondagas. They
are preserved as a most precious treasure by these people at their
agency in Onondaga County, New York. The drawings were made by
Mr. Trill from a series of minute photographs made from the original

belts by General J. S. Clark, of Auburn, New York. These were obtained for me by the Rev. W. M. Beauchamp, of Baldwinsville, New York, who has also very kindly furnished many of the facts embodied in the following descriptions.[1]

These belts are made in the usual manner, and present a great variety of shapes, sizes, and designs. Their full history has never been obtained by the whites, and it is not probable that the Indians themselves have preserved a very full account of their origin and significance. They are all ancient, and, judging by their appearance, must date far back in the history of the League. Many of them are quite fragmentary, and fears are entertained that they will gradually fall to pieces and be lost. It is to be hoped that measures will be taken to have them preserved at least in the form of accurate chromo-lithographs. Mr. Beauchamp, states that they are yearly wasting away, as a little wampum is annually cast into the fire at the burning of the " white dog," and these belts are the source of supply.

The small belt presented in Fig. 1, Plate XXXIX, is somewhat fragmentary, an unknown number of beads having been lost from the ends. It is seven rows wide and at present two hundred beads long. The design consists of a series of five double diamonds worked in dark wampum upon white. At one end a few rows of an additional figure remain, and at the other a small white cross is worked upon a ground of dark beads. The number of figures may be significant of the number of parties to a treaty.

Fig. 2 represents a well preserved belt, seven rows in width and about three hundred and twenty in length. The ground is of dark wampum, on which are worked five hexagonal figures of white wampum. For a short space at the ends alternate rows are white. As was suggested in regard to the preceding belt, the figures in this may represent the parties to a treaty.

The belt shown in Fig 3 differs from the others in being pictographic. It is also quite perfect, although the character of the beads indicates considerable age. It is seven rows in width and three hundred and fifty beads in length. The figures are white, on a dark ground, and consist of a cross near one end, connected by a single row of beads with the head of the figure of a man toward the other end. Beneath the feet of the elementary man the figure of a diamond is worked. The cross is probably significant of the mission of the man who comes from a long distance to the lodge or council of the red man. This is probably a French belt.

The remnant of a very handsome belt is shown in Plate XL. Considerable wampum has been lost from both ends, but the design appears to be nearly perfect, and consists of a trowel or heart-shaped figure in the center with two rectangular figures on the right and two on the left. These are in white upon a dark ground. Mr. Beauchamp states that it

[1] Mr. Beauchamp has published many interesting facts in regard to these belts in the American Antiquarian, Vol. II, No. 3.

WAMPUM BELT BELONGING TO THE ONONDAGAS.

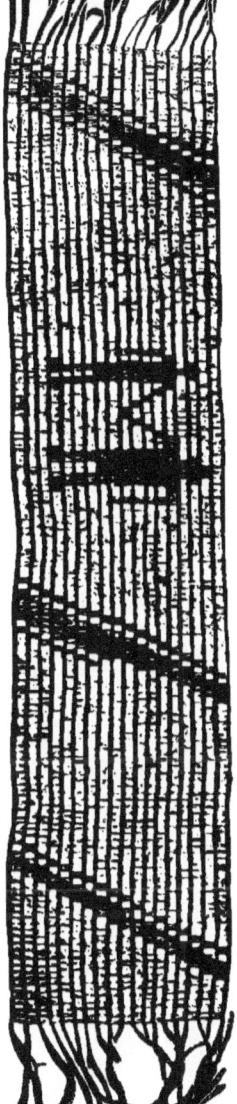

THE PENN BELT. (¼)

is said to be very old, and is thought to represent the formation of the Iroquois league and to signify "one heart for all the nations." He doubts its great antiquity as the beads are too regular for hand-made cylinders. The belt is thirty-eight rows wide and about two hundred beads in length.

The large elaborately figured belt shown in Plate XLI is almost perfect. The lateral margins are white; a broad notched band of dark wampum occupies the middle of this belt; through this from end to end runs a chain of white diamonds, sixteen in number, which may represent States or nations. It is forty-five rows wide and two hundred and forty beads long.

The magnificent belt shown in Plate XLII, is probably the finest example in existence. It is fifteen rows wide and six hundred and fifty in length, making the enormous total of nine thousand seven hundred and fifty beads. Mr. Beauchamp believes that this belt, or one like it, has been described as representing the formation of the League. From Webster's[1] statement, that it was "made by George Washington," he surmises that it is a belt memorizing a covenant between the Indians and the government. In the center is a house which has three gables and three compartments. Next the house on either side are two pictographic men, who appear to stand beneath protecting arms which pass over their heads, connect with the house, and grasp the hands of the first personages immediately on the right and left. In all there are fifteen figures of men, two being connected with the house; of the others, six stand on the right and seven on the left of the central group. It is suggested by Mr. Beauchamp that these figures may represent the thirteen colonies.

Six other belts are shown in the photographs procured by General Price. One of them is thirteen rows wide and two hundred and fifty beads in length. The light ground is decorated with groups of triple chevrons. This belt is somewhat fragmentary. Another is forty-nine rows wide, being the widest example known. The original length cannot be determined, but at present it is two hundred and forty beads in length, and hence contains about twelve thousand beads. The pattern is simple, consisting of a dark ground notched at the edges with triangular figures of white. As the four remaining belts of this fine collection have no features of especial interest, they need not be described here.

The remarkable belt shown in Plate XLIII has an extremely interesting, although a somewhat incomplete, history attached to it. It is believed to be the original belt delivered by the Leni-Lenape sachems to William Penn at the celebrated treaty under the elm tree at Shackamaxon in 1682. Although there is no documentary evidence to show that this identical belt was delivered on that occasion, it is conceded on all hands that it came into the possession of the great founder of Penn-

[1] Present chief of the Onondagas.

sylvania at some one of his treaties with the tribes that occupied the province ceded to him. Up to the year 1857 this belt remained in the keeping of the Penn family. In March, 1857, it was presented to the Pennsylvania Historical Society by Granville John Penn, a great grandson of William Penn. Mr. Penn, in his speech on this occasion,[1] states that there can be no doubt that this is the identical belt used at the treaty, and presents his views in the following language: " In the first place, its dimensions are greater than of those used on more ordinary occasions, of which we have one still in our possession—this belt being composed of eighteen strings of wampum—which is a proof that it was the record of some very important negotiation. In the next place, in the center of the belt, which is of white wampum, are delineated in dark-colored beads, in a rude but graphic style, two figures— that of an Indian grasping with the hand of friendship the hand of a man evidently intended to be represented in the European costume, wearing a hat; which can only be interpreted as having reference to the treaty of peace and friendship which was then concluded between William Penn and the Indians, and recorded by them in their own simple but descriptive mode of expressing their meaning, by the employment of hieroglyphics. Then the fact of its having been preserved in the family of the founder from that period to the present time, having descended through three generations, gives an authenticity to the document which leaves no doubt of its genuineness; and as the chain and medal which were presented by the Parliament to his father, the admiral, for his naval services, have descended amongst the family archives unaccompanied by any written document, but is recorded on the journals of the House of Commons, equal authenticity may be claimed for the wampum belt confirmatory of the treaty made by his son with the Indians; which event is recorded on the page of history, though, like the older relic, it has been unaccompanied in its descent by any document in writing."

It will be seen, by reference to the accompanying illustration, that beside the two figures of men there are three oblique bands of dark wampum, one on the left and two on the right. The one next the central group on the right is somewhat broken, and consists of two long bands and one short one. It is probable that these bands were used to record, by association, some important features of the treaty in which the belt was used. The beads are strung upon cords made of sinew or vegetable fibre, while the longitudinal fillets are of buckskin. This belt may be seen at the rooms of the Historical Society of Pennsylvania.

[1] The proceedings attending the presentation are fully recorded in the Memoirs of the Historical Society of Pennsylvania, volume iii, page 207. A full size lithographic illustration of the belt printed in color is also given.

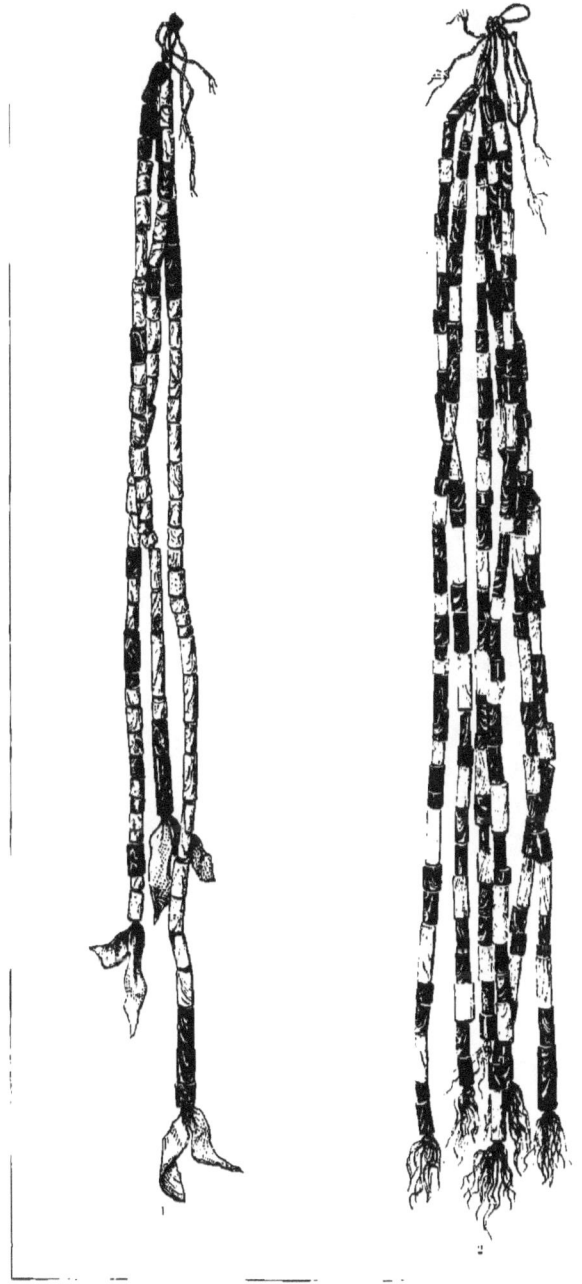

PENDANTS.

It would probably be vain to attempt to determine how pendant ornaments first came into use, whether from some utilitarian practice or
through some superstitious notion. It matters not, however, whether
the first pendant was an implement, a utensil, or a fetichitic talisman;   5
it has developed by slow stages into an ornament upon which has been
lavished the best efforts of culture and skill. The simple gorget of
shell suspended upon the naked breast of the preadamite is the prototype of many a costly jewel and many a princely decoration. With the
American savage it was a guardian spirit, invested with the mystery
and the power of the sea, and among the more cultured tribes became
in time the receptacle of the most ambitious efforts of a phenominal
art. The important place the gorget has taken in ornament and as a
means of displaying personal aggrandizement has made it a most powerful agent in the evolution of the arts of taste.

As a rule the larger and more important pendants are employed as
gorgets, but vast numbers of the smaller specimens are strung with
beads at intervals along the strings, attached as auxiliary pendants to
the larger gorgets, suspended from the nose, ears, and wrists, or form
tinkling borders to head-dresses and garments. These pendants consist either of entire shells, or of parts of shells, pierced or grooved to
facilitate suspension. The purely artificial forms are infinitely varied.
The character of the shell, however, has much to do with the form of
the finished ornaments, deciding their thickness and often their outline.
In size they range from extremely minute forms to plates six or more
inches in diameter. The perforations, in position and number, are greatly
varied, but as a rule the larger discoidal pendants will be found to have
two marginal perforations for suspension.

These nicely-polished shell-disks afforded tempting tablets for the
primitive artist, and retain many specimens of his work as an engraver.
The engraved specimens, however, should be treated separately, according to the class of design which they contain. Plain pendants need but
a brief notice, and may be treated together as one group, with such
subdivisions only as may be suggested by their form, their derivation,
or their geographical distribution.

Plain pendants.—It will be unnecessary to cite authorities to show
that our ancient peoples were fond of pendant ornaments, and wore
them without stint, but to illustrate the manner in which they were
used and the methods of combining them with other articles of jewelry
in necklaces, bracelets, &c., I shall refer briefly to the literature of the
period of American discovery.

The inhabitants of Mexico are said to have been very simple in the
matter of dress, but displayed much vanity in their profuse employment of personal ornament. Besides feathers and jewels, with which

they adorned their clothes, they wore pendants to the ears, nose, and lips, as well as necklaces, bracelets, and anklets. The ear ornaments of the poor were shells, pieces of crystal, amber, and other brilliant stones, but the rich wore pearls, emeralds, amethysts, or other gems, set in gold.[1] The priestly personages so graphically delineated in the ancient Aztec manuscripts are as a rule loaded down with pendant ornaments. In traveling north along the west coast of Mexico the Friar Niza encountered Indians who wore many large shells of mother of pearl about their necks, and farther up toward Cibola the inhabitants wore pearl shells upon their foreheads;[2] and Cabeça de Vaca when among the pueblos of New Mexico noticed beads and corals that came from the "South Sea." Ornaments made from marine shells are found in many of the ancient ruins to-day. They are also highly valued by the modern Indians of this region.

In the earliest accounts of the Indians of the Atlantic coast we find frequent mention of the use of pendants and gorgets, and the manner of wearing them as ornaments. Beverly, after having described beads made of a shell resembling the English buglas, says that they also make "runtees" of the same shell, and grind them as smooth as peak. "These are either large like an oval Bead, drill'd the length of the Oval, or else they are circular and flat, almost an Inch over, and one Third of an Inch thick, and drill'd edgeways. Of this Shell they also make round Tablets of about four Inches Diameter, which they polish as smooth as the other, and sometimes they etch or grave thereon Circles, Stars, a half Moon, or any other Figure suitable to their Fancy. These they wear instead of Medals before or behind their Neck, and use the *Peak*, *Runtees*, and Pipes for Coronets, Bracelets, Belts, or long Strings hanging down before the Breast, or else they lace their Garments with them, and adorn their *Tomahawks*, and every other thing that they value."[3] The "Pipes" here spoken of were probably long, heavy cylindrical beads.

In referring to this class of ornaments, Lafitau says: "The collars which the savages sometimes wear around the neck are about a foot in diameter, and are not different from those which one now sees on some antiques, on the necks of statues of barbarians. The northern savages wear on the breast a plate of hollow shell, as long as the hand, which has the same effect as that which was called *Bulla* among the Romans."[4]

Wood, speaking of the Indians of Northern New England, in 1634, says: "Although they be thus poore, yet is there in them the sparkes of naturall pride, which appeares in their longing desire after many kinds of ornaments, wearing pendants in their eares, as formes of birds, beasts, and fishes carved out of bone, shels, and stone, with long brace-

[1] Clavigero: History of Mexico, Trans. by Cullen, vol. I, p. 437.
[2] Davis: Spanish Conquest of New Mexico, p. 124.
[3] Beverly: History of Virginia, p. 195.
[4] Lafitau: Moeurs des Sauvages Ameriquains, p. 61.

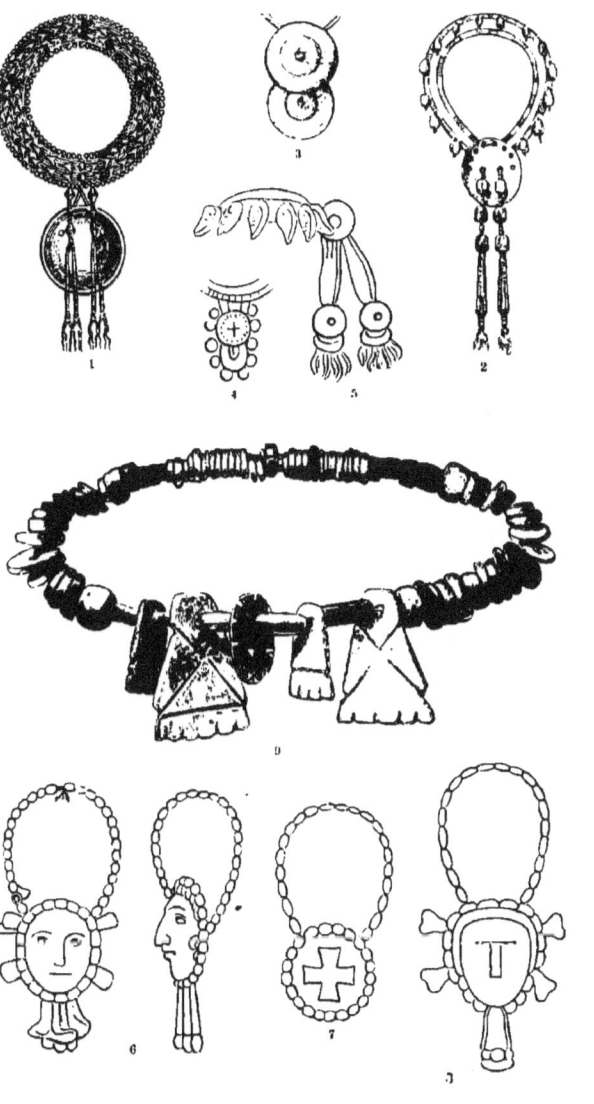

1, 2. Necklaces, from Lafitau.   6, 7, 8. From ancient sculptures.
3. From De Bry.   9. Bracelet from a Peruvian grave.
4, 5. From Mexican paintings.

ANCIENT PENDANTS.

lets of their curious wampompeag and mowhackees, which they put about their necks and loynes."[1]

Kalm says of the Indians of Lorette, near Quebec, Canada, that " round their necks they have a string of violet wampums, with little white wampums between them. These wampums are small, of the figure of oblong pearls, and made of the shells which the *English* call clams. At the end of the wampum strings many of the *Indians* wear a large French silver coin, with the king's effigy, on their breasts; others have a large shell on the breast, of a fine white colour, which they value very high, and is very dear; others, again, have no ornament at all round the neck."[2]

Pendants of metal and medals of European manufacture soon replaced in a great measure the primitive gorgets of shell; and early in the history of the tribes a heterogeneous collection of native beads, silver crosses, and traders' medals, ornamented the breasts of the simple savages.

In studying the habits and customs of our native peoples we look with a great deal of interest upon the earliest historical records, but generally find it prudent to remember that the "personal equation" was unusually large in those days, and in studying the illustrations given in the works of early writers we must make due allowance for the well-known tendency to exaggerate as well as for the fact that the artist has more frequently drawn from descriptions than from sketches made on the spot.

In Plate XLV two examples are given which seem to me to be trustworthy, as they agree with the descriptions given, and are in a general way characteristic of the American aborigines. Fig. 1 is reproduced, original size, from Plate 2, Volume II, of Lafitau, and shows a broad necklace ornamented with figures that resemble arrow heads. From this, by means of a cord, is suspended a large circular disk with concave front, which undoubtedly represents a shell gorget. In front of this and suspended from the necklace are two long strands of beads of various sizes and shapes, which give completeness to a very tasteful ornament. In the same plate is a pretty fair drawing of a native in costume. He is represented wearing a necklace similar to the one just described. An enlarged drawing of this ornament is given in Fig. 2. In Fig. 3 I reproduce a necklace from a plate in De Bry, which consists of a string of beads with two large disks that look more like metal than shell. A similar ornament is shown in Fig. 4, but with figured disks and secondary pendants. It is copied from the Codex of the Vatican. A common form of necklace among the ancient Aztecs consisted of small univalve shells suspended from a string. One of these, with other pendants, is shown in Fig. 5. It is also copied from the Vatican Codex. Others of a much more complex nature may be found

---

[1] Wood: New England Prospect, p. 74.
[2] Kalm: Travels in North America, 1772, vol. ii, p. 320.

258 ART IN SHELL OF THE ANCIENT AMERICANS.

in the same manuscript. Of even greater interest are the beautiful necklaces, with their pendants, found in the sculptures of Mexico and Yucatan.[1] Three of these are shown in Figs. 6, 7, and 8. One has a disk with human features engraved upon it, another has a cross with equal arms, and another a T-shaped cross. All have more or less auxiliary ornamentation. In Fig. 9 I present a bracelet of beads and pendants from Peru which illustrates one of the simpler uses of pendants. I have not learned whether the parts of this ornament were originally arranged as given in the cut or not; the original stringing may have been somewhat different. The beads are mostly of shell, and are of a variety of colors, white, red, yellow, and gray. The discoidal and cylindrical forms are both represented. The former range from one eighth to three-eighths of an inch in diameter; the latter are one-eighth of an inch in thickness and three-eighths in length. The larger pendants, made of whitish shell, are carved to represent some life form, probably a bird; a large perforation near the upper end passes through the head, two oblique notches with deep lines at the sides, define the wings, and a series of notches at the wide end represent the tail. Two smaller pendants are still simpler in form, while another, with two nearly central perforations and notched edges, resembles a button.

Eastern forms.—The great number of elaborately carved and engraved gorgets of shell found among the antiquities of the Atlantic slope, all of which need careful descriptions, so overshadow the simple forms illustrated in Plate XLVI, that only a brief description of the latter need be given. Rudeness of workmanship and simplicity of form do not in any sense imply greater antiquity or a less advanced state of art. The simpler forms of plain pendants constituted the every-day jewelry of the average people and, like beads, were probably used freely by all who desired to do so. Many forms are found—circular, oval, rectangular, triangular, pear-shaped, and annular. The more ordinary forms are found in mounds and graves in all parts of the country; other forms are more restricted geographically, and probably exhibit features peculiar to the works of a particular clan, tribe, or group of tribes. Even these simple forms may have possessed some totemic or mystic significance; it is not impossible that the plainer disks may have had significant figures painted upon them. Such of the forms as are found to have definite geographic limits become of considerable interest to the archæologist. In method of manufacture they do not differ from the most ordinary implements or beads, the margins being trimmed, the surfaces polished and the perforations made in a precisely similar manner.

In Plate XLVI I present a number of plain circular disks. The larger specimens are often as much as four or even five inches in diameter and the smaller fraternize with beads, as I have shown in Plate XLV. Figs. 1 and 2 are from a mound at Paint Rock Ferry, Tenn. They are neat, moderately thin, concavo-convex disks, with smooth sur-

[1] *Vide* Kingsborough, Waldeck, Bancroft, &c.

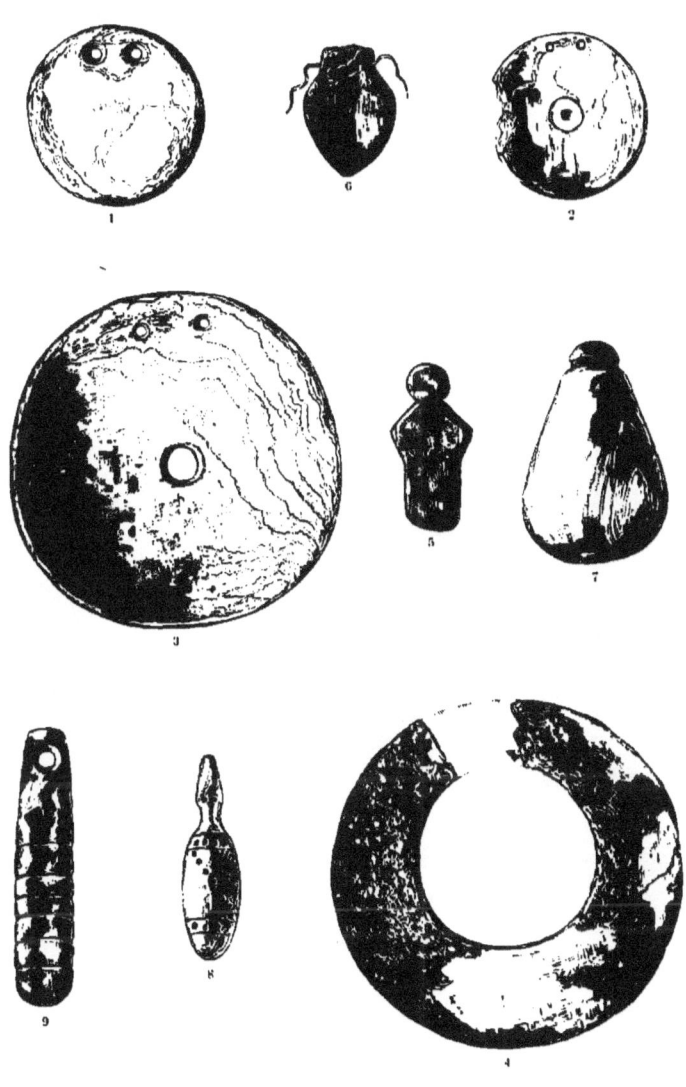

PENDANT ORNAMENTS—EASTERN FORMS.

faces and rounded edges. The first has two perforations at the upper edge, while the other has similarly placed but much smaller ones, besides a small central perforation surrounded by an incised circle. The national collection contains similar specimens from most of the Atlantic States; they differ from the larger discoidal beads only in the method of perforation. A typical specimen of this class, four and a half inches in diameter, is shown in Fig. 3. It was associated with the remains of a number of children in a mound in Hardin County, Ohio. Disks of this class were usually suspended upon the breast with the concave side out. That many of the specimens described were suspended in this way is indicated by the character of the abrasion produced by the cords. On the concave side the cord of suspension has worn deep grooves between the perforations, and on the opposite or convex side similar grooves extend obliquely upward from the holes toward the margin of the disk, indicating the passage of the cord upward and outward around the neck of the wearer.

A large white disk, similar to the one just described, was obtained from a grave at Accotink, Va. It is five inches in diameter and has one central and three marginal perforations. It is made from a *Busycon perversum*, and is neatly shaped and well polished.

A fine specimen two inches in diameter was obtained from a mound on the French Broad River, Tenn., and, with many other similar specimens, is now in the national collection.

The central perforation is often very much enlarged. A number of specimens, recently sent to the National Museum, from a mound in Auglaize County, Ohio, show several stages of this enlargement. One specimen five inches across has a perforation nearly one inch in diameter, while in another the perforation is enlarged until the disk has become a ring. These gorgets show evidences of long use, the surfaces and edges being worn and the perforations much extended in the manner described above. They have been derived from the *Busycon perversum*.

In Fig. 4 I illustrate an annular gorget from a mound in Alexander County, Ill. It was found associated with ornaments of copper by the side of a human skull, and is hence supposed to have been an ear ornament. It is fragmentary and has suffered greatly from decay, the surface being mostly covered with a dark film of decomposed shell substance, which when broken away, exposes the chalky surface of the shell. These shell rings, so far as I can learn, have been found in the States of Ohio and Illinois only.

Rectangular pendants are much more rare. The national collection contains one rude specimen from Texas. It is about two inches wide by two and a half long, and is made from the base of some large dextral-whorled shell. A similar but much more finished specimen comes from Georgia, and is preserved in the New York Natural History Museum.

A large keystone-shaped gorget with rounded corners was obtained from an ancient burial place at Beverly, Canada. It is illustrated in Plate L, Fig. 1.

The small pendant shown in Fig. 5 is given by Schoolcraft in "Notes on the Iroquois." It represents rudely the human figure, and is ornamented with eight perpendicular and four or five transverse dots. It was found on the site of an old fort near Jamesville, N. Y. In the same work Mr. Schoolcraft illustrates another small pendant, which is reproduced in Fig. 6. The body is heart-shaped, the perforation being made through a rectangular projection at the upper end. It was found at Onondaga, N. Y.

The small pendant presented in Fig. 7 is from West Bloomfield, N. Y. It has been suspended by means of a shallow groove near the upper end. It is made from the basal point of a dextral-whorled shell.

The handsome little pendant shown in Fig. 8 was found with similar specimens in Monroe County, New York—probably on some ancient village site. It is well preserved and has been made from the columella of a dextral-whorled shell. An ornamental design, consisting of lines and dots, is engraved upon the face. A small, deeply countersunk perforation has been made near the upper end. These objects have apparently been strung with beads, as the perforations show evidence of such abrasion as beads would produce. Many of the New York specimens have a new look, and their form suggests the possibility of civilized influence. They are certainly more recent than the western and southern specimens.

A small cylindrical pendant is illustrated in Fig. 9. A large, neat perforation has been made at the upper end, and the middle portion of the body is ornamented by a series of encircling grooves. This specimen has been made from a large *Unio* and was obtained from a mound in Union County, Ky.

Western forms.—In variety of form the plain pendants of the California coast excel all others. Specimens from the graves are generally well preserved, not having lost their original iridescence, although so much decayed as to suffer considerably from exfoliation.

As indicated by the present well preserved condition of these shell ornaments, they are probably not of very ancient date; indeed it is highly probable that many of them are post-Columbian.

Cabrillo visited the island of Santa Rosa in 1542 and found a numerous and thriving people. In 1816 only a small remnant of the inhabitants remained, and these were removed to the main-land by Catholic priests. Their destruction is attributed to both war and famine. The history of the other islands is doubtless somewhat similar.

Articles made from shell are found to resemble each other very closely, whether from the islands or the main-land. All probably belong to the same time, and although the peoples of the islands are said to have spoken a different language from those of the main-land, their arts were

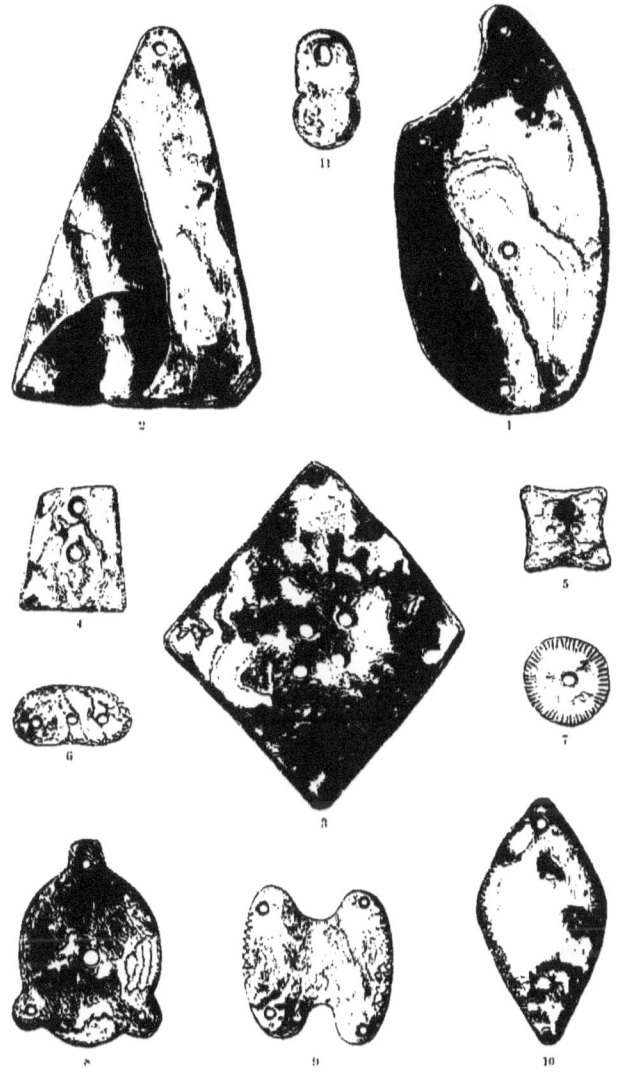

PLAIN PENDANTS—PACIFIC COAST FORMS.

apparently pretty much the same. They do not differ, as far as works in shell are concerned, from the modern tribes of the main-land. There is also a noticeable resemblance between the art of the ancient California Islanders and that of the present inhabitants of the great Pacific archipelagoes.

The record of many of the specimens obtained from these islands seems to be very incomplete, scarcely more being known than the fact that they were obtained from the ancient graves. Since, however, they are almost exclusively ornaments belonging probably to a single period, detailed accounts of their methods of occurrence would not add greatly to their value.

In previous chapters vessels, hooks, and beads made of the *Haliotis* have been described, and the high estimation in which they are everywhere held briefly noted. The variety of ways in which this shell is utilized is indeed remarkable and the multitude of forms into which it is worked for ornament is a matter of surprise. All are neatly and effectively worked, and evince no little skill and taste on the part of the makers.

The *Haliotis* is not the only shell used, but it has no rival in point of beauty. Bivalve shells are utilized to a considerable extent, many tasteful things being made from the *Fissurella*, the *Mytilus*, the *Pachydesma*, and the *Pecten*. The perforations are generally neatly made and are more numerous than in similar eastern specimens; besides those for suspension there are frequently many others for the attachment of secondary pendants and for fastening to the costume. Many specimens are ornamented with edgings of notches and crossed lines but very few have been found on which significant characters have been engraved, and we look in vain for parallels to the curious designs characteristic of the gorgets of the mound-builders.

A glance at the numerous examples given in Plates XLVII, XLVIII, and XLIX will give a good idea of the multiplicity of forms into which these ornaments are wrought.

A rather remarkable group of pendants is represented by Fig. 1. They are characterized by a deep scallop at the left, with a long curved hook-like projection above. They take their form from the shape of the lip of the *Haliotis*, from which they are made—the hook being the upper point of the outer lip where it joins the body, and the scallop the line of the suture. The body of the ornament is formed from the lip of the shell. In size they vary to some extent with the shells from which they are derived. The body is at times quite oval and again slender and hooked like the blade of a sickle. The perforations are generally very numerous, a fact that indicates their use as central pieces for composite pendants. It is apparent that the wearers thought more of the exquisite coloring of these ornaments than of the outline or surface finish. This is only one of many instances that prove the innate and universal appreciation of beauty of color by savage peoples.

In Fig. 2 a fine example of the subtriangular or keystone shaped pendants is presented. The edges are very neatly cut and the corners slightly rounded. The back is ground smooth, but on the front the original surface of the shell is preserved, the colors being extremely rich and brilliant. A single perforation has been drilled near the upper end. It is made from a *Haliotis rufescens*, and was obtained from the island of Santa Rosa.

The handsome specimen shown in Fig. 3 was obtained from a grave on the island of San Miguel. It has suffered much from decay. There are four neatly made perforations near the center. It has apparently been cut from the same shell as the preceding.

Fig. 4 is a small keystone-shaped specimen having two perforations.

Fig. 5 represents a small, delicate specimen of rectangular shape, having two minute perforations. This, as well as the preceding, was obtained from a grave on the island of San Miguel.

Fig. 6 illustrates a small oval, wafer-like specimen, the edges of which have been ornamented with a series of crossed lines. It has three neat perforations on the line of the longer axis. It is from the island of Santa Cruz.

Fig. 7 represents a small button-like disk with a central perforation; the margin is ornamented with a series of radiating lines. It was obtained from Santa Barbara.

A pendant of very peculiar form is shown in Fig. 8. The oval body has three marginal projections, all of which are perforated; there is also a perforation near the center. The surface retains a heavy coating of some dark substance, which gives the ornament much the appearance of corroded metal. It was obtained from San Miguel Island.

In a number of cases advantage has been taken of the natural perforations of the shell, both to give variety to the outline of small pendants and to save the labor of making artificial perforations. A very handsome little specimen is shown in Fig. 9. The two indentations above and below represent two of the natural perforations of the shell; artificial perforations are made in each of the four corners or wings. It was also obtained from the island of San Miguel.

Fig. 10 represents a leaf-shaped pendant with notched edges and a single perforation. It comes from the island of Santa Cruz.

The examples given are typical of the very large class of ornaments derived from the *Haliotidæ*. The striking specimens shown in Plate XLVIII are, with one exception, made from shells of this class. The two sickle-shaped pendants illustrated in Figs. 1 and 2 are made from the broadened inner lip of the *Haliotis californianus* (?). In one a single perforation has been made near the upper end; in the other there are two, one near each end. The faces have been neatly dressed and the corners ornamented with minute notches. They are from graves on Santa Cruz Island. Two exquisite specimens, also from Santa Cruz Island, are presented in Figs. 3 and 4. They have been cut from the body of a

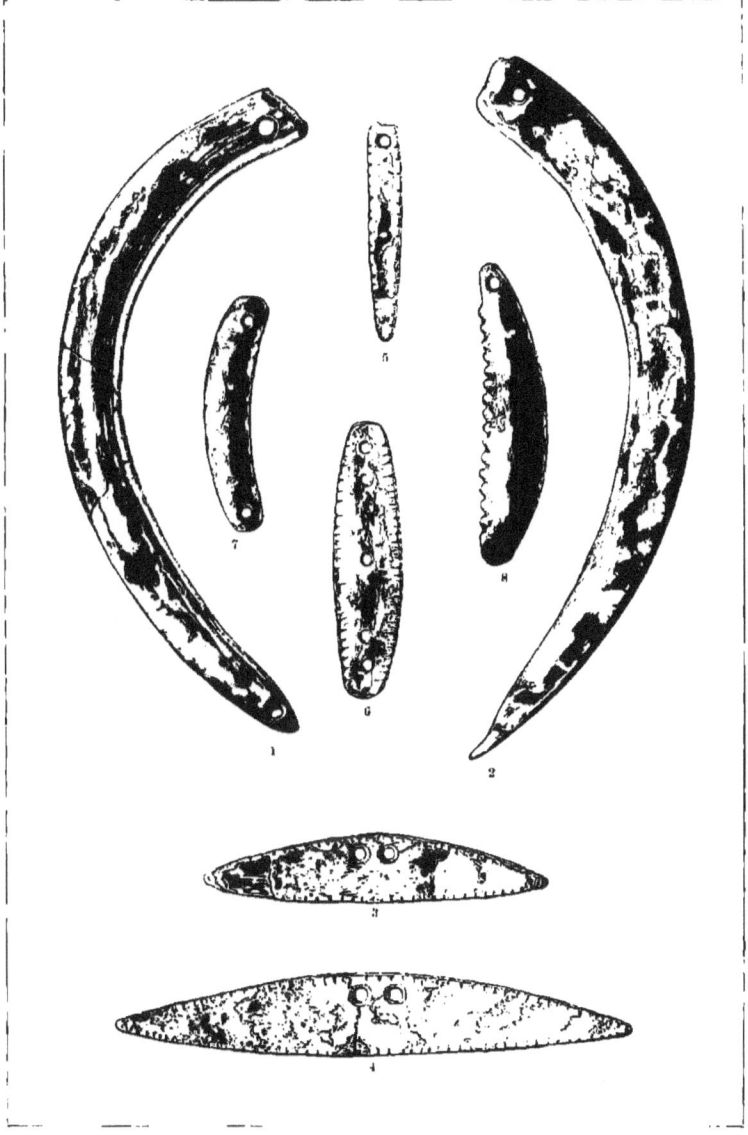

1-7. Pendants made of the Haliotis. (½)   8. Pendant made of a Cyprea. (½)

PENDANT ORNAMENTS OF THE PACIFIC COAST.

Haliotis splendens (?), and finished with much care. Two perforations have been made near the upper margin, which is arched or curved while the lower is nearly straight. The edges are neatly notched. Although somewhat altered by exposure these objects are still very pretty.

A very neat, well preserved little pendant is shown in Fig. 5. The specimen presented in Fig. 6 is peculiar in having a series of five perforations, one near the middle and the others near the ends. The example given in Fig. 7 has two perforations, one at each end. These are all made from species of the *Haliotis*.

The specimen presented in Fig. 8 is made from the lip of a *Cyprea spadicea* with very little change except the carefully made perforation. It is from the island of San Miguel. The idea of beautifying ornaments made from the *Haliotis* and other shells by notching the edges may have been suggested by the natural notches characteristic of the *Cyprcas*.

Figs. 1, 2, and 3, Plate XLIX, illustrate a group of small, delicate, ladle-shaped pendants. The perforation for suspension is at the upper end of the handle and the body has an oval or circular perforation, which is often so enlarged as to leave only a narrow ring, like the rim of an eyeglass. The specimen shown in Fig. 3 has two lobes, with a large perforation or opening in each. In one instance the handle is quite wide at the upper end and ornamented by two deep lateral notches. The edges of these specimens are nearly always adorned with notches or crossed lines. All are fashioned from the *Haliotis*, and although considerably stained are still well enough preserved to show the pearly lusters of that shell.

Circular and oval disks are also numerous and vary much in finish; some have a great number of perforations or indentations, and nearly all are neatly notched around the margins. Examples are given in Figs. 4 and 5.

The national collection contains a number of rings and pieces of rings made from the valves of a large clam, probably a *Pectunculus*, one example of which is shown in Fig. 6. The convex back of the shell is ground off until a marginal ring only remains. A perforation is made near the angle of the beak. The shell is from the California coast, but the rings were collected mostly if not entirely from Arizona and New Mexico. It is not impossible that the tribes of the interior procured these articles from white traders, as they are known to have secured other shell ornaments in this way.

The natives of the California coast were not slow in taking advantage of natural forms to aid their art or to save labor. The shells of the *Fissurellidæ* as well as of the *Haliotidæ* have been in great favor. They have been used as beads and pendants in their natural state or the natural perforations have been enlarged until only a ring has been left, or the margin and sides have been ground down until nothing of the original form or surface remained. Two of these forms are shown in Figs. 7

and 8. They are from graves on San Miguel Island, and are made from the *Lucupina crenulata*; others come from Santa Cruz Island, and probably also from the adjoining islands as well as from the main land. Rings are also made from other shells. Examples made from the *Acmæa mitra* and *Cyprea spadicea* are shown in Figs. 9, 10, and 11. They come from San Miguel.

PERFORATED PLATES.

We find that pendant gorgets grade imperceptibly into another group of objects, the use or significance of which have not be fully determined. These objects are more frequently made of stone or copper, but good examples in shell have been found. As a rule they take the form of thin oblong plates which exhibit great variety of outline. The perforations are peculiar, and have not been designed for ordinary suspension, but are placed near the middle of the specimen as if for fixing it to the person or costume by means of cords. Many theories have been advanced in attempting to determine their use. They have been classed as gorgets, badges of authority, shuttles, armor plates, wrist protectors, and as implements for sizing sinews and twisting cords.

Objects of this class in stone have been frequently illustrated and described. They are made of many varieties of stone, some of which seem to have been selected on account of their beauty. They have been neatly shaped and often well-polished. The edges are occasionally notched and the surfaces ornamented with patterns of incised lines. The perforations vary from one to four, the greater number of specimens, however, having only two. In the early days of mound exploration objects of this class were even greater enigmas, if possible, than they are to-day. Even the material of which a number of them were formed remained for a long time undetermined. Schoolcraft has published an illustration of a large specimen from the Grave Creek Mound, Va. This drawing is reproduced in Fig. 3, Plate L. The original was six inches long, one and three-tenths inches wide, and three-tenths of an inch in thickness. He expresses the opinion that it was one of those ancient badges of authority formerly in such general use among the Indians.[1]

Another specimen, very much like the last in size and shape, but made of shell, supposed at the time of discovery to be ivory, was found associated with human remains in the Grave Creek Mound. It is described by Mr. Tomlinson in the American Pioneer,[2] and the cut given in Plate L, Fig. 4, is copied from that work.

A remarkable specimen of this class is given in Fig. 5. It is made

[1] Schoolcraft, in Trans. Am. Eth. Soc., Vol. II, Plate 1.
[2] Tomlinson, in The American Pioneer, Vol. II, p. 200.

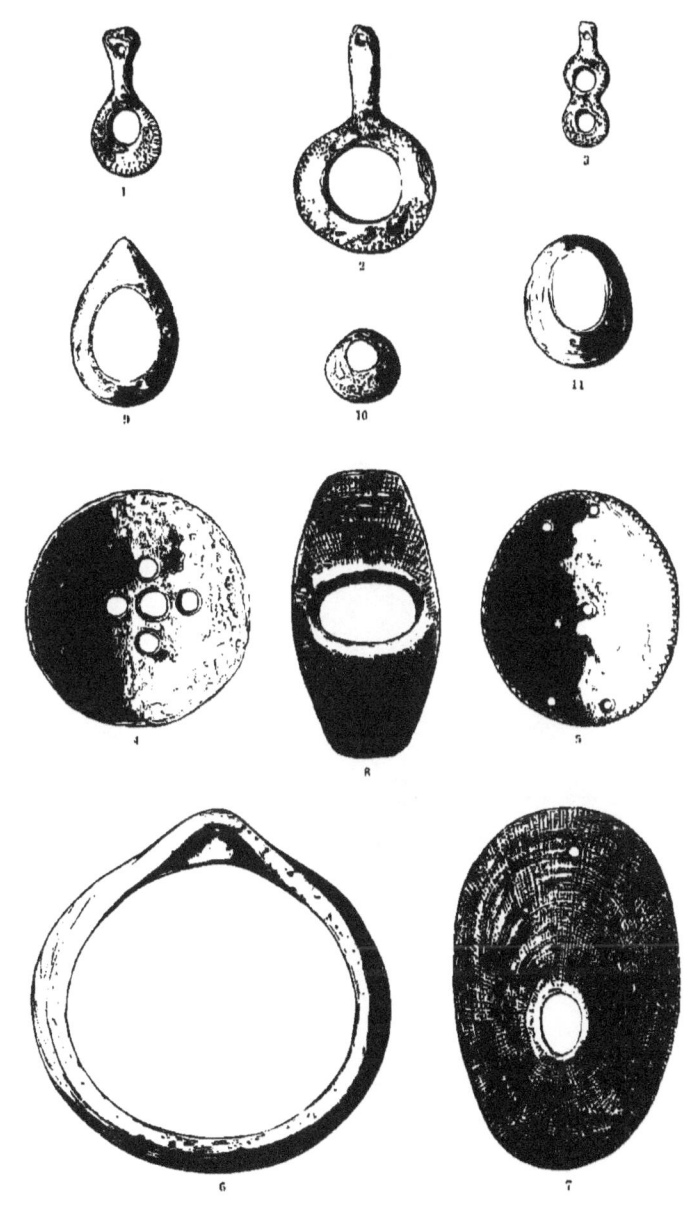

PLAIN PENDANTS—PACIFIC COAST FORMS.

(1)

from the body of a large *Busycon perversum*, and is nine and a half inches long by three inches in width at the widest part. The concave surface has been highly polished, but is now somewhat roughened by weathering; the back has been slightly ground to take off the rougher ridges of growth: the edges are even and rounded and in many places quite thin. The peculiarity of its shape is such as to give it very much the appearance of the sole of a sandal. The perforations are three in number, one being near the middle and the others near the broader end, about one and a half inches apart; they are very neatly made and are slightly bi-conical and a little countersunk. There appears to be no evidence whatever of abrasion by use. It was found associated with human remains in a mound at Sharpsburg, Mercer County, Ohio. A similar specimen from the same locality is nearly nine inches in length, and lacks but a little of three and a half inches in width. As in the specimen illustrated, one perforation is placed near the middle and two others near the broader end. This specimen is highly polished on the broader part of the back, and is evenly smoothed on the concave side. It bears evidence of considerable use, and the two holes are much worn by a string or cord, which, passing from one hole to the other on the concave side of the plate, gradually worked a deep groove between them. On the back or convex side, the perforations show no evidence of wear. The central perforation is not worn on either side. The letter of Mr. Whitney, transmitting this relic to the National Museum, states that there were in the mound "about ten pairs of the shell sandals of different sizes, and made to fit the right and left feet." From the latter remark I should infer that some were made from dextral and others from sinistral shells; the two described are made from the *Busycon perversum*.

An extremely fine specimen, much like the preceding, was exhumed from an ancient mound in Hardin County, Ohio. It was found on the head of a skeleton which occupied a sitting posture near the center of the mound. It is nine inches in length by three and one-half inches in width, and in shape resembles the sole of a moccasin, being somewhat broader and less pointed than the specimen presented in Fig. 5. It had been placed upon the skull with the wider end toward the back, but whether laid there as a burial offering simply or as constituting a part of the head-dress of the dead savage we have no means of determining. The perforations are three in number, and are placed similarly to those in the specimen illustrated in Fig. 5. Two other skeletons had similar plates associated with them, which differed from the one described in size only, the smaller one being less than six inches in length. Lithographs of two of these specimens are given by Mr. Matson, in whose very excellent report they were first described.[1]

The gorget presented in Fig. 1 of this plate is copied from Schoolcraft.[2] It was taken, along with many other interesting relics, from

---

[1] Matson, in Ohio Centennial Report, p. 131.

[2] Schoolcraft: History of the Indian Tribes, &c., part I, plate XIX.

one of the ossuaries at Beverly, Canada West. It is formed from some large sea shell, and is three inches in width by three and three-fourths inches in length. Its perforations are four in number, and are so placed as to be conveniently used either for suspension by a single cord or for fixing firmly by means of two or more cords. It seems to hold a middle place between pendants proper and the pierced tablets under consideration.[1]

The unique specimen given in Fig. 2 is from Cedar Keys, Florida, but whether from a grave or a shell-heap I am at present unable to state. In its perforations, which are large and doubly conical, it resembles very closely the typical tablet of stone. The outline is peculiar; being rounded at the top, it grows broader toward the base like a celt, and terminates at the outer corners in well-rounded points, the edge between being ornamented with a series of notches or teeth. It has been cut from the wall of a *Busycon perversum*, and is sharply curved. The surface is roughened by time, but there is no evidence of wear by use either in the perforations or in the notches at the base.

In studying these remarkable specimens the fact that they so seldom show marks of use presents itself for explanation. Dr. Charles Rau, whose opinions in such matters are always worthy of consideration, remarks " that at first sight one might be inclined to consider them as objects of ornament, or as badges of distinction; but this view is not corroborated by the appearance of the perforations, which exhibit no trace of that peculiar abrasion produced by constant suspension. The classification of the tablets as ' gorgets,' therefore, appears to be erroneous."[2]

The same argument could, however, be brought with equal force against their use for any of the other purposes suggested. The perforations, if not used for suspension or attachment, would be subject to wear from any other use to which they could be put. But, as we have already seen, one of the specimens in shell exhibits well-defined evidence of wear, and that of such a character as to indicate the passage of a cord between the perforations in a position that would produce abrasion between the holes on the concave side of the plate, but would leave the back entirely unworn. This peculiar result could only be produced by attachment in a fixed position, concave side out, to some object perforated like the plate, the cord passing directly through both. The perforations of pendants necessarily show wear on both sides; a like result would follow from the use of these plates in any of the other ways mentioned. Those made of shell could not, on account of their warped

[1] The ossuaries here mentioned are in the township of Beverly, twenty miles from Dundas, at the head of Lake Ontario. They are situated in a primitive forest, and were discovered upwards of thirty years ago through the uprooting of a tree. Large numbers of skeletons had been deposited longitudinally in trenches, with many implements, utensils, and ornaments. Two brass kettles were found in one of the graves. (Schoolcraft: Red Races of America, p. 326.)

[2] Rau: Archaeological Collection of the National Museum, p. 33.

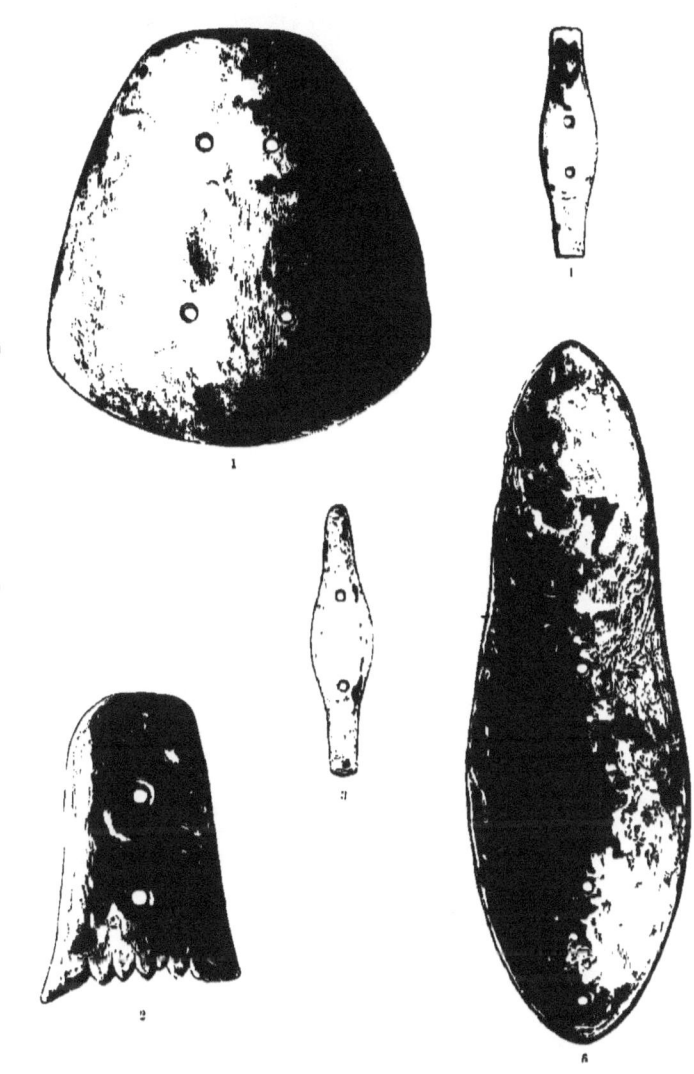

1. Ornament from Beverly, C. W.   3, 4. Objects from the Grave Creek Mound, Va.
2. Ornament from Florida.   5. Perforated plate from Ohio.

PERFORATED PLATES.

shape, be used for shuttles; besides, they show no evidence of marginal wear, such as would result from this use. The fact, too, that the material had to be brought from the distant sea-shore would seem to render it too rare and precious to be employed in the ordinary arts when wood, stone, and bone would serve the purpose as well. Owing to the carelessness or negligence of collectors we have but little information in regard to their relation to the human remains with which they were deposited. Such facts as we have, however, tend, I believe, to show that they were used for personal decoration. Again, the material of which they are formed is, on account of its beauty, especially adapted for ornament, and for this use it has been almost exclusively reserved by peoples as distant from the sea as were the ancient peoples of the Ohio Valley.

ENGRAVED GORGETS.

It has already been suggested that the simpler forms of pendants with plain surfaces may have had particular significance to their possessors, as insignia, amulets, or symbols, or that they may have received painted designs of such a character as to give significance to them. For ornament the natural or plainly polished surface of the shell possessed sufficient beauty to satisfy the most fastidious taste—a beauty that could hardly be enhanced by the addition of painted or incised figures. But we find that many of the larger gorgets obtained from the mounds and graves of a large district have designs of a most interesting nature engraved upon them, which are so remarkable in conception and execution as to command our admiration. Such is the character of these designs that we are at once impressed with the idea that they are not products of the idle fancy, neither is it possible that they had no higher office than the gratification of barbarian vanity. I have given much time to their examination, and, day by day, have become more strongly impressed with the belief that no single design is without its significance, and that their production was a serious art which dealt with matters closely interwoven with the history, mythology and polity of a people gradually developing a civilization of their own.

Although these objects were worn as personal ornaments they probably had specialized uses as insignia, amulets, or symbols.

As *insignia*, they were badges of office or distinction. The devices engraved upon them were derived from many sources and were probably sometimes supplemented by numeral records representing enemies killed, prisoners taken, or other deeds accomplished.

As *amulets*, they were invested with protective or remedial attributes and contained mystic devices derived from dreams, visions, and many other sources.

As *symbols* they possessed, in most cases, a religious character, and were generally used as *totems* of clans. They were inscribed with characters derived chiefly from mythologic sources. A few examples contain geometric designs which may have been *time-symbols*, or they may have indicated the order of ceremonial exercises.

That these objects should be classed under one of these heads and not as simple ornaments engraved with intricate designs for embellishment alone is apparent when we consider the serious character of the work, the great amount of labor and patience shown, the frequent recurrence of the same design, the wide distribution of particular forms, the preservation of the idea in all cases, no matter what shortcomings occur in execution or detail, and the apparent absence of all lines, dots, and figures not essential to the presentation of the conception.

In describing these gorgets I have arranged them in groups distinguished by the designs engraved upon them.[1] They are presented in the following order:

The Cross,
The Scalloped Disk,
The Bird,
The Spider,
The Serpent,
The Human Face,
The Human Figure: and to these I append The Frog,

which is found in Arizona only, and although carved in shell does not appear to have been used as a pendant, as no perforations are visible.

Within the United States ancient tablets containing engraved designs are apparently confined to the Atlantic slope, and are not found to any extent beyond the limits of the district occupied by the stone-grave peoples. Early explorers along the Atlantic coast mention the use of engraved gorgets by a number of tribes. Modern examples may be found occasionally among the Indians of the northwest coast as well as upon the islands of the central Pacific.

THE CROSS.

The discoverers and early explorers of the New World were filled with surprise when they beheld their own sacred emblem, the cross, mingling with the pagan devices of the western barbarian. Writers have speculated in vain—the mystery yet remains unsolved. Attempts to connect the use of the cross by prehistoric Americans with its use in the East have signally failed, and we are compelled to look on its occurrence here as one of those strange coincidences so often found in the practices of peoples totally foreign to each other.

If written history does not establish beyond a doubt the fact that the cross had a place in our aboriginal symbolism, we have but to turn

[1] The handsome illustrations presented in the accompanying plates were mostly drawn by Miss Kate C. Osgood, who has no superior in this class of work.

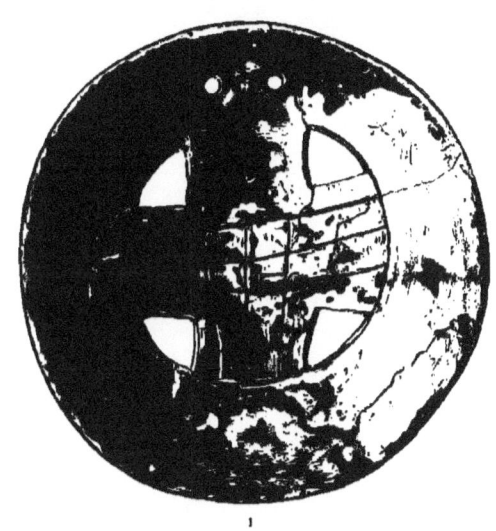

1

2

1. From a mound, Union County, Ill.   2. From Charleston, Mo.

SHELL GORGETS—THE CROSS.

to the pages of the great archæologic record, where we find that it occupies a place in ancient American art so intimately interwoven with conceptions peculiar to the continent that it cannot be separated from them. It is found associated with other prehistoric remains throughout nearly the entire length and breadth of America.

I have the pleasure of presenting a few new examples of this emblem, obtained from the district at one time occupied by the mound-builders. The examples are carved in shell or engraved upon disks of shell which have been employed as pendant gorgets. In the study of these particular relics, one important fact in recent history must be kept constantly in mind. The first explorers were accompanied by Christian zealots, who spared no effort to root out the native superstitions and introduce a foreign religion, of which the cross was the all-important symbol. This emblem was generally accepted by the savages as the only tangible feature of a new system of belief that was filled with subtleties too profound for their comprehension. As a result, the cross was at once introduced into the regalia of the natives; at first probably in a European form and material attached to a string of beads in precisely the manner that they had been accustomed to suspend their own trinkets and gorgets; but soon, no doubt, delineated or carved by their own hands upon tablets of stone and copper and shell, in the place of their own peculiar conceptions. From the time of La Salle down to the extinction of the savage in the middle Mississippi province, the cross was kept constantly before him, and its presence may thus be accounted for in such remains as post-date the advent of the whites. Year after year articles of European manufacture are being discovered in the most unexpected places, and we shall find it impossible to assign any single example of these crosses to a prehistoric period, with the assurance that our statements will not some day be challenged. It is certainly unfortunate that the American origin of any work of art resembling European forms must rest forever under a cloud of suspicion. As long as a doubt exists in regard to the origin of a relic, it is useless to employ it in a discussion where important deductions are to be made. At the same time it should not be forgotten that the cross was undoubtedly used as a symbol by the prehistoric nations of the South, and consequently that it was probably also known in the North. A great majority of the relics associated with it in ancient mounds and burial places are undoubtedly aboriginal. In the case of the shell gorgets, the tablets themselves belong to an American type, and are highly characteristic of the art of the Mississippi Valley. A majority of the designs engraved upon them are also characteristic of the same district.

We find at rare intervals designs that are characteristically foreign; these, whether Mexican or European, are objects of special interest and merit the closest possible examination. That the design under consideration, as well as every other engraved upon these tablets, is symbolic or otherwise significant, I do not for a moment doubt; but the probabilities as to the European or American origin of the symbol of the cross found in this region are pretty evenly balanced. In its delineation there is certainly nothing to indicate its origin. By reference to Plate LIII it will be seen that in all the examples given it is a simple and symmetrical cross, which might be duplicated a thousand times in the religious art of any country. A study of the designs associated with the cross in these gorgets is instructive, but does not lead to any definite result. In one case the cross is inscribed upon the back of a great spider; in another it is surrounded by a rectangular framework of lines, looped at the corners, and guarded by four mysterious birds, while in others it is without attendant characters; but the workmanship is purely aboriginal. I have not seen a single example of engraving upon shell that suggested a foreign hand, or a design, with the exception of this one, that could claim a European derivation.

Some very ingenious theories have been elaborated in attempting to account for the presence of the cross among American symbols. Brinton believes that the great importance attached to the points of the compass—the four quarters of the heavens—by savage peoples has given rise to the sign of the cross. With others the cross is a phallic symbol, derived, by some obscure process of evolution, from the veneration accorded to the reciprocal principle in nature. It is also frequently associated with sun-worship, and is recognized as a symbol of the sun—the four arms being remaining rays left after a gradual process of elimination. Whatever is finally determined in reference to the origin of the cross as a religious symbol in America will probably result from the exhaustive study of the history, language, and art of the ancient peoples, combined with a thorough knowledge of the religious conceptions of modern tribes, and when these sources of information are all exhausted it is probable that the writer who asserts more than a probability will overreach his proofs.

Such delineations of the cross as we find embodied in ancient aboriginal art represent only the final stages of its evolution, and it is not to be expected that its origin can be traced through them. In one instance, however, a direct derivation from nature is suggested. The ancient Mexican pictographic manuscripts abound in representations of trees, conventionalized in such a manner as to resemble crosses; these apparently take an important part in the scenes depicted. By a comparison of these curious trees with the remarkable cross in the Palenque tablet, I have been led to the belief that they must have a common significance and origin. The analogies are indeed remarkable. The tree-cross in the paintings is often the central figure of a group in which priests offer sacrifice, or engage in some similar religious rite. The cross holds the same relation in the Palenque group. The branches of these cross-shaped trees terminate in clusters of symbolic fruit, and the arms of the cross are loaded down with symbols which, although highly conventionalized, have not yet entirely lost their vege-

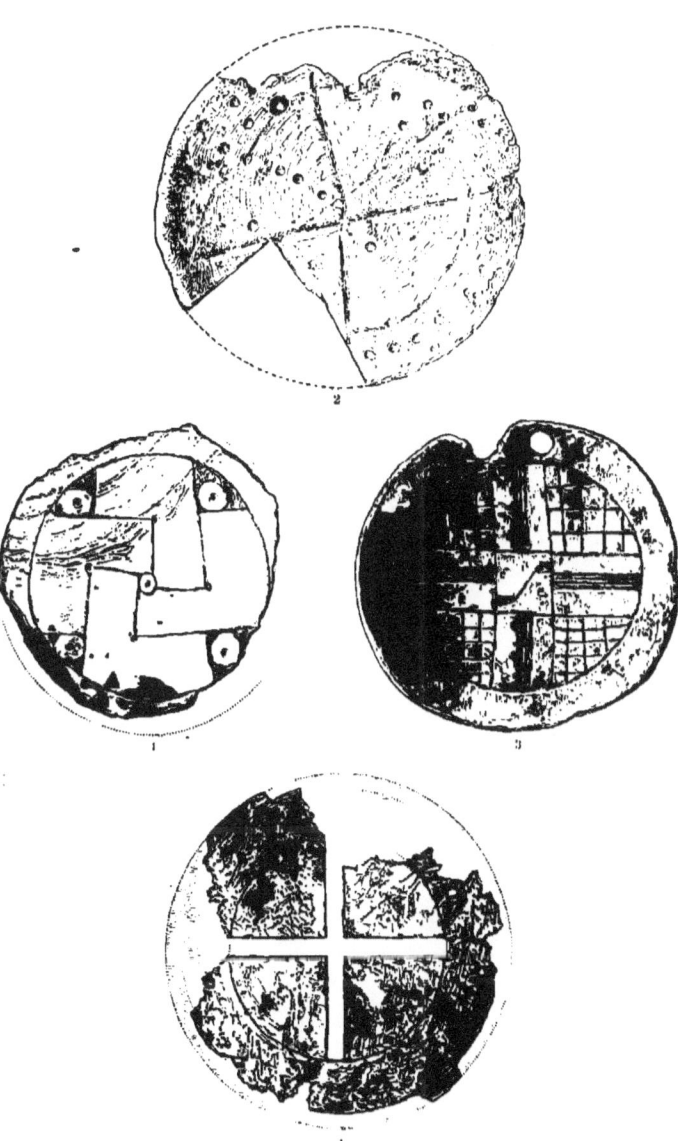

1. Shell gorget, Fain's Island, Tenn.   3. Shell gorget, Lick Creek, Tenn.
2. Shell gorget, Lick Creek, Tenn.   4. Copper plate, Ohio.

THE CROSS OF THE MOUND-BUILDERS.

tuble character. The most remarkable feature, however, is not that the crosses resemble each other in these respects, but that they perform like functions in giving support to a symbolic bird which is perched upon the summit. This bird appears to be the important feature of the group, and to it, or the deity which it represents, the homage or sacrifice is offered. These analogies go still farther; the bases of the cross in the tablet and of the crosses in the paintings are made to rest upon a highly conventionalized figure of some mythical creature. A consideration of these facts seems to me to lead to the conclusion that the myths represented in all of these groups are identical, and that the cross and cross-like trees have a common origin. Whether that origin is in the tree on the one hand or in a cross otherwise evolved on the other I shall not attempt to say.

The gorget presented in Fig. 1., Plate LI, belongs to the collection of Mr. F. M. Perrine, and was obtained from a mound in Union County, Ill. It is a little more than three inches in diameter and has been ground down to a uniform thickness of about one-twelfth of an inch. The surfaces are smooth and the margin carefully rounded and polished. Near the upper edge are two perforations for suspension. The cord used passed between the holes on the concave side, wearing a shallow groove. On the convex side, or back, the cord marks extend upward and outward, indicating the usual method of suspension about the neck. The cross which occupies the center of the concave face of the disk, is quite simple. It is partially inclosed on one side by a semicircular line, and at present has no other definition than that given by four triangular perforations which separate the arms. The face of the cross is ornamented with six carelessly drawn incised lines, which interlace in the center, as shown in the cut—three extending along the arm to the right and three passing down the lower arm to the inclosing line. I have not been able to learn anything of the character of the interments with which this specimen was associated.

Fig. 2 of the same plate represents a large shell cross, the encircling rim of which has been broken away. The perforations are still intact. The cross is quite plain. This specimen is very much decayed, and came to the National Museum inside of a skull obtained from a grave at Charleston, Mo. Beyond this there is no record of the specimen.

In Fig. 1, Plate LII, I present a large fragment of a circular shell ornament, on the convex surface of which a very curious ornamental design has been engraved. The design, inclosed by a circle, represents a cross such as would be formed by two rectangular tablets or slips, slit longitudinally and interlaced at right angles to each other. Between the arms of the cross in the spaces inclosed by the circular border line are four annular nodes, having small conical depressions in the center. These nodes have been relieved by cutting away portions of the shell around them. In the center of the cross is another small node or ring similarly relieved. The lines are neat and deeply incised.

The edge of the shell has been broken away nearly all around. The accompanying cut represents the ornament natural size—one and a half inches in diameter and one-sixteenth of an inch in thickness. It was obtained from a mound on Fain's Island, Tennessee.

The small gorget presented in Fig. 2, Plate LII, is of inferior workmanship and the lines and dots seem to have a somewhat haphazard arrangement. The cross, which may or may not be significant, consists of two shallow irregular grooves which cross each other at right angles near the center of the disk and terminate near the border. There are indications of an irregular, somewhat broken, concentric line near the margin. A number of shallow conical pits have been drilled at rather irregular intervals over most of the surface. One pair of perforations seems to have been broken away and others drilled, one of the latter has also been broken out. A triangular fragment is lost from the lower margin of the disk. This specimen was obtained from a mound on Lick Creek, East Tennessee, by Mr. Dunning.

The gorget shown in Fig. 3 contains a typical example of the cross of the mound-builder. The cut was made from a pencil sketch and is probably not quite accurate in detail. The border of the disk is plain, with the exception of the usual perforations at the top. The cross is inclosed in a carelessly drawn circle, and the spaces between the arms, which in other crosses are entirely cut out, or are filled with rays or other figures, are here decorated with a pattern of crossed lines. The lines which define the arms of the cross intersect in the middle of the disk. The square figure thus produced in the center contains a device that is probably significant. A doubly-curved or S-shaped incised line, widened at the ends, extends obliquely across the square from the right upper to the left lower corner. This figure appears to be an elementary or unfinished form of the device found in the center of many of the more elaborate disks. Intersected by a similar line it would form a cross like that upon the back of one of the spiders shown in Plate LXI, or somewhat more evenly curved, it would resemble the involuted figure in the center of the circular disks given in Plate LIV. This specimen was obtained from a mound on Lick Creek, Tenn., and is now in the Peabody Museum.

In Fig. 4 a large copper disk from an Ohio mound is represented. The specimen is eight inches in diameter, is very thin, and has suffered greatly from corrosion. A symmetrical cross, the arms of which are five inches in length, has been cut out of the center. Two concentric lines have been impressed in the plate, one near the margin and the other touching the ends of the cross. It is now in the Natural History Museum at New York.

In Plate LIII I present a large number of crosses, most of which have been obtained from the mounds, or from ancient graves, within the district occupied by the mound-builders. Eight are engraved upon shell gorgets (illustrations of which are given in the accompanying

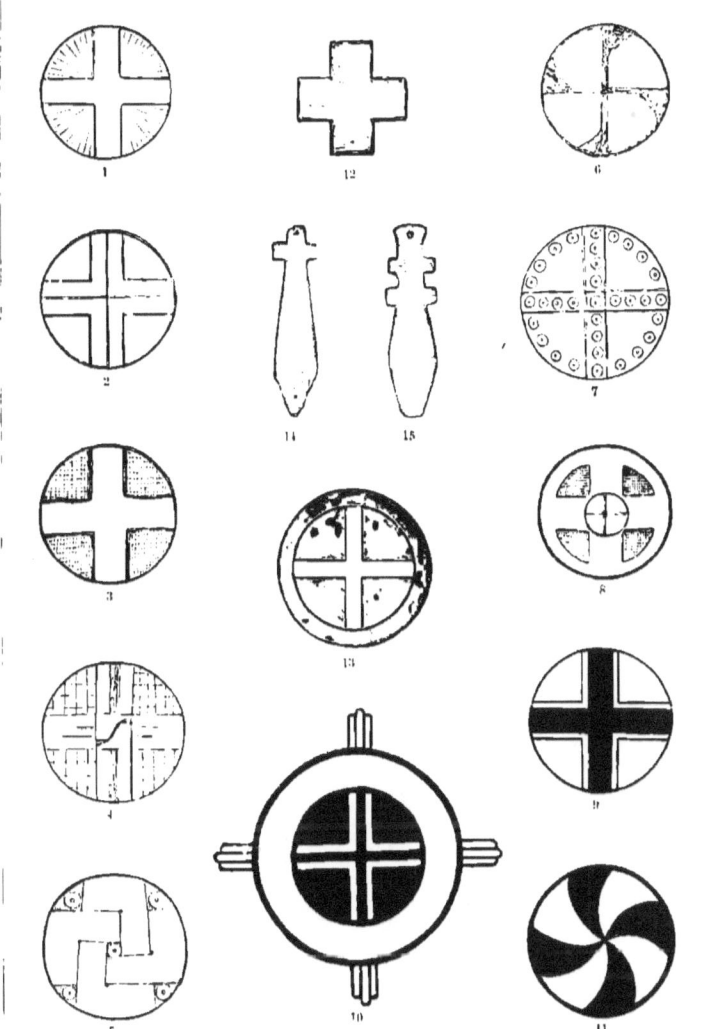

THE CROSS.

plates), one is cut in stone, three are painted upon pottery, and four are executed in copper. With two exceptions they are inclosed in circles, and are hence symmetrical Greek crosses, the ends being rounded to conform to the circle; the remaining two (Figs. 14 and 15) represent forms of the Latin cross, and resemble the crosses attached to the rosaries of the Catholic priesthood. A silver cross similar to the last given was obtained from a mound in Ohio.

The plate itself is instructive, and may be presented without further remark.

SCALLOPED DISKS.

In making a hasty classification of the many engraved gorgets, I have found it convenient to place in one group a numerous and somewhat extraordinary class of designs which have been engraved upon scalloped disks. Like the cross, the symbol here represented is one that cannot with certainty be referred to an original. The general shape of the disks is such as to suggest to most minds a likeness to the sun, the scallops being suggestive of the rays. As this orb is known to be an object of first importance in the economy of life—the source of light and heat —it is naturally an object of veneration among many primitive peoples. It is well known that the barbarian tribes of Mexico and South America had well-developed systems of sun-worship, and that they employed symbols of many forms, some of which still retained a likeness to the original, while others had assumed the garb of animals or fanciful creatures. These facts being known, it seems natural that such a symbol as the one under consideration should be referred to the great original, which it suggests.

The well-known fact that the district from which these gorgets come, was, at the time of discovery by the whites, inhabited by a race of sun-worshipers—the Natchez—gives to this assumption a shadow of confirmation. So far as I am aware, however, no one has ventured a positive opinion in regard to their significance, but such suggestions as have been made incline toward the view indicated above. I feel the great necessity of caution in such matters, and while combating the idea that the designs are ornamental or fanciful only, I am far from attributing to them any deeply mysterious significance. They may in some way or other indicate political or religious station, or they may even be cosmogenic, but the probabilities are much greater that they are time symbols. Before venturing further, however, it will be well to describe one of these disks, a typical example of which is presented in Plate LIV.

The specimen chosen as a type of these rosette-like disks was obtained from a mound near Nashville, Tenn., by Professor Powell. It was found near the head of a skeleton, which was much decayed, and had been so disturbed by recent movements of the soil as to render it difficult to determine its original position. The shell used is apparently a large specimen of the *Busycon perretsum*, although the lines

18 E

of growth are not sufficiently well preserved to permit a positive deter-
mination of the species. The substance of the shell is well preserved;
the surface was once highly polished, but is now pitted and discolored
by age. The design is engraved on the concave surface as usual, and
the lines are accurately drawn and clearly cut. The various concentric circles are drawn with geometric accuracy around a minute shallow pit as a center. These circles divide the surface into five parts—a
small circle at the center surrounded by four zones of unequal width.
The central circle is three-eighths of an inch in diameter, and is surrounded by a zone one-half an inch in width, which contains a rosette
of three involuted lines; these begin on the circumference of the inner
circle in three small equidistant perforations, and sweep outward to the
second circle, making upwards of half a revolution. These lines are
somewhat wider and more deeply engraved than the other lines of the
design. In many specimens they are so deeply cut in the middle part
of the curve as to penetrate the disk, producing crescent-shaped perforations. The second zone is one-fourth of an inch in width, and in
this, as in all other specimens, is quite plain.' The third zone is one-
half an inch in width, and exhibits some very interesting features.
Placed at almost equal intervals we find six circular figures, each of
which incloses a circlet and a small central pit; the spaces between the
circular figures are thickly dotted with minute conical pits, somewhat
irregularly placed; the number of dots in each space varies from thirty-
six to forty, which gives a total of about two hundred and thirty.

The outer zone is subdivided into thirteen compartments, in each of
which a nearly circular figure or boss has been carved, the outer edges
of which form the scalloped outline of the gorget. Two medium sized
perforations for suspension have been made near the inner margin of
one of the bosses next the dotted zone; these show slight indications of
abrasion by the cord of suspension. These perforations, as well as the
three near the center, have been bored mainly from the convex side of the
disk. Whatever may be the meaning of this design, we cannot fail to
recognize the important fact that it is significant—that an idea is expressed. Were the design ornamental, we should expect variation in
the parts or details of different specimens resulting from difference of
taste in the designers; if simply copied from an original example for
sale or trade to the inhabitants we might expect a certain number of
exact reproductions; but in such a case, when variations did occur, they
would hardly be found to follow uniform or fixed lines; there would also
be variation in the relation of the parts of the conception as well as in
the number of particular parts; the zones would not follow each other
in exactly the same order; particular figures would not be confined to
particular zones; the rays of the volute would not always have a sinistral turn, or the form of the tablet be always circular and scalloped.
It cannot be supposed that of the whole number of these objects at one
time in use, more than a small number have been rescued from decay,

SCALLOPED SHELL DISK.

Nashville, Tenn.

(½)

and these have been obtained from widely scattered localities and doubtless represent centuries of time, yet no variants appear to indicate a
leading up to or a divergence from the one particular type. A design
of purely ornamental character, even if executed by the same hand,
could not, in the nature of things, exhibit the uniformity in variation
here shown. Fancy, unfettered by ideas of a fixed nature, such as
those pertaining to religious or sociologic customs, would vary with the
locality, the day, the year, or the life. I have examined upwards of
thirty of these scalloped disks, the majority of which are made of shell.
I shall not attempt to describe each specimen, but shall call attention to
such important variations from the type as may be noticed.

In Fig. 1, Plate LV, we have a well-preserved disk which has four
involute lines, the others having three only; these lines are deeply cut
and, for about one-third of their length, penetrate the shell, producing
four crescent-shaped perforations. The circles in the third or dotted
zone are neatly made and evenly spaced, and inclose circlets and conical pits. The dots in the intervening spaces are closely and irregularly
placed, and in number range from forty to forty-five, giving a total of
about three hundred and forty. Other features are as usual. The specimen was obtained from a stone grave in Kane's Field, near Nashville,
Tenn., and is now in the Peabody Museum.

It is possible that the specimen presented in Fig. 2, Plate LV, should
not be placed in this group; but as there are many points of resemblance to the type, it may be described here. At first sight it appears
that one of the outer zones is lacking, but it will be seen that through
some unknown cause the two have been merged together, alternating
bosses of the outer line being carried across both zones. The whole design has been carelessly laid out and rudely engraved. The lines of the
involute are arranged in four groups of two each and occupy an unusually wide belt. There are near the margin two sets of perforations for
suspension. The specimen was obtained from the Brakebill mound, near
Knoxville, Tenn., and is in an advanced stage of decay.

In Plate LVI, Fig. 4, I present a small specimen, which has the appearance of being unfinished. The zones are all defined, but, with the
exception of the outer, which has thirteen bosses, are quite plain. The
lines are deeply but rudely cut. It was obtained from a stone grave at
Oldtown, Tenn., and is now in the Peabody Museum.

Besides the type specimen already presented, there may be seen in the
National Museum two very good examples, from a mound near Franklin, Tenn. The smaller is about three inches in diameter and is nearly
circular; it has suffered much from decay, but nearly all the design can
be made out. The lines of the involute penetrate the disk producing
short crescent-shaped perforations; the circles in the dotted zone are
seven in number and inclose the usual circlets and conical pits; the
dots in the intervening spaces are too obscure to be counted. The spec-

imen has sixteen marginal scallops. The larger specimen is somewhat fragmentary, portions being broken away from opposite sides. It is nearly four and a half inches in diameter, and the design has been drawn and engraved with more than ordinary precision. The central circle incloses a perforated circlet, and the involute lines are long and shallow. The dotted zone has seven circles with inclosed circlets and pits. The outer zone contains fifteen oval figures.

Another example of these shell disks is illustrated by Professor Putnam, in the eleventh annual report of the Peabody Museum, page 310. It is said to have been found near Nashville, Tenn., although its pedigree is not well established. According to Professor Putnam, it is made from the shell of a *Busycon*, and is apparently in a very good state of preservation. It is about four inches in diameter and is inscribed with the usual design, a central circle and dot surrounded by a triple involute and three concentric zones. The narrow inner zone is plain, as usual; the middle dotted zone has six circles with central dots, the spaces between being closely dotted, and the outer zone contains thirteen of the oval figures, the outer edges of which form the scalloped margin of the disk. The perforations for suspension are placed as usual near the inner margin of the outer zone in the spaces between the oval figures.

A fine example of engraved disks has been figured by Dr. Joseph Jones, from whose work the illustrations given in Figs. 1 and 2, Plate LVI, have been taken. As his description is one of the first given and quite graphic, I make the following quotation: "In a carefully constructed stone sarcophagus, in which the face of the skeleton was looking toward the setting sun, a beautiful shell ornament was found resting upon the breast-bone of the skeleton. This shell ornament is 4.4 inches in diameter, and it is ornamented on its concave surface, with a small circle in the center, and four concentric bands, differently figured, in relief. The first band is filled by a triple volute; the second is plain, while the third is dotted, and has nine small round bosses carved at unequal distances upon it. The outer band is made up of fourteen small elliptical bosses, the outer edges of which give to the object a scalloped rim. This ornament on its concave figured surface had been covered with red paint, much of which was still visible. The convex smooth surface is highly polished and plain, with the exception of three concentric marks. The material out of which it is formed was evidently derived from a large flat sea-shell. * * * The form of the circles or '*suns*' carved upon the concave surface is similar to that of the paintings on the high rocky cliffs on the banks of the Cumberland and Harpeth. * * * This ornament, when found, lay upon the breast bone, with the concave surface uppermost, as if it had been worn in this position suspended around the neck, as the two holes for the thong or string were in that portion of the border which pointed directly to the chin or central portion of the lower jaw of the skeleton. The marks of the thong by which it was suspended are manifest upon both the au-

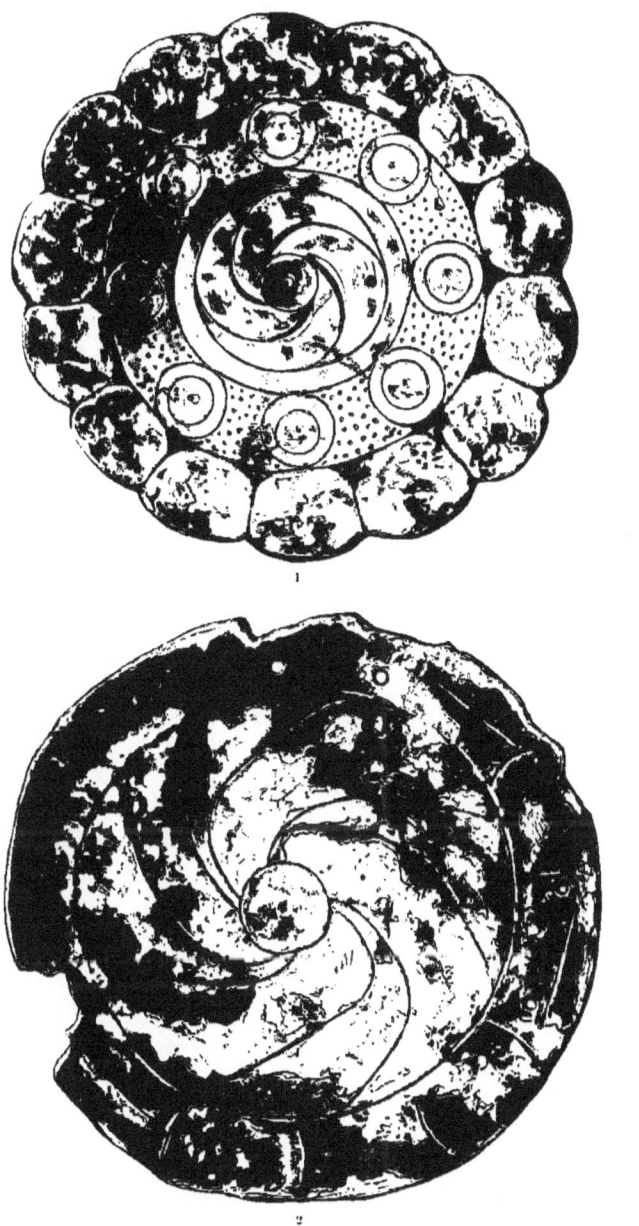

1. From a mound near Nashville. (½)   2. From the Brakebill Mound. (½)

SHELL DISKS.

Tennessee.

terior and posterior surfaces, and in addition to this the paint is worn off from the circular space bounded below by the two holes." [1]

Fig. 2 represents the back or convex side of the disk, the long curved lines indicate the laminations of the shell, and the three narrow crescent-shaped figures near the center are perforations resulting from the deep engraving of the three lines of the volute on the concave side. The stone grave in which this ornament was found occupied the summit of a mound on the banks of the Cumberland River opposite Nashville, Tennessee. Professor Jones, also represents in the same work, page 109, a large fragment of a similar ornament which has apparently had seven circlets in the dotted zone and thirteen marginal bosses. This specimen, which is three and one half inches in diameter, was exhumed by Dr. Grant, from "a small rock mound" near Pulaski, Giles County, Tennessee.

Prof. C. C. Jones describes a number of stone disks containing designs which evidently belong to the class under consideration. He inclines to the opinion that they were designed for some sacred office, and suggests that they were used as plates to offer food to the sun god. The specimen of which I present an outline in Fig. 3, Plate LVII, is figured by Mr. Jones, and his description is as follows: It is "circular in form, eleven inches and a half in diameter, an inch and a quarter in thickness, and weighing nearly seven pounds. It is made of a close-grained, sea-green slate, and bears upon its surface the stains of centuries. Between the rim, which is scalloped, and the central portion, are two circular depressed rings, running parallel with the circumference and incised to the depth of a tenth of an inch. This circular basin, nearly eight inches in diameter, is surrounded by a margin or rim a little less than two inches in width, traversed by the incised rings and beveled from the center toward the edge. The lower surface or bottom of the plate is flat, beveled upward, however, as it approaches the scalloped edge, which is not more than a quarter of an inch in thickness. * * * The use of these plates from the Etowah Valley may, we think, be conjectured with at least some degree of probability. It is not likely that they were employed for domestic or culinary purposes. Their weight, variety, the care evidenced in their construction, and the amount of time and labor necessarily expended in their manufacture, forbid the belief that they were intended as ordinary dishes from which the daily meal was to be eaten, and suggest the impression that they were designed to fulfill a more unusual and important office. The common vessels from which the natives of this region ate their prepared food were bowls and pans fashioned of wood and baked clay, calabashes, pieces of bark, and large shells. Flat platters, made of an admixture of clay and pounded shells, well kneaded and burnt, were ordinarily employed for baking corn-cakes and frying meat ; but it does

[1] Jones: Aboriginal Remains of Tennessee, pp. 42–3.

not anywhere appear that ornamental stone plates were in general use."[1]

This specimen, or one identical with it, is in the possession of the Natural History Museum in New York. It was plowed up in 1859 on the lower terrace of a large mound near Cartersville, Ga.

Other specimens somewhat similar to the one described by Professor Jones have been obtained from the same region, two of which are now in the National Museum. One of these from a mound on the Warrior Riv. is made of gray slate, and is about eight inches in diameter. It is smooth, symmetrical, and doubly convex. There are three shallow, irregular lines near the border, and the periphery is ornamented with twenty-one scallops. Another specimen, a cut of which has already been published by Dr. Rau in "The Archæological Collection of the National Museum," p. 37, is illustrated in Plate LVII, Fig. 1. It is nearly one-half an inch in thickness, and about ten inches in diameter. A single incised line runs parallel with the circumference, which is ornamented with nine rather irregularly placed notches. The stone disk, of which an outline is given in Fig. 2, Plate LVII, was obtained from the Lick Creek mound, in East Tennessee. Its resemblance to the shell disks is so striking that it must be regarded as having a similar origin if not a similar use. The division into zones is the same as in the shell disks; the outer is divided into twelve lobes, and the cross in the center takes the place of the involute rosette with its central circle. The fact that this particular design is engraved on heavy plates of stone as well as upon shell gorgets is sufficient proof that its origin cannot be attributed to fancy alone.

I have seen at the National Museum a curious specimen of stone disk, which should be mentioned in this place, although there is not sufficient assurance of its genuineness to allow it undisputed claim to a place among antiquities. It is a perfectly circular, neatly-dressed sandstone disk, twelve inches in diameter and one-half an inch in thickness. Upon one face we see three marginal incised lines, as in the example just described, while on the other there is a well-engraved design which represents two entwined or rather knotted rattlesnakes. An outline of this curious figure is given in Plate LXVI. Within the circular space inclosed by the bodies of the serpents is a well-drawn hand in the palm of which is placed an open eye; this would probably have been omitted by the artist had he fully appreciated the skeptical tendencies of the modern archæologist. The margin of the plate is divided into seventeen sections by small semicircular indentations. This object is said to have been obtained from a mound near Carthage, Ala. The reverse is shown in Fig. 4, Plate LVII. A similar specimen from a mound near Lake Washington, Mississippi, is described by Mr. Anderson.[2]

The short time at my disposal has barely permitted me to collect the

---

[1] Jones: Antiquities of the Southern Indians, pp. 373-5.

[2] Anderson, in the Cincinnati Quarterly Journal of Science, October, 1875, p. 378.

1. Nashville, Tenn.
2. Nashville, Tenn. (reverse).
3. Nashville, Tenn.

4. Oldtown, Tenn.
5. Nashville, Tenn.
6. Pulaski, Tenn.

SCALLOPED SHELL DISKS.

facts, and I shall have to leave it to the future or to others to follow out fully the suggestions here presented. I had expected to find some uniformity in the numbers or ratios of the various zones, circles, and dots, and by that means possibly to have arrived at some conclusion as to their significance. I have already shown that certain elements of the design are fixed in position and number, while others vary, and the following table is presented that these facts may be made apparent. The list is quite incomplete.

It will be seen by reference to the fourth column that the involute symbol of the inner zone is, with one exception, divided into three parts. The second zone is not given in the table, as it is always plain. The third or dotted zone contains circlets which range from six to nine, while the dots, which have been counted in a few cases only, have a wide range, the total number in some cases reaching three hundred and forty. The bosses of the outer zone range from thirteen to eighteen. The examples in stone seem to have a different series of numbers.

The student will hardly fail to notice the resemblance of these disks to the calendars or time symbols of Mexico and other southern nations of antiquity. There is, however, no absolute identity with southern examples. The involute design in the center resembles the Aztec symbol of day, but is peculiar in its division into three parts, four being the number almost universally used. The only division into three that I have noticed occurs in the calendar of the Muyscas, in which three days constitute a week. The circlets and bosses of the outer zones gives them a pretty close resemblance to the month and year zones of the southern calendars.

My suggestion that these objects may be calendar disks will not seem unreasonable when it is remembered that time symbols do very often make their appearance during the early stages of barbarism. They are the result of attempts to fix accurately the divisions of time for the regulation of religious rites, and among the nations of the south constituted the great body of art. No well-developed calendar is known among the wild tribes of North America, the highest achievements in this line consisting of simple pictographic symbols of the years, but there is no reason why the mound-builders should not have achieved a pretty accurate division of time resembling, in its main features, the systems of their southern neighbors.

SHELL.

Illustrated in	Collection.	Locality.	Divisions of invo- lute.	Circlets in 2d zone.	Bosses in marginal zone.	Dots in 2d zone.	Peculiar features.
Pl. LIV	N. M., 32000	Tenn	3	6	13	340 (?)	Three central per- forations.
Pl. LV, 1	P. M., 15247	..do	4	8	14	....	
Pl. LVI, 1	J. Jones	do. ...	3	9	14	....	Three incisions.
Pl. LVI, 3	P. M., 1180?	..do.....	3	6	13	....	
Pl. LVI, 4	P. M., 15960	..do.....	3	Plain...	13	....	Unfinished (?)
	P. M., 15896	do.....	3	8	17	....	
	P. M	do.....	3	6	16	....	
	P. M., 15906	do.....	3	8	13	100 (?)	Two central per- forations.
	P. M., 15835	do.....	3	6	14	250 (?)	
	P. M., 15916	do.....	3	6	18	....	Three crescent per- forations.
	N. M., 19076	do.	3	7	16	....	
	N. M., 19075	do.....	3	7	15	280 (?)	

STONE.

Illustrated in	Collection.	Locality.		Circlets		Bosses	Peculiar features.
Pl. LVII, 1	N. M., 9334	Ga	....	Plain....		9	....
Pl. LVII, 2	P. M., 2963	do.....	....	do.....		12	...... Cross in center.
Pl. LVII, 3	N. Y. Nat. Hist. M.	do.....	....	do.		24	....
	N. M., 9332	do.....	....	do.....		21	....
Pl. LXVI	N. M	Ala	....	do.....		17	.... Serpent, obverse.
	Anderson	Miss	....	do.....		18	.... Serpent, center.

N. M., National Museum.   P. M., Peabody Museum.

THE BIRD.

With all peoples the bird has been a most important symbol. Possessing the mysterious power of flight, by which it could rise at pleasure into the realms of space, it naturally came to be associated with
the phenomena of the sky—the wind, the storm, the lightning, and the
thunder. In the fervid imagination of the red man it became the actual ruler of the elements, the guardian of the four quarters of the
heavens. As a result the bird is embodied in the myths, and is a
prominent figure in the philosophy of many savage tribes. The eagle,
which is an important emblem with many civilized nations, is found to
come much nearer the heart of the superstitious savage; its plumes
are the badge of the successful warrior; its body a sacred offering to
his deities, or an object of actual veneration. The swan, the heron,
the woodpecker, the paroquet, the owl, and the dove were creatures of
unusual consideration; their flight was noted as a matter of vital importance, as it could bode good or evil to the hunter or warrior who
consulted it as an oracle.

The dove, with the Hurons, is thought to be the keeper of the souls

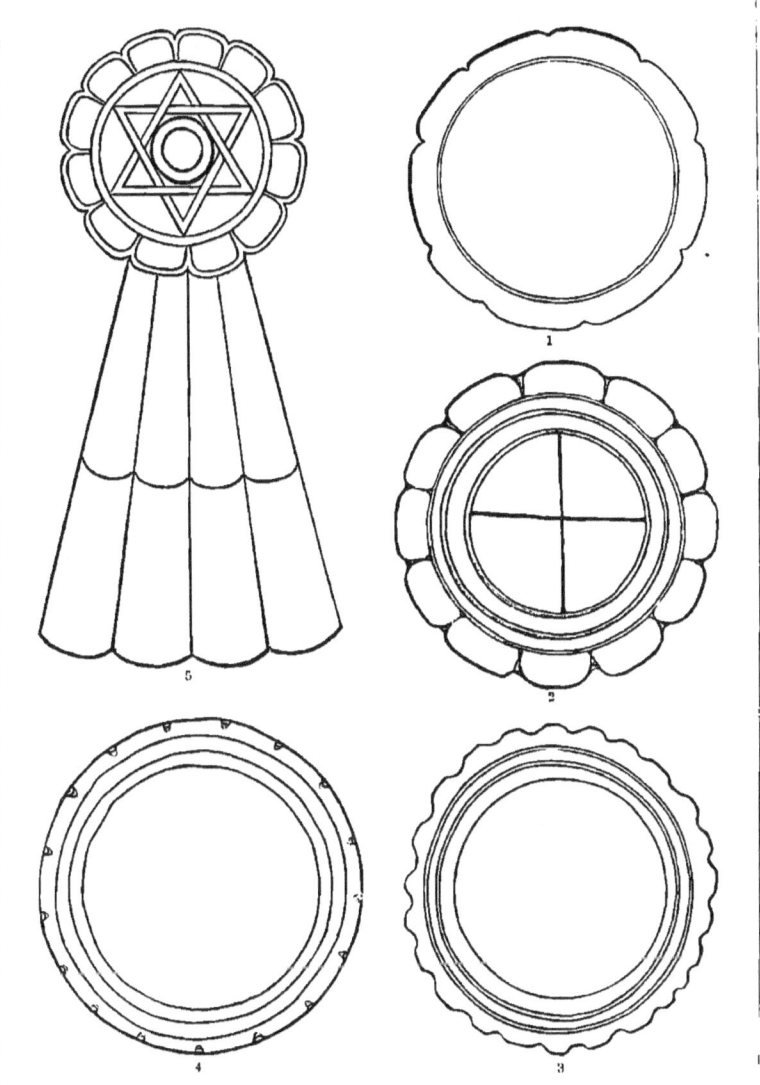

1. Stone, Warrior River, Ala.
2. Stone, Lick Creek Mound, Tenn.
3. Stone, Etowah Valley, Ga.
4. Stone, Carthage, Ala.
5. Stone, Sun symbol, Uxmal.

SCALLOPED DISKS.

of the dead, and the Navajos are said to believe that four white swans dwell in the four quarters of the heavens and rule the winds.

The storm-bird of the Dakotas dwells in the upper air, beyond the range of human vision, carrying upon its back a lake of fresh water; when it winks its eyes there is lightning; when it flaps its wings we hear the thunder; and when it shakes out its plumage the rain descends. Myths like this abound in the lore of many peoples, and the story of the mysterious bird is interwoven with the traditions which tell of their origin. A creature which has sufficient power to guide and rule a race is constantly embodied in its songs, its art, and its philosophy. Thus highly regarded by the modern tribes, it must have been equally an object of consideration among prehistoric races. We know that the Natchez and the Creeks included the bird among their deities, and by the relics placed within his sepulchers we know that it held an important place in the esteem of the mound-builder.

Our prehistoric peoples seem to have taken special delight in carving its form in wood and stone, in modeling it in clay, in fashioning it in copper and gold, and in engraving it upon shell. One of the most interesting of all the specimens preserved to us is illustrated in Plate LVIII. The design with which this relic is embellished possesses no little artistic excellence, and doubtless embodies some one of the many charming myths of the heavens.

I am perfectly well aware that a scientific writer should guard against the tendency to indulge in flights of fancy, but as the myths of the American aborigines are highly poetical, and abound in lofty rhetorical figures, there can be no good reason why their graphic art should not echo some of these rhythmical passages. To the thoughtful mind it will be apparent that, although this design is not necessarily full of occult mysteries, every line has its purpose and every figure its significance. Yet of these very works one writer has ventured the opinion that "they do but express the individual fancy of those by whom they were made;" that they are even without "indications of any intelligent design or pictographic idea." I do not assume to interpret these designs; they are not to be interpreted. Besides, there is no advantage to be gained by an interpretation. We have hundreds of primitive myths within our easy reach that are as interesting and instructive as these could be. All I desire is to elevate these works from the category of trinkets to what I believe is their rightful place—the serious art of a people with great capacity for loftier works. What the gorgets themselves were, or of what particular value to their possessors, aside from simple ornament, must be, in a measure, a matter of conjecture. They were hardly less than the totems of clans, the insignia of rulers, or the potent charms of a priesthood.

The gorget in question is unfortunately without a pedigree. It reached the National Museum through the agency of Mr. C. F. Williams, and is labeled "Mississippi." On it face, however, there is sufficient evidence to establish its aboriginal origin. The form of the object, the character of the design and the evident age of the specimen, all bespeak the mound-builder. It was in all probability obtained from one of the multitude of ancient sepulchers that abound in the State of Mississippi. The disk is four and a quarter inches in diameter, and is made from a large, heavy specimen of the *Busycon perversum*. It has been smoothly dressed on both sides, but is now considerably stained and pitted. The design has in this case been engraved upon the convex side, the concave surface being plain. The perforations are placed near the margin and are considerably worn by the cord of suspension. In the center is a nearly symmetrical cross of the Greek type inclosed in a circle one and one-fourth inches in diameter. The spaces between the arms are emblazoned with groups of radiating lines. Placed at regular intervals on the outside of the circle are twelve pointed pyramidal rays ornamented with transverse lines. The whole design presents a remarkable combination of the two symbols, the cross and the sun. Surrounding this interesting symbol is another of a somewhat mysterious nature. A square framework of four continuous parallel lines, symmetrically looped at the corners, incloses the central symbol, the inner line touching the tips of the pyramidal rays. Outside of this again are the four symbolic birds placed against the side of the square opposite the arms of the cross. These birds, or rather birds' heads, are carefully drawn after what, to the artist, must have been a well recognized model. The mouth is open and the mandibles long, slender, and straight. The eye is represented by a circlet which incloses a small conical pit intended to represent the iris, a striated and pointed crest springs from the back of the head and neck, and two lines extend from the eye, down the neck, to the base of the figure. In seeking an original for this bird we find that it has perhaps more points of resemblance to the ivory-billed woodpecker than to any other species. It is not impossible, however, that the heron or swan may have been intended. That some particular bird served as a model is attested by the fact that other specimens, from mounds in various parts of Tennessee, exhibit similar figures. I have been able to find six of these specimens, all of which vary to some extent from the type described, but only in detail, workmanship, or finish. The specimen presented in Fig. 2, Plate LIX, was obtained by Mr. Cross from a stone grave on Mr. Overton's farm near Nashville, Tenn. Professor Putnam, who secured it from Mr. Cross, has published a cut of it in the Eleventh Annual Report of the Peabody Museum. It is made from a large marine shell, probably a *Busycon*, and is represented natural size both by Mr. Putnam and myself.

SHELL GORGET—THE BIRD.

Mississippi.

($\frac{1}{1}$)

The design is essentially the same as that shown in the type specimen, but is much more rudely executed. A circlet with a central pit takes the place of the cross and sun. The looped rectangular figure has but two lines and the birds' heads are not so full of character as those on the other specimens; they resemble the heads of chicks with a few pin-feathers sprouting from the back and top of the head rather than full-fledged birds. The design is engraved on the concave side. The perforations are much worn. This specimen is now in the Peabody Museum.

The same collection contains a large fragment of another small disk about two inches in diameter. The central part seems to be plain, but the looped figure, which has four lines, resembles very closely that engraved on the other plates. It is mentioned by Professor Putnam, on page 309 of the Eleventh Annual Report of the Peabody Museum. It is said to have been found on the surface in Humphrey County, Tennessee.

A much larger specimen, which resembles my type specimen very closely, is shown in Fig. 1, Plate LIX. It was obtained by Professor Putnam and Dr. Curtis from a stone grave on Mrs. Williams' farm, Cumberland River, Tennessee. It is nearly circular, and about two and a half inches in diameter. A small piece has been lost from the upper margin. It is neatly made and quite smooth, and the lines of the design are clearly and evenly engraved. The small cross in the center is inclosed by a plain narrow zone, and is defined by four triangular perforations between the arms. In this respect it resembles other shell crosses found within the Mississippi Valley. Surrounding the plain zone are eight pyramidal rays with cross-bars; in this feature, and in the drawing of the looped square and the birds' heads, there is but little variation from the type specimen. The surface upon which the engraving is made seems to be slightly convex.

Another specimen of this class was obtained from a stone grave near Gray's mound, at Oldtown, Tenn. It is shown in Fig. 3, Plate LIX. The design is very much like that of the type specimen, from which it differs in having four large perforations near the center. Although the engraved design which once occupied the central space is almost totally effaced, one or two of the tips of the pyramidal rays may be detected. It is probable that the four round perforations correspond to the four triangular ones by which the arms of the cross in the preceding example are defined. The perforations for suspension are near one margin, and seem to be very much worn by use. The whole object is fragile from decay. This specimen is also in the Peabody Museum.

One more very imperfect specimen obtained from a stone grave in the Cumberland Valley is nearly five inches in diameter and very irregular in outline. Barely enough of the engraved design remains to show that it belongs to the class under consideration.

It will be observed that the specimens of this class obtained from

Tennessee are confined to a limited area. It thus seems especially unfortunate that so little is known of the history of the type specimen given in Plate LVIII, as without assurance of the correctness of the statement that it is from Mississippi we cannot make use of it to show geographical distribution. In reference to this point, however, we have a few very interesting facts which make the occurrence of specimens in localities as widely separated as the "Cumberland River" and "Mississippi" seem inconsequential. I refer now to two specimens described by Dr. Abbott in "Primitive Industry." One of these is a remarkable slate knife, the striking features of which are a "series of etchings and deeply incised lines of perhaps no meaning. Taken in order, it will be noticed that at the back of the knife are four short lines at uniform distances apart, and a fifth near the end of the implement. Besides these are fifteen shorter parallel lines near the broader end of the knife and about the middle of the blade. A series of five zigzag lines are also cut on the opposite end of the blade. * * * More prominent than the numerous lines to which reference has been made, are the clearly defined, unmistakable birds' heads, placed midway between the two series of lines. * * * Did we not learn from the writings of Heckewelder, that the Lenapé had 'the turkey totem,' we might suppose that this drawing of such bird heads originated with the intrusive southern Shawnees, who, at one time, occupied lands in the Delaware Valley, and who are supposed by some writers to have been closely related to the earliest inhabitants of the Southern and Southwestern States. Inasmuch as we shall find that, not only on this slate knife, but upon a bone implement also, similar heads of birds are engraved, it is probable that the identity of the design is not a mere coincidence, but that it must be explained either in accordance with the statements of Heckewelder, or be considered as the work of southern Shawnees after their arrival in New Jersey. In the latter event, the theory that these disks were the work of a people different from and anterior to the Indians found in the Cumberland Valley at the time of the discovery of that region by the whites is, apparently, not sustained by the facts."[1]

A cut of the bone implement referred to above is reproduced from Dr. Abbott's work, in Plate LIX, Fig. 4. It has probably been made from a portion of a rib of some large mammal and is thought to be somewhat fragmentary. "The narrow portion has been cut or ground away to some extent, and the edges are quite smoothly polished. Near the end of this handle-like portion, there is a countersunk perforation, and upon the concave side of the wider part there are rudely outlined the heads of two birds."[2] These resemble somewhat closely the heads depicted on the other specimen described by Dr. Abbott. The specimens referred to are both from New Jersey, and are probably surface finds.

[1]Abbott: Primitive Industry, pp. 70, 72, and 73.
[2]Ibid., p. 207.

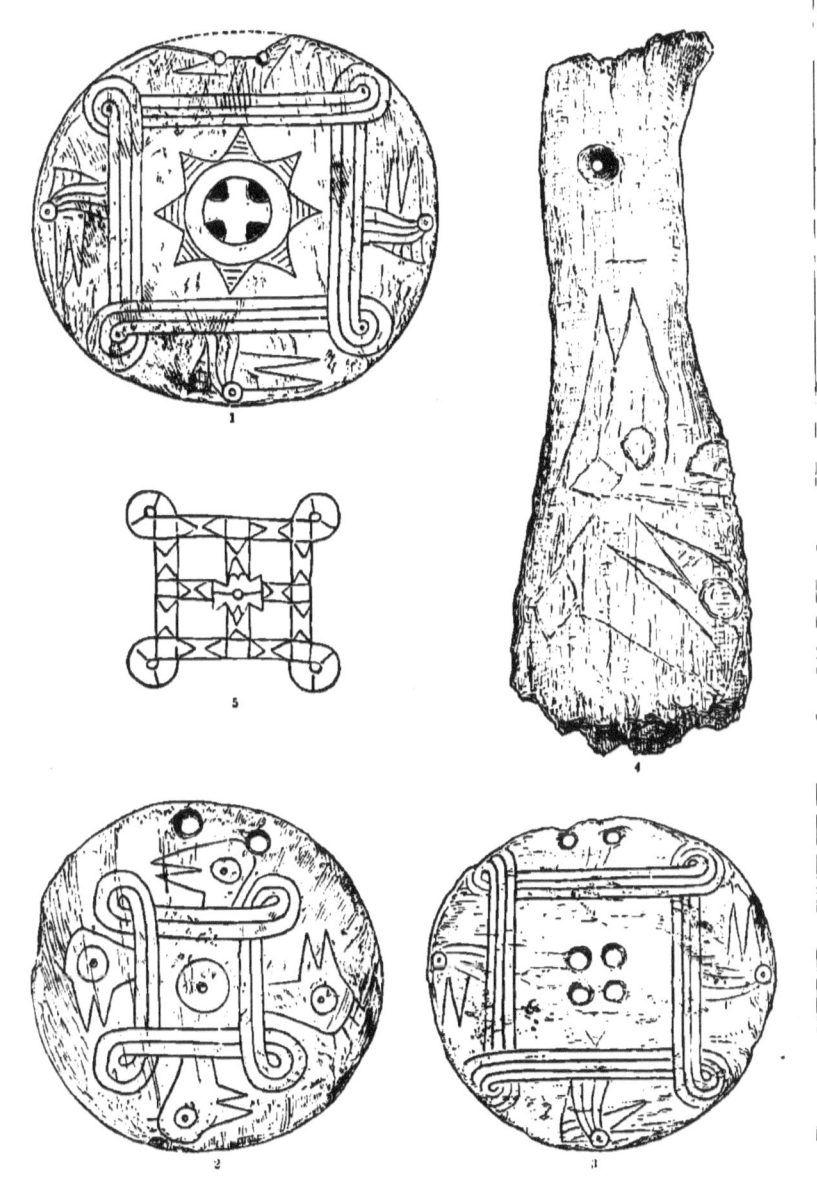

1. Shell gorget from stone grave, Tenn.
2. Shell gorget from stone grave, Tenn.
3. Shell gorget from stone grave, Tenn.
4. Bone implement, N. J.
5. Design from Aztec painting.

THE BIRD.

Although the heads represented on these specimens do certainly in some respects suggest that of the turkey, the characters are not sufficiently pronounced to make it impossible that some other bird was intended, so that the original in the mind of the ancient artist may have been the same as that from which the examples on shell were drawn.

In comparing the northern examples with those of Tennessee I observe another feature that is more conclusive as to the identity of origin than the rather obscure resemblance of the birds' heads delineated. I have not had the opportunity of examining the specimen illustrated in Fig. 4; but in the cut given by Dr. Abbott a rather indefinite figure can be traced which has a striking resemblance to the looped rectangle characteristic of the designs on shell. This resemblance could hardly be owing to accident, and if the peculiar figure mentioned is actually found in conjunction with the birds' heads upon the New Jersey specimen, it will certainly be safe to conclude that the bone, stone, and shell objects belonged to the same people, and that they constituted the totems of the same clan, or were the insignia of corresponding offices or orders.[1]

As bearing upon the question of the species of bird represented in the preceding specimens, I present in Plate LX an illustration published by Dr. Rau in the Smithsonian Report for 1877. This remarkable ornament (represented in Fig. 3) was obtained from a mound in Manatee County, Florida. It is a thin blade of gold, pointed at one end and terminating at the other in a highly conventionalized representation of a bird's head, the general characteristics of which are much like those of the examples engraved upon shell. The crest is especially characteristic, and, as pointed out by Dr. Rau, suggests a prototype in the ivory-billed woodpecker, an inhabitant of the Gulf States.

The significance of the looped figure which forms so prominent a feature in the designs in question has not been determined. I would offer the suggestion, however, that, from the manner of its occurrence, it may represent an inclosure, a limit, or boundary. It may be well to point out the fact that a similar looped rectangle occurs several times in the ancient Mexican manuscripts. One example, from the Vienna Codex,[2] is presented in Fig. 5, Plate LIX. It is not a little remarkable that a cross occupies the inclosed area in all these examples.

I shall close this very hasty review of the bird in the art of the Mound Builders by presenting the remarkable example of shell carving shown in Fig. 1, Plate LX. Like so many of the National Museum specimens, it is practically without a record—a stray. It is labeled " B. Pybas, Tuscumbia, Ala." It is old and fragmentary, the shell substance being, however, quite well preserved. It is the right hand half of a

---

[1] Since this paragraph has been in type I have seen the specimen, and find that the looped figure is clearly defined.

[2] Kingsborough: vol. II, Plate 20.

gorget which represents an eagle's head in profile. The skill of the ancient artist is shown to great advantage; nothing can be found, even in the most elaborately carved pipes, equal to the treatment of this remarkable head. To overcome the difficulty of cutting the flinty and massive shell was no small triumph for a people still in the stone age. To conceive and execute such a graphic work is a still more marvelous achievement.[1] The lines of the mandibles and protruding tongue are strongly and correctly drawn. The eye and the markings of the head are executed in smooth, deeply incised lines, and are conventionalized in a manner peculiar to the American aborigines.

THE SPIDER.

Among insects the spider is perhaps best calculated to attract the attention of the savage. The tarantula is in many respects a very extraordinary creature, and is endowed with powers of the most deadly nature, which naturally places it along with the rattlesnake in the category of creatures possessing supernatural attributes. Its curiously constructed house with the hinged door and smoothly plastered chamber must ever elicit the admiration of the beholder. But the spider, which spins a web and projects in mid-air a gossamer structure of marvelous symmetry and beauty, and builds an ambush from which to spring upon his prey, was probably one of the first instructors of adolescent man, and must have seemed to him a very deity. It is not strange, therefore, that the spider appears in the myths of the savages. With the great Shoshone family, according to Professor Powell, the spider was the first weaver, and taught that important art to the fathers. The Cherokees, in their legend of the origin of fire, "represent a portion of it as having been brought with them and sacredly guarded. Others say that after crossing wide waters they sent back for it to the Man of Fire from whom a little was conveyed over by a spider in his web."[2]

The spider occurs but rarely in aboriginal American art, occasionally it seems, however, to have reached the dignity of religious consideration and to have been adopted as a totemic device. Had a single example only been found we would not be warranted in giving it a place among religious symbols. Four examples have come to my notice; these are all engraved on shell gorgets and are illustrated in Plate LX. Two are from Illinois, one from Missouri, and the other from Tennessee.[3] The example shown in Fig. 1 was obtained by Mr. Croswell from a mound near New Madrid, Mo. It is described as a circular ornament,

[1] Let any one who thinks lightly of such a work undertake, without machinery or well-adapted appliances, to cut a groove or notch even, in a moderately compact specimen of *Busycon*, and he will probably increase his good opinion of the skill and patience of the ancient workman if he does nothing else.

[2] E. G. Squier: Serpent Symbol, page 69, quoting MSS. of J. H. Payne.

[3] I am very much indebted to Prof. F. F. Hilder, of Saint Louis, for photographs of three of these specimens as well as for much information in regard to their history.

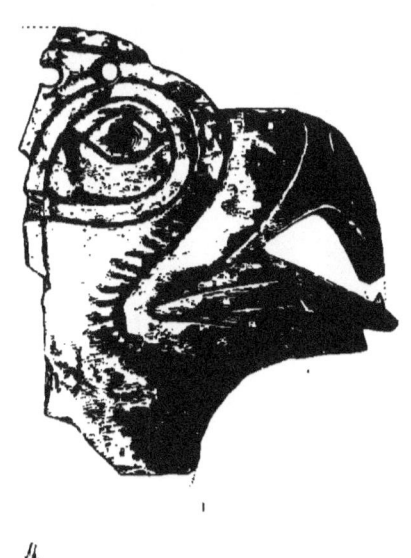

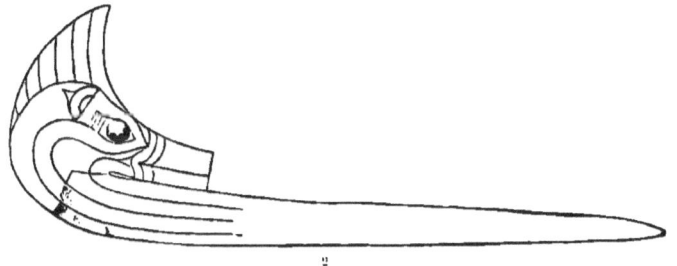

1. Fragment of shell gorget, Alabama. (⅓)   3. Head of ivory-billed woodpecker.
2. Gold ornament, Florida. (⅓)

THE BIRD.

three inches in diameter, that had, apparently, been cut from a *Busy-con*. Mr. Crosswell says that "the convex face was entirely plain, but the concave side bears the figure of a tarantula, or large spider, very skillfully engraved, the body being formed by a circle inclosing a cross, showing beyond doubt its sacred and symbolic character. This orna-ment, when found, lay on the breast-bone of a skeleton, with the concave or ornamented side uppermost. Two holes in the upper part were evi-dently intended for the thong or string by which it had been suspended from the neck. A circumstance that renders this relic still more inter-esting is the fact that two other shell ornaments, bearing precisely simi-lar devices, have recently been found in Illinois within seven miles of this city, thus proving that the figures were not a mere fanciful inven-tion, but had some symbolic meaning."[1]

The disk thus briefly described by Mr. Crosswell is so much like the example shown in Fig. 3 that I shall not describe it further, but shall refer to its peculiarities in the descriptions of others that follow.

The handsome gorget illustrated in Fig. 3 was obtained from a mound in Saint Clair County, Illinois, seven miles from the city of Saint Louis. It was found upon the breast of a skeleton, and was very much discol-ored and quite fragile from decay, but no part of the design, which is engraved upon the concave side, has been obliterated. Near the margin and parallel with it three lines have been engraved. The spider is drawn with considerable fidelity to nature and covers nearly the entire disk, the legs, mandibles, and abdomen reaching to the outer marginal line. As in the specimen described above, the thorax is placed in the center of the disk, and is represented by a circle; within this a cross has been engraved, the ends of which have been enlarged on one side, producing a form much used in heraldry, but one very rarely met with in aboriginal American art. The head is somewhat heart-shaped and is armed with palpi and mandibles, the latter being ornamented with a zigzag line and prolonged to the marginal lines of the disk. The eyes are represented by two small circles with central dots. The legs are correctly placed in four pairs upon the thorax, and are very graph-ically drawn. The abdomen is large and heart-shaped, and is orna-mented with a number of lines and dots, which represent the natural markings of the spider. The perforations for suspension are placed near the posterior extremity of the abdomen. It will be observed that this is also the case with the three other specimens. Having described this specimen somewhat carefully, it will be unnecessary to give a de-tailed description of the very similar specimen shown in Fig. 2. The latter was found in a stone grave in Saint Clair County, Illinois, and does not differ in any essential feature from either of the other specimens, one of which was found near by, and the other about one hundred miles farther south.

In reference to the cross it has been suggested that it may have been

---

[1] Croswell, in Transactions Academy of Science of Saint Louis, vol. III, p. 537.

derived from the well-defined cross found upon the backs of some species of the genus *Atta*, but there appears to be good reason for believing otherwise. The cross here shown has a very highly conventionalized character, quite out of keeping with the realistic drawing of the insect, and, what is still more decisive, it is identical with forms found upon many other objects. The conclusion is that the cross here, as elsewhere, has a purely symbolic character. Spider gorgets are also mentioned by A. J. Conant in the Kansas City Review, Vol. I, page 400, and in his work on the Commonwealth of Missouri, page 96, but no details are given. It is probable that the objects referred to by Mr. Conant are the same as those more definitely placed by Prof. Hilder.

The specimen shown in Fig. 4 was obtained from a mound on Fain's Island, Tennessee. The disk is somewhat more convex on the front than is indicated in the engraving. It is two and a half inches in diameter, and is quite thin and fragile, although the surface has not suffered much from decay. The margin is ornamented with twenty-four very neatly made notches or scallops. Immediately inside the border on the convex side are two incised circles, on the outer of which two small perforations for suspension have been made; inside of these, and less than half an inch from the margin, is a circle of seventeen sub-triangular perforations, the inner angle of each being much rounded. Inside of this again is another incised circle, about one and one-fourth inches in diameter, which incloses the highly conventionalized figure of an insect resembling a spider. In a general way—in the number and arrangement of the parts—this figure corresponds pretty closely to the very realistic spiders of the three other disks; in detail however, it is quite unlike them. It is much more highly conventionalized—the natural markings of the body being nearly all omitted, and the legs being without joints and square at the tips. The cross does not appear on the body, but its place is taken by a large conical perforation, made entirely from the convex side. The central segment of the body is round, as in the other cases; to this the four pairs of legs are attached. Without reference to the other specimens, it would be difficult to distinguish the anterior from the posterior extremity, and even with this aid we cannot be quite certain. The larger extremity is somewhat triangular in outline and is ornamented with two cross lines and two eyes. Were it not for the fact that these eyes resemble so closely those found in the other specimens I should call this the posterior extremity, as the opposite end terminates in a pair of well-shaped mandibles, the triangular space between them being cut quite through the disk. The section of the body between this and the central circle also resembles the head, which suggests the conclusion either that the eyes are misplaced or that, as drawn, they are only intended to represent the bright spots of the insect's body.

The rarity of these spider gorgets makes it seem rather remarkable that specimens should occur in localities so widely separated as Fain's

1. From a mound, Missouri.   3. From a mound, Illinois.
2. From a stone-grave, Illinois.   4. From a mound, Tennessee.

SPIDER GORGETS.

(⁴⁄₄)

Island and Saint Louis, but the races inhabiting this entire region, are known to have had many arts in common, and besides this it is not impossible that the same tribe or clan may, at different times, have occupied both of these localities. The marked differences in the design and execution of these specimens, however, indicate a pretty wide distinction in the time or art of the makers.

THE SERPENT.

The serpent has had a fascination for primitive man hardly surpassed by its reputed power over the animals on which it preys. In the minds of nearly all savages it has been associated with the deepest mysteries and the most potent powers of nature. No other creature has figured so prominently in the religious systems of the world, few of which are free from it; and as art, in a great measure, owes its existence to an attempt to represent or embellish objects which are supposed to be the incarnations of spirits, the serpent is an important element in all art. Wherever the children of nature have wandered its image may be found engraved upon the rocks, or painted or sculptured upon monuments of their own construction. It is found in a thousand forms; beginning with those so realistic that the species can be determined, we may pass down through innumerable stages of variation until all semblance of nature is lost. Beyond this it becomes embodied in the conventional forms of art or looks back from its obscure place in an alphabet through a perspective of metamorphism as marvelous as that visible to the creature itself could it view the course of its evolution from the elements of nature.

So well is the serpent known as a religious symbol among the American peoples that it seems hardly necessary to present examples of the curiously interesting myths relating to it. We are not surprised to find the bird, the wolf, or the bear placed among representatives of the "Great Spirit," and hence to find them embodied in art; but it would be a matter of surprise if the serpent were ever absent.

With the mound-builders it seems to have been of as much importance as to other divisions of the red race, ancient or modern. It is of very frequent occurrence among the designs engraved upon gorgets of shell, a multitude of which have been thus dedicated to the serpent-god.

It is a well-known fact that the rattlesnake is the variety almost universally represented, and we find that these engravings on shell present no exception to this rule. From a very early date in mound exploration these gorgets have been brought to light, but the coiled serpent engraved upon their concave surfaces is so highly conventionalized that it was not at once recognized. Professor Wyman appears to have been the first to point out the fact that the rattlesnake was represented; others have since made brief allusion to this fact. Two examples only have been illustrated; one by Professor Jones,[1] who regards it as being without intelligent design, and the other by Dr. Rau,[2] who does not sug-

---

[1] Jones: Antiquities of the Southern Indian, plate XXX.
[2] Archæological Collection of the National Museum, p. 69.

gest an interpretation. Among the thirty or forty specimens that I have examined, the engraving of the serpent is, with one exception, placed upon the concave side of the disk, which is, as usual, cut from the most distended part of the *Busycon percersum*, or some similar shell. The great uniformity of these designs is a matter of much surprise. At the same time, however, there is no exact duplication; there are always differences in position, detail, or number of parts. The serpent is always coiled, the head occupying the center of the disk. With a very few exceptions the coil is sinistral. The head is so placed that when the gorget is suspended it has an erect position, the mouth opening toward the right hand.

As at first glance it will be somewhat difficult for the reader to make out clearly the figure of the serpent, even with the well defined lines of the drawing before him, I will present the description pretty much in the order in which the design revealed itself to me in my first attempt to decipher it.

The saucer-like disks are almost circular, the upper edge being mostly somewhat straightened—the result of the natural limit of the body of the shell above. All are ground down to a fairly uniform thickness of from one-eighth to one-fourth of an inch. The edges are evenly rounded and smooth. Two small holes for suspension occur near the rim of the straighter edge, and generally on or near the outline of the engraved design, which covers the middle portion of the plate. The diameter ranges from one to six inches.

To one who examines this design for the first time it seems a most inexplicable puzzle; a meaningless grouping of curved and straight lines, dots and perforations. We notice, however, a remarkable similarity in the designs, the idea being radically the same in all specimens, and the conclusion is soon reached that there is nothing haphazard in the arrangements of the parts and that every line must have its place and purpose. The design is in all cases inclosed by two parallel border lines, leaving a plain belt from one-fourth to three-fourths of an inch in width around the edge of the disk. All simple lines are firmly traced, although somewhat scratchy, and are seldom more than one-twentieth of an inch in width or depth.

In studying this design the attention is first attracted by an eye-like figure near the left border. This is formed of a series of concentric circles, the number of which varies from three in the most simple to twelve in the more elaborate forms. The diameter of the outer circle of this figure varies from one-half to one inch. In the center there is generally a small conical depression or pit. The series of circles is partially inclosed by a looped band one-eighth of an inch in width, which opens downward to the left; the free ends extending outward to the border line, gradually nearing each other and forming a kind of neck to the circular figure. This band is in most cases occupied by a series of dots or conical depressions varying in number from one to thirty. The

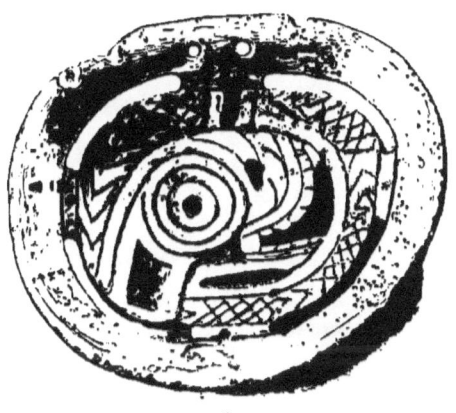

1. Shell gorget from Georgia. (½)   1. McMahan Mound, Tenn. (½)

RATTLESNAKE GORGETS.

1. McMahan Mound, Tenn.
2. McMahan Mound, Tenn.

RATTLESNAKE GORGETS.

(⅔)

neck is decorated in a variety of ways; by dots, by straight and curved lines, and by a cross-hatching that gives a semblance of scales. A curious group of lines occupying a crescent-shaped space at the right of the circular figure and inclosed by two border lines, must receive particular attention. This is really the front part of the head—the jaws and the muzzle of the creature represented. The mouth is always clearly defined and is mostly in profile, the upper jaw being turned abruptly upward, but, in some examples, an attempt has been made to represent a front view, in which case it presents a wide V-shaped figure. It is, in most cases, furnished with two rows of teeth, no attempt having been made to represent a tongue. The spaces above and below the jaws are filled with lines and figures, which vary much in the different specimens; a group of plume-like figures, extends backward from the upper jaw to the crown, or otherwise this space is occupied by an elongated perforation. The body is represented encircling the head in a single coil, which appears from beneath the neck on the right, passes around the front of the head, and terminates at the back in a pointed tail with well defined rattles. It is engraved to represent the well-known scales and spots of the rattlesnake, the conventionalized figures being quite graphic. In the group of specimens represented in Plate LXIV areas of cross-hatched lines, representing scales, alternate with circular figures, containing two or three concentric circles and a central dot. In some cases one or more incised bands cross the body in the upper part of the curve.

The examples shown in Plate LXV have many distinctive features. The markings of the body consist of alternating areas of scales and chevrons or of chevrons alone. These figures are interrupted in the upper part of the coil by a number of lines which cross the body at right angles. The body is in many cases nearly severed from the rim of the disk by four oblong perforations, which follow the border line of the design. In most cases three other perforations occur about the head; one represents the mouth, one defines the forehead and upper jaw, and the third is placed against the throat. These may be intended merely to define the form more clearly. The curious plume-like figures that occur upon the heads of both varieties may indicate the natural or reputed markings of the animal represented. It is possible that the group shown in this plate may be intended to represent the common yellow rattlesnake, the *Crotalus horridus*, of the Atlantic slope, the characteristic markings of which are alternating light and dark chevrons, while the diamond rattlesnake, the *Crotalus adamanteus*, of the Southern States may have served as a model for the other group.

In Plate LXII I present two of these rattlesnake gorgets. The specimens shown in Fig. 1 is from Georgia and is the smallest example that has come to my notice. It is represented natural size. The design is quite obscure, but enough remains to show that it does not differ es-

sentially from the type already presented. There appear to be no holes
for suspension, but it is probable that two of the oblong perforations
upon the border of the design had been used for that purpose.

The handsome specimen given in Fig. 2 was obtained from the great
mound at Sevierville, Tenn., and is in a very good state of preservation. It is a deep, somewhat oval plate, made from a *Busycon perversum*.
The surface is nicely polished and the margins neatly beveled. The
marginal zone is less than half an inch wide and contains at the upper
edge two perforations, which have been considerably abraded by the
cord of suspension. Four long curved slits or perforations almost
sever the central design from the rim; the four narrow segments that
remain are each ornamented with a single conical pit. The serpent is
very neatly engraved and belongs to the chevroned variety. The eye
is large and the neck is ornamented with a single rectangular intaglio
figure. The mouth is more than usually well defined. The upper jaw
is turned abruptly upward and is ornamented with lines peculiar to this
variety of the designs.

The body opposite the perforations for suspension is interrupted by a
rather mysterious cross band, consisting of one broad and two narrow
lines. As this is a feature common to many specimens it probably has
some important office or significance.

In Plate LXIII I present two of the best examples of these serpent
gorgets yet brought to light. They were obtained from the McMahan
Mound, at Sevierville, Tenn., in 1871, and are in an excellent state of
preservation. Both are made from large heavy specimens of the *Busycon perversum*. The example given in Fig. 1 is but slightly altered by
decomposition, the transluceney of the shell being still perceptible. The
back retains the strongly marked ridges of growth. The interior has
been highly polished, but is now somewhat marked, apparently by some
fine textile fabric which has been buried with it and has, in decaying,
left its impress upon the smooth surface of the shell. The design is very
much like the type described, but has some peculiar features about the
neck and under the head of the serpent.

The specimen shown in Fig. 2 may be regarded as a type of these
gorgets, and is the one chiefly used in the general description given on
a preceding page. It is six inches long by five wide, and has been
neatly dressed and polished on both sides. As every detail is clearly
and correctly shown in the cut I shall not describe it further.

For convenience of comparison I have arranged two plates of outlines.
The specimen shown in Fig. 1, Plate LXIV, is almost identical with the
one last mentioned in size and shape. This, with the similar but somewhat smaller specimen given in Fig. 2, is also from the McMahan Mound.
Figs. 3 and 4 are outlines of the specimens already given in Plate LXIII.

The fine specimen shown in Fig. 5 is from the Brakebill Mound, near
Knoxville, Tenn., and is now in the Peabody Museum. It is five inches
in length and a little more than four and one-half in width. It is very

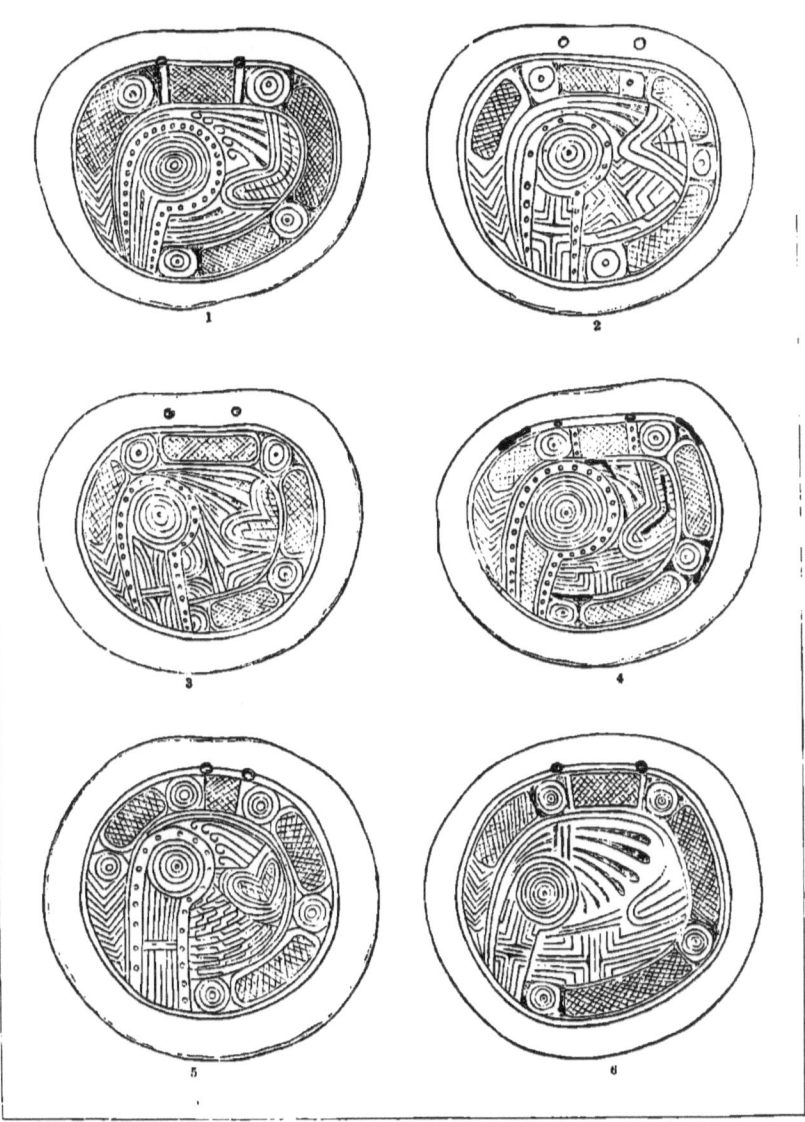

1. McMahan Mound.
2. McMahan Mound.
3. McMahan Mound

4. McMahan Mound.
5. Brakebill Mound.
6. Williams Island.

RATTLESNAKE GORGETS.

Tennessee.

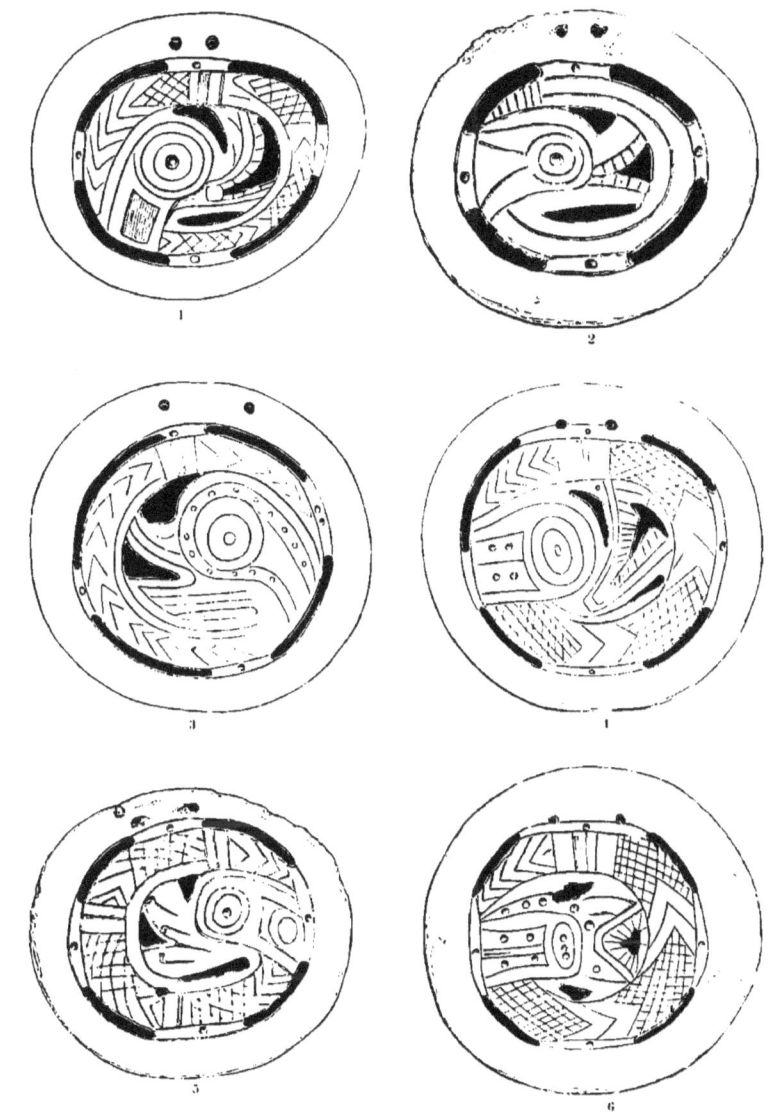

1. McMahan Mound.
2. Lick Creek Mound.
3. McMahan Mound.

4. McMahan Mound.
5. Green County Mound
6. Lick Creek Mound.

RATTLESNAKE GORGETS.

Tennessee.

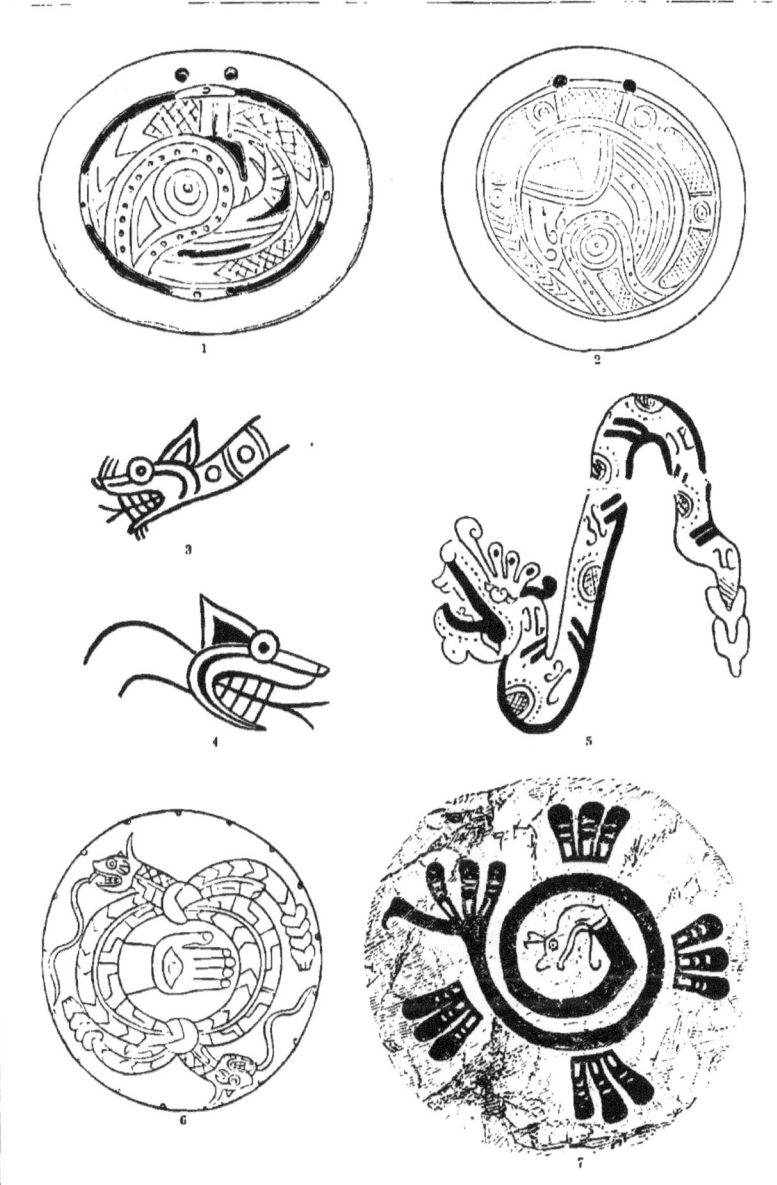

1. Shell gorget, Georgia.
2. Shell gorget, Tennessee.
3, 4. Painting, Peru.
5. From an Aztec painting.
6. Stone disk, Carthage, Ala.
7. Painted on rock, Nicaragua.

THE SERPENT.

much like the Sevierville specimens and is made of the same species of
shell. The markings of the space beneath the head are peculiar, and
in some other details it differs from the other specimens.

Fig. 6 illustrates a large specimen now in the National Collection. It
is also from Tennessee, and resembles the preceding examples quite
closely.

The specimens illustrated in Plate LXV represent a somewhat different type of design, but are found associated with the others. The three
shown in Figs. 2, 6, and 7 belong to the Peabody Museum, and are
from mounds in East Tennessee. The others are in the National Collection, and come from the same region.

It was my intention to pursue this study somewhat further, and the
illustrations presented in Plate LXVI were partially prepared for the
purpose of instituting comparisons between these northern forms and
others of the south, but the time at my disposal will not permit of it.

Fig. 1 is an outline of a rattlesnake gorget, probably from Georgia,
which is preserved in the Natural History Museum of New York. It
is four inches in length by three and one-half in width. The same specimen is figured by Jones in Plate XXX of his "Antiquities of the Southern Indians."

Fig. 2 represents a large specimen from Tennessee, which is now preserved in the National Collection. The design is placed upon the gorget
somewhat differently from the other specimens, the mouth of the serpent being near the top and the neck below at the right. There is also
a dotted belt at the right of the head which is not found in any of the
specimens described.

Figs. 3 and 4 represent drawings of serpents' heads found in the ancient city of Chimu, Peru.[1]

Fig. 5 is copied from one of the codices of Goldsborough, and is a
very spirited representation of a plumed and spotted rattlesnake.

The tablet shown in Fig. 6 has already been described under "scalloped disks."

The remarkable plumed and feathered serpent given in Fig. 7 is painted
upon the rocks at Lake Nijapa, Nicaragua.[2]

THE HUMAN FACE.

A very important group of shell ornaments represent, more or less
distinctly, the human face. By a combination of engraving and sculpt-
ure a rude resemblance to the features is produced. The objects are
generally made from a large pear-shaped section of the lower whorl of
heavy marine univalves. The lower portion, which represents the neck
and chin, is cut from the somewhat restricted part near the base of the
shell, while the broad outline of the head reaches the first suture of the
noded shoulder of the body whorl. The simplest form is represented

[1] Squier: Peru, p. 1-6.
[2] Bancroft: Native Races of the Pacific States, vol. IV., p. 37.

by a specimen from a mound at Sevierville, Tenn. It is a plain, pear-shaped fragment, with evenly dressed margin and two perforations, which take the position of the eyes. A sketch of this is presented in Fig. 1, Plate LXIX. Similar specimens have been obtained from mounds in other States. A little further advance is made when the surface of the most convex part is ground away, with the exception of a low vertical ridge, which represents the nose. Further on a boss or node appears below the nose, which takes the place of the mouth, as seen in Fig. 2.

From the elementary stages exhibited in these specimens a gradual advance is made by the addition of details and the elaboration of all the features. A corona encircles the head, the ears are outlined (Fig. 5, Plate LXX), the eyes are elaborated by adding one or more concentric circles or ovals, brows are placed above, and groups of notched and zigzag lines extend downward upon the cheeks. The node at the mouth is perforated or cut in intaglio in circular or oblong figures, and the chin is embellished by a variety of incised designs. Illustrations of the various forms are given in Plates LXIX and LXX.

These objects are especially numerous in the mounds of Tennessee, but their range is quite wide, examples having been reported from Kentucky, Virginia, Illinois, Missouri, and Arkansas, and smaller ones of a somewhat different type from New York. In size they range from two to ten inches in length, the width being considerably less. They are generally found associated with human remains in such a way as to suggest their use as ornaments for the head or neck. There are, however, no holes for suspension except those made to represent the eyes, and these, so far as I have observed, show no abrasion by a cord of suspension. Their shape suggests the idea that they may have been used as masks, and as such may have been placed upon the faces of the dead in the same manner that metal masks were used by some oriental nations.

Among the large number of interesting objects of shell obtained from the McMahon Mound at Sevierville, Tenn., were a number of these shell masks. In the notes of the collector they are mentioned as having been found on the breast or about the heads of skeletons. The example shown in Fig. 1, Plate LXVII, is a medium-sized, rather plain specimen from the above-named locality. It is seven and one-fourth inches long and nearly six inches wide, and has been made from a *Busycon perversum*. The margins are much decayed, and the convex surface is pitted and discolored. The inside is smooth, and has a slight design rudely engraved upon it. Of a very different type is the specimen shown in Fig. 2. It is new looking, and well preserved. The slightly translucent surface is highly polished, and the engraved lines are quite fresh looking. It was collected by J. D. Lucas, and is labeled Aquia Creek, Va. It is five and one-half inches in length by five in width, and is apparently made from some dextral-whorled shell. The outline is somewhat rec-

1. Mask-like ornament, Tennessee. (⅔)

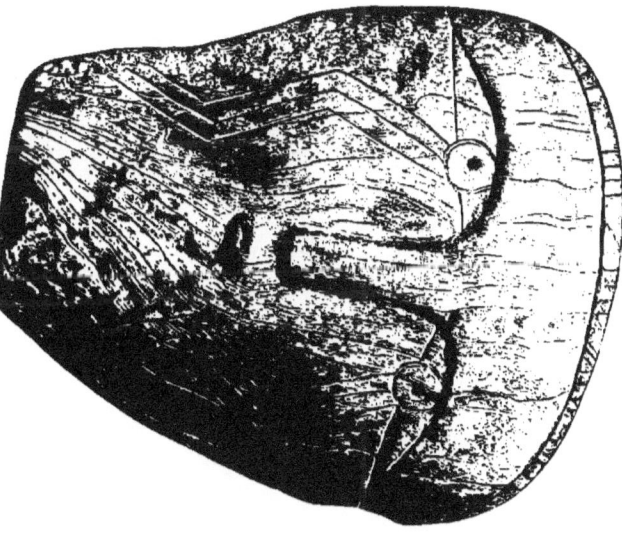

2. Mask-like ornament, Virginia. (⅓)

THE HUMAN FACE.

SHELL MASK.

Virginia.

$(\frac{1}{2})$

tangular, the upper surface being pretty well rounded and ornamented with a corona of incised lines, which are arranged in six groups of four each. Inside of these a single incised line runs parallel with the edge, from temple to temple. The eyes are represented by small circles with small central pits, and the lids are indicated by long, pointed ellipses. From each of the eyes a group of three zigzag lines extends downward across the cheek, terminating near the edge of the plate, opposite the mouth. These lines may be interpreted in two ways: First, if the object is a mourning mask, made with especial reference to its use in burial, they may signify tears, since, in the pictographic language of many tribes, tears are represented by lines descending from the eyes, and, with other nations, running water is symbolized by curved or zigzag lines; in the second place, these lines may represent figures painted upon the face during the period of mourning, or they may simply represent the characteristic lines of the painting or tattooing of the clan or tribe to which the deceased belonged. It is not at all improbable that these objects were further embellished by painted designs which have been obliterated.

The nose is represented by a flat ridge, which terminates abruptly below, the nostrils being indicated by two small excavations. The mouth is represented by an oval node, in which a horizontal groove has been made.

The most elaborately engraved example of these masks yet brought to the notice of the public is shown in Plate LXVIII. It was obtained by Mr. Lucien Carr from a large mound, known as the Ely Mound, near Rose Hill, Lee County, Virginia, and is described and illustrated by that gentleman in the tenth annual report of the Peabody Museum.[1] Wishing to present this fine specimen to the best advantage possible, I have had a large cut made from a photograph furnished by Professor Putnam, curator of the Peabody Museum. Parts of the design which were obscure I have strengthened, following the guidance of such fragments of lines as were still traceable, or by simply duplicating the lines of the opposite side, as these designs are in all cases bi symmetrical.

Having described a great number of relics exhumed from this mound, Mr. Carr goes on to say "that the most interesting of the articles taken from this grave was an engraved shell made from the most dilated portion of the *Strombus gigas*, and carved on the convex side into the likeness of a human face." It measures 138 millimeters in length, by 120 in breadth. It is perforated with three holes, "the two upper of which are surrounded with circles, and represent eyes; between these is a raised ridge of shell, in place of the nose, and below this is a third hole, which is just above a series of lines that were probably intended as the mouth. Four lines, parallel to each other during three-fourths of their length, begin at the outer corner of the eye and are zigzaged to the lower jaw, where they are drawn to a point. The concave side of the

[1] Carr, in Tenth Annual Report Peabody Museum, p. 87.

shell is perfectly plain, and still preserves its high polish, though the right portion of the face on the carved or convex side shows the sad effects of time and exposure."

Although I have not had an opportunity of examining this specimen closely, I am inclined to the opinion, judging by its outlines, that the shell from which it was made has been sinistrally whorled, and hence a *Busycon perversum*. I should also prefer to consider the hole beneath the nose as representing the mouth, as it certainly does in many other cases, and the peculiar figure—the three vertical lines which extend downward from the hole and the two banded figures that cross them at right angles—as a representation of some painted or tatooed design characteristic of the builders of the mound.

Other examples of these objects are represented in Plate LXIX. Of especial interest I may mention the specimen shown in Fig. 4, obtained, with other similar examples, by Professor Putnam, from the Lick Creek mound, in East Tennessee. The perforations which represent the eyes are surrounded by two concentric circles, and the zigzag lines beneath are supplemented by two sets of pendant figures formed of notched lines, the two longer of which extend down the sides of the nose, the others being connected with the lower margin of the eye. In one example four parallel lines pass from the mouth downward over the chin.

Fig. 3 represents a specimen from the Brakebill Mound, East Tennessee. The mouth is not indicated, and the nose is but slightly relieved. Each eye, however, is inclosed by a figure which extends downward over the cheek, terminating in three sharp points.

So far as the specimens at hand show, this peculiar embellishment of the eyes and mouth is characteristic of Virginia and East Tennessee. A small specimen from Georgia, now preserved in the Natural History Museum at New York, has a somewhat similar ornamentation of the eyes. This specimen is shown in Fig. 6, Plate LXX.

In Fig. 8 of the same plate we have the representation of a face modeled in clay, on which a number of incised lines, similar to those engraved on shell, have been drawn. The crown of notches is also present. The specimen has been illustrated by Professor Jones.[1] It is now in the museum of Natural History at New York, and was probably obtained from the Etowah Valley, Georgia. Examples in stone are also numerous, and show certain features in common with those in shell.

Fig. 9 is from Northern Ohio, and is carved from a nodule of iron ore.

The very beautiful little head shown in Figs. 1 and 2 is from a cave at Mussel Shoals, Ala. It is made of shell, and is somewhat altered by decay. The crown is peculiarly notched, and resembles a very common Mexican form. The notch in the middle of the forehead can be traced to a division in the head-dress noticed in the more elaborately carved Mexican specimens.

The example shown in Figs. 3 and 4 is copied from a rather rude cut

---

[1] Jones: Antiquities of the Southern Indians, p. 430.

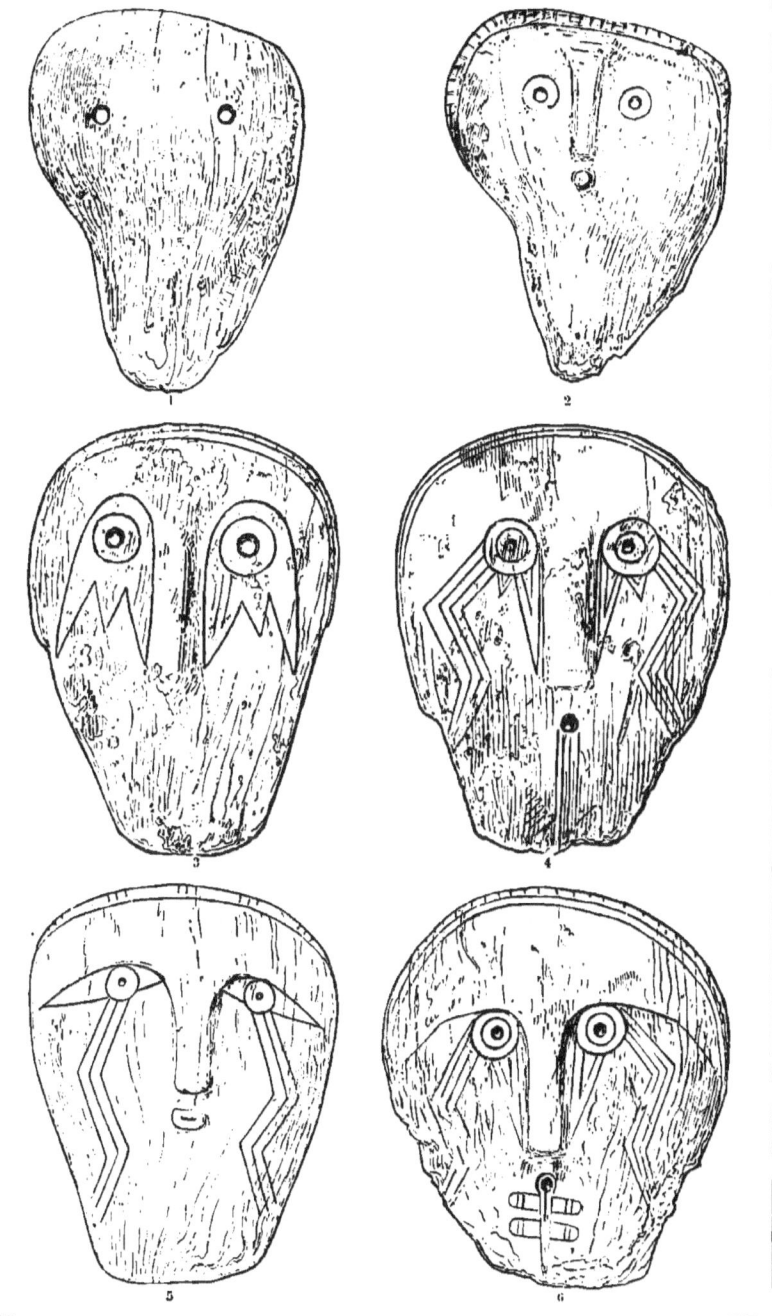

1. McMahan Mound, Tenn.
2. McMahan Mound, Tenn.
3. Brakebill Mound, Tenn.

4. Lick Creek Mound, Tenn.
5. Acquia Creek, Va.
6. Mound, Ely County, Va.

THE HUMAN FACE.

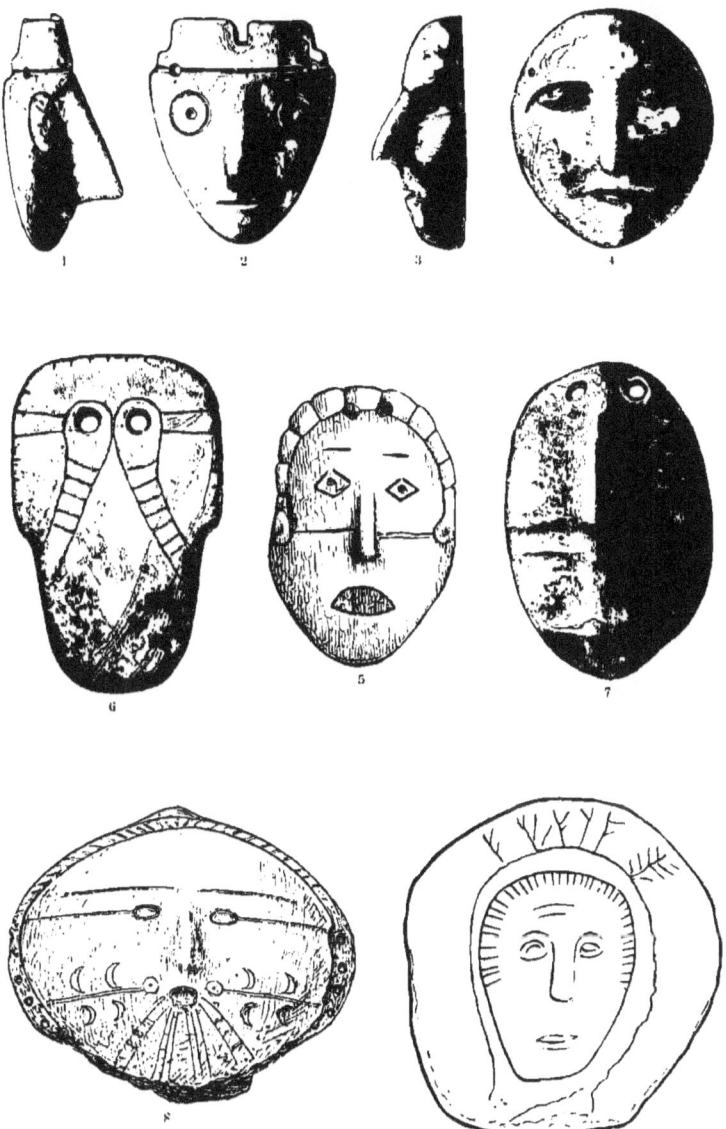

1. 2. Shell ornament from a cave, Alabama. (⅓)
3. 4. Shell ornament from New York. (⅓)
   5. Shell ornament, stone grave, Tennessee.
   6. Shell ornament from Georgia. (⅓)

7. Shell ornament from Tennessee. (⅓)
8. Face modeled in clay, Georgia.
9. Face carved in iron ore, Ohio.

THE HUMAN FACE.

given by Schoolcraft, who describes it as follows: "This well-sculptured article was discovered in the valley of the Kasanda Creek, Onondaga County. The material is a compact piece of sea-shell. It still preserves in a considerable degree the smoothness and luster of its original finish. * * * At the angle of the temples are two small orifices for suspending it around the neck. The entire article is finished with much skill and delicacy."[1]

The very rude specimen presented in Fig. 7 is from a mound at Franklin, Tenn. It seems to have been some natural form, but slightly changed by art. A somewhat similar specimen from a mound in Tennessee may be seen in the Peabody Museum.

The cut presented in Fig. 5 is taken from Jones's Antiquities of Tennessee, page 48. The specimen was obtained from the stone grave of a child at the foot of a mound near Nashville, Tenn. It has diamond-shaped eyes, a feature of very rare occurrence in the art of this region.

THE HUMAN FIGURE.

I now come to a class of works which are new and unique, and in more than one respect are the most important objects of aboriginal art yet found within the limits of the United States. These relics are four in number, and come from that part of the mound-building district occupied at one time by the "stone grave" peoples—three from Tennessee and one from Missouri. Similar designs are not found in other materials, and, indeed, nothing at all resembling them can be found, so far as I know, either in stone or in clay. If such have been painted or engraved on less enduring materials they are totally destroyed. I shall first describe the specimens themselves, and subsequently dwell at some length upon their authenticity, their significance, and their place in art.

First, I present, in Plate LXXI, a shell gorget on which is engraved a rather rude delineation of a human figure. The design occupies the concave side of a large shell disk cut from a *Busycon perversum*. Near the upper margin are the usual holes for suspension. The engraved design fills the central portion of the plate and is inclosed by two approximately parallel lines, between which and the edge of the shell there is a plain belt three-fourths of an inch wide. A casual observer would probably not recognize any design whatever in the jumble of half obliterated lines that occupies the inclosed space. It will first be noticed that a column about three-fourths of an inch in width stands erect in the center of the picture; from this spring a number of lines, forming serpentine arms, which give the figure as much the appearance of an octopus crowded into a collector's alcohol jar as of a human creature. A little study will convince one, however, that the central column represents the human body, and the tangle of lines surrounding it will be found to represent the arms, legs, hands, feet, and their appendages—no line within the border being without its

[1] Schoolcraft: Notes on the Iroquois, p. 235.

office. The upper extremity of the body is occupied by a circle one-eighth of an inch in diameter, which represents the eye. The head is not distinguished from the body by any sort of constriction for the neck, but has evidently been crowned by a rude aurora-like crest similar to that found in so many aboriginal designs. This does not appear in the engraving given, as it, as well as other features, was so nearly obliterated as to escape observation until the idea was suggested by the study of other similar designs. The mouth is barely suggested, being represented by three shallow lines placed so low on the trunk that they occupy what should be the chest. From the side of the head a number of lines, probably meant for plumes, extend across the bordering lines almost to the edge of the shell; below this are two perforated loops, which seem to take the place of ears; the one on the right is doubly perforated and has a peculiar extension, in a bent or elbowed line, across the border. The arms are attached to the sides of the body near the middle in a haphazard sort of way and are curiously double-jointed; they terminate, however, in well-defined hands against the right and left borders, the thumb and fingers being, in each case, distinctly represented. The legs and feet are at first exceedingly hard to make out, but when once traced are as clear as need be. The body terminates abruptly below within an inch of the base of the inclosed space. One leg extends directly downward, the foot resting upon the border line; the other extends backward from the base of the trunk and rests against the border line at the right; the legs have identical markings, which probably represent the costume. Each foot terminates in a single well-defined talon or claw, which folds upward against the knee. This is a most interesting feature, and one which this design possesses in common with the three other drawings of the human figure found in Tennessee. The spaces between the various members of the figure are filled in with ornamental appendages, which seem to be attached to the hands and feet, and probably represent plumes. The numerous perforations in this specimen are worthy of attention: within the border line there are twenty-six, which vary from one-fourth to one-sixteenth of an inch in diameter. They are placed mostly at the joints of the figure or at the junction of two or more lines. Such perforations are of frequent occurrence in this class of gorgets and may have had some particular significance to their possessors. This specimen was found in the great mound at Sevierville, Tenn., upon the breast of a skeleton, and is now in the National Collection. It has suffered considerably from decay, the surface being deeply furrowed, pitted, and discolored. The holes are much enlarged and the lines in places are almost obliterated.

I began the study of this design with the thought that, in reference to this specimen at least, Professor Jones was right, and that the confused group of lines might be the meaningless product of an idle fancy, but ended by being fully satisfied that no single line or mark is without its place or its significance.

SHELL GORGET—THE HUMAN FIGURE.

McMahan Mound, Tennessee.

(i)

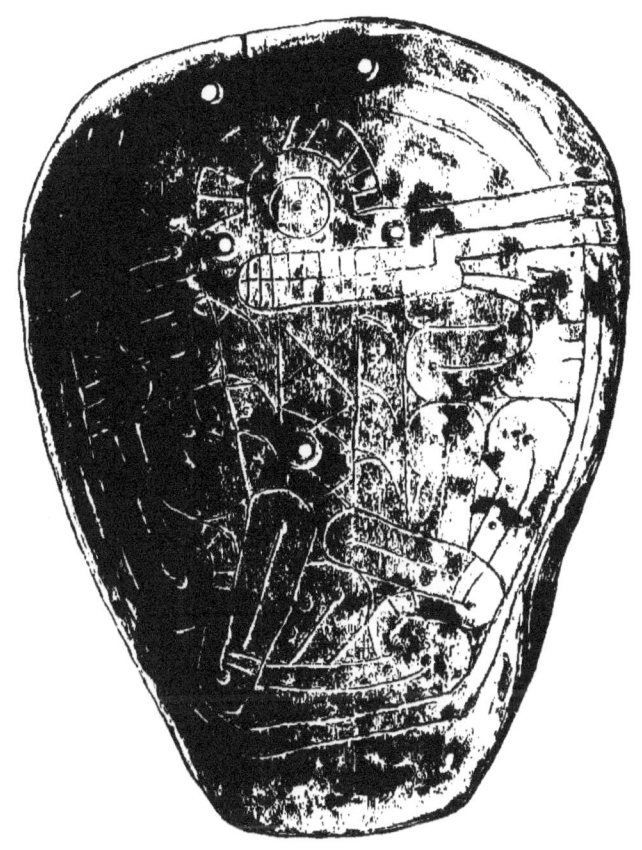

SHELL GORGET—THE HUMAN FIGURE

Mound, Tennessee.

(¼)

After having examined this design so critically, it will be an easy matter to interpret that engraved upon the tablet illustrated in Plate LXXII. Although found in widely separated localities, and engraved in a somewhat different style, they are identical in type, and exhibit but slight differences in detail. At the top of the plate we have the two doubly conical perforations for suspension, but the double border line is not completed above, being interrupted by the plumes from the head. The head itself is decorated with the usual crown of radiating lines, a small circle with a central pit represents the eye, and below this is a well-defined mouth with a double row of teeth. Extending to the right from the mouth is an appendage consisting of one straight and two interrupted lines, which may be a part of the costume, or, since it issues from the mouth, may possibly symbolize speech. The body, which is short and straight, is divided vertically into three parts; the central space contains a large conical perforation, and is covered with a lace-work of lines; the lateral spaces are ornamented with rows of buttons or scales, which consist of meagerly outlined circles with central dots. The curiously folded arms have precisely the same relative positions as the corresponding members in the other specimen, and the fingers touch the bordering line on the right and left, the thumb being turned backward against the elbow. The legs are represented in a manner that suggests a sitting posture, the rounded knees coming in front of and joining the base of the body; in position and decoration they repeat the other specimen. The feet, or the rounded extremities that represent them, rest upon the border line, as in the case previously described, and terminate in upturned talons that are long, curved, and jointed, and terminate in square or blunt tips. Plume-like appendages are attached to the arms and legs, and fill the spaces not occupied by the members of the body; these plumes or pendants are always represented by folded bands or fillets which are ornamented on one side with dots. A plume attached to the left side of the head is represented by two curved lines, which reach to the edge of the shell. There are five perforations, two for suspension, two at the sides of the face, and one near the middle of the trunk. This specimen is in a very perfect state of preservation, the surface being smooth and but little stained. It is somewhat pear-shaped, resembling in this respect the mask-like gorgets previously described. It is about seven inches in height and five in width, and has been made from a very thick and compact shell, probably a *Busycon*. It was obtained from a mound in Meigs County, Tennessee, and is preserved in the Peabody Museum. In mechanical execution this specimen is much superior to the preceding one; the edges and surface of the shell are nicely dressed, although the lines of the design are indifferently cut.

Another unique shell gorget is presented in Plate LXXIII. It was obtained from a mound in Southeastern Missouri, and is now in the possession of Professor Potter, of Saint Louis. The disk is about four and a half inches in diameter, and was originally nearly circular, but the edges are now much decayed and battered. A cut with a brief description is given by Mr. A. J. Conant in his recent work, "Foot-prints of Vanished Races," page 95. My cut is made from a photograph obtained from Professor Putnam, of the Peabody Museum. This is probably the same photograph used by Mr. Conant. The engraved design is of a totally distinct type from the last, and evinces a much higher grade of skill in the artist. It is encircled by six nearly parallel lines, which occupy about half an inch of the border of the disk. Portions of these still remain, the inner one being nearly entire. Between this and the second line are two perforations for suspension. The idea first suggested by a glance at the engraved design is that it strongly resembles the work of the ancient Mexicans, and the second idea of many archæologists will probably be that there may be a doubt of its genuineness. Setting this question aside for the present, let us examine the engraving in detail. Placing the plate so that the two perforations are at the left, we have the principal figure in an upright posture. This figure apparently represents a personage of some importance, as he is decked from head to foot with a profusion of ornaments and symbols. He is shown in profile with the arms extended in action, and the feet separated as if in the act of stepping forward. The head is large, occupying about one-third of the height of the design. The elaborate head-dress fills the upper part of the inclosed space, pendant plumes descend to the shoulders before and behind, and circular ornaments are attached to the hair and the ear. The conventionalized eye is lozenge or diamond shaped, with a small conical pit for the pupil.

The profile shows a full forehead, a strong nose, and a prominent chin. Two lines extend across the cheek from the bridge of the nose to the base of the ear. In and projecting from the mouth is a symbolic figure, the meaning of which can only be conjectured. The shoulders and body are but meagerly represented. From the waist a peculiar apron-like object is suspended, which reaches to the knees; it may be a part of the costume or a priestly symbol. The legs and feet are dwarfed, but quite well outlined. There are encircling bands at the knees and ankles, and a fan-like extension of the costume, somewhat resembling the tail of a bird, descends between the legs. Attached to the back, is a figure of a rather extraordinary character. Similar figures may be seen in some of the Mexican paintings, and seem to represent a contrivance for carrying burdens, in which at times elfish figures are accommodated. The right arm is extended forward, and the hand grasps a singular shaft, with which a blow is aimed at the severed head of a victim, which is held face downward by the left hand of the standing figure. The severed head still retains the plumed cap, from which a long pendant descends in front of the face. The eye is lozenge-shaped. A zigzag line crosses the cheek from the ear to the bridge of the nose, and a curious symbolic figure. is represented

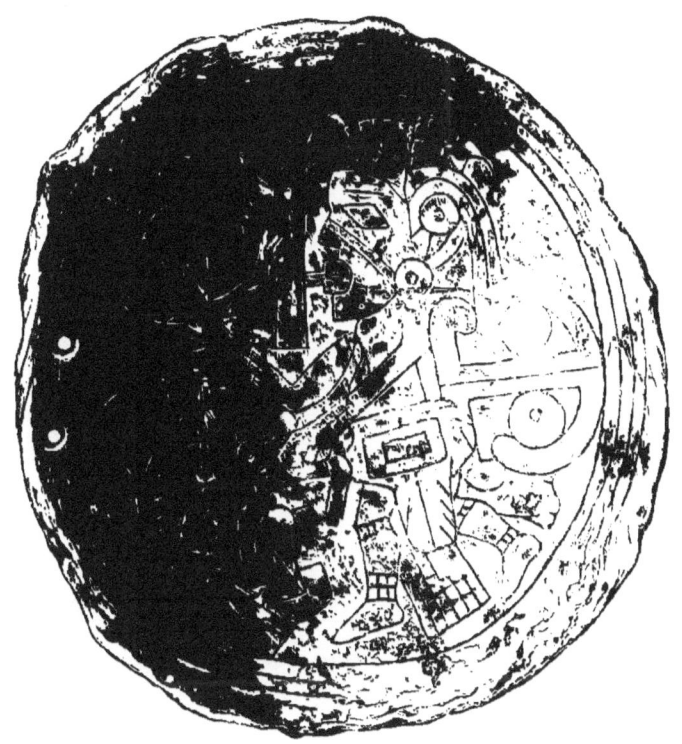

SHELL GORGET—THE HUMAN FIGURE

Missouri.

(⅓)

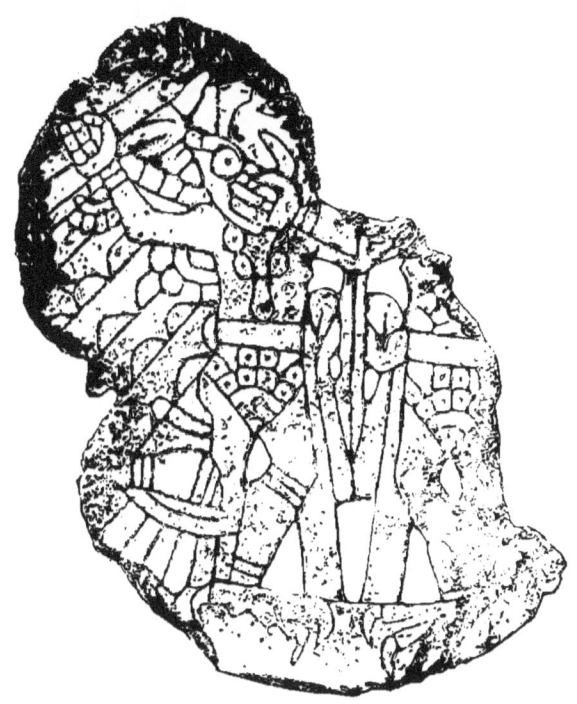

ENGRAVED GORGET—FIGHTING FIGURES.

Tennessee.

as issuing from the mouth. The shaft held in the right hand seems
to issue from a circular figure, doubtless of symbolic character, which
occupies the space in front of the head of the standing figure. It is
possible that the figure which issues from the mouth of the victim
represents the point of this mystic shaft which has penetrated the
head, although we should have to allow some inaccuracies in the drawing if this were the case. Any one at all familiar with the curious
pictographic manuscripts of the ancient Mexicans will see at a glance
that we have here a sacrificial scene, in which a priest seems to be engaged in the sacrifice of a human being. In the extraordinary manuscripts of the ancient Aztecs we have many parallels to this design.
So closely does it approach the Aztec type that, although no duplicate
can be found in any of the codices, there is not a single idea, a single
member or ornament that has not its analogue in the Mexican manuscripts. To make this clear to every one I present, in Plate LXXV,
Fig. 4, a single example for comparison. This one is selected from the
manuscript of M. De Féjerváry, preserved at Budapest, Hungary.[1]
Fortunately for the credit of this Missouri relic we do not find its duplicate—there are only family resemblances; there are similar plumes,
with similar ornaments and pendants, similar costume and attitudes;
there are similar features and similar symbols; but there is no absolute
identity, except in motive and conception.

Among the multitude of works of art collected within the last de-
cade very few will be found to surpass in interest the fragment of a shell
gorget from the McMahon Mound, at Sevierville, Tenn. The disk, when
entire, has been nearly five inches in diameter. A little more than one-
third had crumbled away, and the remaining portion was only preserved
by the most careful handling, and by immediate immersion in a thin solution of glue. This specimen is the first of the kind ever brought to
light in this country, and must certainly be regarded as the highest example of aboriginal art ever found north of Mexico. The design, as in
the other cases, has been engraved on the convex surface of a polished
shell disk, and represents two human figures, plumed and winged and
armed with eagles' talons, engaged in mortal combat. As in the last
specimen described, this has, at first sight, an exotic look, bearing certainly in its conception a general resemblance to the marvelous bas-
reliefs of Mexico and Central America; but the resemblance goes no
further, and we are at liberty to consider it a northern work *sui generis.*
The design has apparently covered the entire tablet, leaving no space
for encircling lines. The two figures are in profile and face each other
in a fierce onset. Of the right-hand figure only the body, one arm, and
one leg remain. The left-hand figure is almost complete; the outline of
the face, one arm, and one foot being obliterated. The right hand is
raised above the head in the act of brandishing a long double-pointed

---

[1] Kingsborough, Vol. III, pl. 22.

knife. At the same time this doughty warrior seems to be receiving a blow in the face from the right hand of the other combatant, in which is clutched a savage-looking blade, with a curved point. The hands are vigorously drawn, the joints are correctly placed, and the thumb presses down upon the outside of the forefinger in its natural effort to tighten and secure the grasp. Two bands encircle the wrists and probably represent bracelets. The arms and shoulders are plain. The head is decorated with a single plume, which springs from a circular ornament placed over the ear; an angular figure extends forward from the base of this plume and probably represents what is left of the head-dress proper; forward of this, on the very edge of the crumbling shell, is one-half of the lozenge-shaped eye, the dot intended to represent the pupil being almost obliterated. It is certainly a great misfortune that both faces are completely gone; their exact character must remain conjectural. A neat pendant ornament is suspended upon the well-formed breast, and a broad belt encircles the waist, beneath which, covering the abdomen, is a design that suggests the scales of a coat of mail. The legs are well-defined and perfectly proportioned; the left knee is bent forward and the foot is planted firmly on the ground, while the right is thrown gracefully back against the rim at the left. Double belts encircle the knees and ankles. The legs terminate in wonderfully well-drawn eagle's feet, armed with vigorously curved talons. A very interesting feature of the design is the highly conventionalized wing, which is attached to the shoulder behind, and fills the space beneath the uplifted arm. A broad many-feathered tail is spread out like a fan behind the legs. The right hand figure, so far as seen, is an exact duplicate of the left. A design of undetermined significance occupies the space between the figures beneath the crossed arms; it may represent conventionalized drapery, but is more probably symbolic in its character. The heads probably been a little too large for good proportion, but the details of the anatomy are excellent. The muscles of the shoulder, the breast and nipple, the waist, the buttock, and the calves of the legs are in excellent drawing. The whole group is most graphically presented. A highly ideal design, it is made to fill a given space with a directness of execution and a unity of conception that is truly surprising.

Let us turn for a moment from this striking effort of the mound-builders to the early efforts of other peoples in the engraver's art. Here are the drawings of the Troglodytes of France, scintillations of paleolithic genius, which appear as a flash of light in the midst of a midnight sky. They are truly remarkable. The clear-cut lines that shadow forth the hairy mammoth suggest the graphic and forcible work of the Parisian of to-day. The rude Esquimaux of our own time engraves images of a great variety of natural objects on his ornaments and implements of ivory in a manner that commands our admiration. But these shell tablets have designs of a much higher grade. They not only represent natural

1. Shell gorget, McMahan Mound, Tenn   4. Figure from an Aztec painting.
2. Sculptured in stone, Mexico.   5. Shell gorget, McMahan Mound, Tenn.
3. Shell gorget, mound, Missouri.   6. Shell gorget, Lick Creek Mound, Tenn.

THE HUMAN FIGURE.

1. Design on Zuñi war-shield, painting.   2. Thunder-bird of the Haidahs, painting.

COMPOSITE FIGURES.

objects with precision, but they delineate conceptions of mythical creatures of composite character for which nature affords no model. In execution the best of these tablets will not compare with the wonderful works in stucco and stone of Palenque, or the elaborate sculptures of the Aztecs, but they are, like them, vigorous in action and complete in conception.

In case the authenticity of these relics be questioned, the facts in regard to them, so far as known, are here presented for reference. As to the two specimens from Sevierville, Tenn. (Plates LXXI and LXXIII), the shadow of a doubt cannot be attached to them. Were there no record whatever of the time or place of discovery, the evidence upon the faces of the relics themselves would show satisfactorily that they are genuine. They were taken from the great mound, which I have called the McMahon Mound, at Sevierville, Tenn. This mound was opened in 1881 by one of our most experienced collectors, Dr. E. Palmer. The specimens when found were in a very advanced stage of decay; pitted, discolored, and crumbling, and had to be handled with the utmost care to prevent total disintegration. They were dried by the collector, immersed in a weak solution of glue, and forwarded immediately to the National Museum at Washington. In this mound a multitude of relics were found, a large number being of shell, many of which are figured and described in this paper. These two gorgets, as well as many others of more ordinary types were found on or near the breasts of skeletons, and it is highly probable that they were suspended about the necks of the dead just as they had been worn by the living. By accurately ascertaining the authenticity of one of these specimens we establish, so far as need be, the genuineness of all of the same class. If one is genuine that is sufficient; the others may or may not be so, without seriously effecting the questions at issue, yet the occurrence of duplicate or closely related specimens in widely separated localities furnishes confirmatory evidence of no little importance. I do not wish to be understood as casting a doubt upon any of the four specimens described, as I am thoroughly convinced that there is no cause for suspicion.

The Missouri gorget, which has already been described and figured, was obtained by unknown persons in Southeastern Missouri. Several years back it came into the hands of Colonel Whitley, and from him it was obtained by its present owner, Professor Potter, of Saint Louis. There has never been a question as to its genuineness, and according to Professor Hilder, who saw it shortly after its discovery, the appearance and condition of the specimen were such that it could not have been of fraudulent manufacture. It was chalky and crumbling from decay, the lines of the design bearing equal evidence with the general surface of the shell of great age. Beside this, even if it were possible to produce such a condition in a recently carved shell, there existed no motive for such an attempt. Nothing was to be made by it; no benefit could accrue to the perpetrator to reward him for his pains, and, further, there was no precedent, there was extant nothing that could serve as a model for such a work.

In Plate LXXV I have arranged a number of figures for convenience of comparison, Figs. 1, 3, 5, and 6, being outlines of the four examples just described. In regard to the restored part of the outline in Fig. 1, I wish to say that my only object in filling out the figure on the right was to secure as far as possible the full effect of the complete original. Observing that all that remains of the right hand figure—the arm, the body, the leg and foot, is a duplicate of the left, it is safe to conclude that the design has been approximately bi-symmetrical, slight discrepancies probably occurring in the details of head and arm, in the expression of face, or in the character of the weapon. It is much to be regretted that the faces are totally destroyed.

In Fig. 3 I present a group of two figures from the so-called "sacrificial stone" found in the Plaza Mayor, city of Mexico. It seems to represent the submission of one warrior or ruler to his victorious opponent, and is one of many designs that might be presented to illustrate the analogies of the Tennessee relic with the interesting works of the far South. There is what might be called a family resemblance, a similarity in idea and action, but little analogy of detail. The northern work is by far the more spirited, and is apparently superior in all the essentials of artistic excellence.

In the composite character of the personages represented this picture finds no parallel. Composite figures are of frequent occurrence in Peruvian art, as in the running figures sculptured on the great monolith at Tiahuanuco, or the mythical combats of the gods of the earth and sea painted on the pottery of Chimu. They are also found in the manuscripts of the ancient Mexicans, as well as in the paintings of the modern Pueblos of New Mexico (Fig. 1, Plate LXXVI), and in the totemic art of the Haidahs (Fig. 2, Plate LXXVI). The most frequent combinations are of birds with men, the inspiration of the work in all cases being derived from the mythology of the people. The wearing of masks has doubtless given rise to many such conceptions, and where the head alone of the human creature has undergone metamorphosis, we may suspect that a mask has originated the conception; but the Tennessee example appears to be the only one in which wings are added independently of the arms or in which bird's feet are attached to the otherwise perfect human creature.

And now we come to the question of the origin of these objects, and especially of the example most closely resembling Mexican work. The Missouri gorget is in many respects quite isolated from known works of the Mississippi Valley. Must it be regarded as an exotic, as an importation from the South, or does it belong to the soil from which it was exhumed? In order to answer this question we must not only determine its relations to the art of Mexico, but we must know just what affinities it has to the art of the mound-builders.

www.ingramcontent.com/pod-product-compliance
Lightning Source LLC
Chambersburg PA
CBHW020111030726
47498CB00006B/2051